D1016971

A WYATT BOOK *for*

W

ST.
MARTIN'S
PRESS

Michael

Powell

and

Emeric

Pressburger

The Red Shoes

A Wyatt Book for St. Martin's Press ❧ New York

THE RED SHOES. Copyright © 1978 by Michael Powell and Emeric
Pressburger. All rights reserved. Printed in the United States of America.
No part of this book may be used or reproduced in any manner
whatsoever without written permission except in the case of brief
quotations embodied in critical articles or reviews. For information,
address A Wyatt Book for St. Martin's Press, 175 Fifth Avenue, New
York, N.Y. 10010.

Design by Jaye Zimet

Library of Congress Cataloging-in-Publication Data

Powell, Michael.
    The red shoes: a novel/by Michael Powell and Emeric
  Pressburger.
        p. cm.
    "A Wyatt book for St. Martin's Press."
    ISBN 0-312-14034-7
    1. Ballet dancers—Fiction.   I. Pressburger, Emeric.   II. Title.
PR6066.0935R43   1996
823'.914—dc20   95-36147
                                                                CIP

THE RED SHOES was originally published by Avon Books, a division of
the Hearst Corporation.

First edition: January 1996

10   9   8   7   6   5   4   3   2   1

London

One

UPON A SPRING EVENING IN LONDON in the twenties of this twentieth century of ours, the Ballets Lermontov was at long last at Covent Garden Opera House. In the third week of their season, Boris Lermontov, the world-famous impresario—whose company's Russian names fronted for half a dozen nationalities (that well-known dancer Hilda Boot became Tamara Butsova overnight)—was presenting a gala performance of a new ballet with music commissioned from an English composer. The queue for the cheap gallery seats had started forming last night; now, by 5:00 P.M., the line extended down the stage door side of Floral Street, and up the other side as well. Buskers, under the tolerant supervision of the police, had been entertaining the queue. The night was cool, but the street performers

Three

had a better audience than usual. Archie, a stocky, bald little man with stentorian voice and reddened nose, was booming:

> Cherries so red,
> Strawberries ripe,
> At home of course they'll be storming!
> Never mind the abuse,
> You've had the excuse:
> You've been to Covent Garden in the morning!

In the midst of his song, a closed black Rolls-Royce turned from Bow Street into Floral Street. Two young policemen made vain attempts to stop it. It was the rush hour; to order the car to back up onto Bow Street would have brought traffic to a halt—a prospect daunting to the young constables. One of them lost his temper and shouted at the driver, "This street is closed! Didn't you see my signal?"

The stolid-looking driver, obviously an experienced factotum, stared straight ahead as he answered, "No, sir. Very sorry, sir. Stage door, sir." He spoke with a Russian accent and jerked his head toward his passenger: "Mr. Lermontov's car, sir."

A senior police officer, in charge of traffic arrangements, arrived on the scene and peered through the window at the dim figure in white tie and tails. He was rewarded with a brief but dazzling smile. Impressed and satisfied, he touched his cap and turned on his subordinate. "Well? What are you waiting for? Can't you see who it is? Let him through!"

The two young policemen rushed about, clearing a lane for the Rolls. The queue pressed against the huge granite blocks that supported the theatre and condescended to carry a few flimsy theatre posters as well.

The buskers went on busking, rather faster than usual, with a wary eye on the police; and a few passersby, who had been hoping to see a celebrity emerge, scattered.

"Move along there, please! Move along!"

The black Rolls sighed fifty yards down Floral Street and stopped at the stage door, so close to the curb that, with a single, quick stride, its passenger was able to reach the safety of the doors. Even so, one of the more knowledgeable balletomanes in the queue, recognizing the tall, slim figure, the amber-headed cane, the glossy hat, shouted, "Lermontov! It's Boris Lermontov!"

His female companion squealed as well, and people craned their necks—but Lermontov had vanished, followed by his driver.

Inside, they were greeted by Jerry, the stage-door keeper: "You're bright and early, Mr. Lermontov. Here's your letters. Lots of telegrams."

Lermontov's man took the mail, passed the telegrams and cables to his master, and kept the letters. Lermontov stood under the naked gas-flame, flaring in its wire cage in the corridor, and rapidly scanned the telegrams.

The door that led to the stage banged. It was the Administration—or rather the assistant to the administrator. He saw Lermontov and was all apologies. "I'm sorry, Lermontov. I had one of my men looking out for you, but he must have missed you. The police decided to close Floral Street. I hope you didn't have far to walk."

"No, thank you, Freddie."

The young man peered out into the street and saw the Rolls blocking his view, large and impressive, like the rump of an elephant. "You got here! Didn't the police stop you, Dmitri?"

Five

"No."

Without looking up from his telegram, Lermontov corrected him: "Dmitri made a little speech. Tell Mr. Freddie what you said."

"It was nothing." Dmitri was bashful.

"Tell him, all the same." Lermontov tore open another cable as if he were cutting a throat.

Dmitri obeyed. Boris Lermontov had told him to speak. So he spoke. "When we were dancing at the Teatro Colón in Rio de Janeiro—"

Lermontov's abstracted voice corrected him: "—in Buenos Aires—"

"—in Buenos Aires, a Russian immigrant, who had lived in London for two months, told me, 'When you're in London, don't drive on the right side of the street. The right side is the wrong side. And most important, call every policeman *Sir*.'"

The thin line of Lermontov's moustache twitched ever so slightly.

"Bravo!" Mr. Freddie clapped Dmitri on the shoulder. "And it works?"

"It works. What time do you want the car, Boris Lermontov?"

His master didn't want the car. He was going to supper with Professor Palmer, composer of the music for the new ballet.

Jerry the doorkeeper, who had been hovering in the background, said, "Professor Palmer's waiting for you in the Green Room."

Lermontov nodded and was gone. Jerry addressed Mr. Freddie: "Excuse me mentioning it. But I wonder if he knows that none of the corps de ballet has clocked in yet. Bit odd, isn't it?"

"After six o'clock they will come." Dmitri explained, "On our first nights they are forbidden to come earlier, to prevent Grisha Ljubov from making any more changes in his choreography."

The others nodded. They knew the fiery-tempered Ljubov.

Dmitri handed a note to Mr. Freddie. "Please give this to Boris Lermontov. It is the address of our new flat. We have moved out of the hotel. I gave it to him already, but he has changed his suit since then."

THEY WERE LEGENDARY CHARACTERS, these Russian impresarios: yet to call them impresarios was like calling Rembrandt a portrait painter, Mozart a musician, Einstein a mathematician. First came Diaghilev. He started it all; the others followed. It takes years to train and create a ballet dancer, but impresarios drop from the clouds like angels, rise from the gutter like gods. They come in all shapes: cultured and barbarous, proud and meek, ruthless and gentle, continuously in need of funds and rolling in luxury. In their breasts burns a sacred flame of passion for their chosen art; and whereas artists are prepared to sacrifice themselves for their art, these impresarios are ready to sacrifice everybody else.

Does it have something to do with the role of dancing, of rhythm, and of music, so often identified in primitive times with sacrifice to the gods? Is this why dancing has remained something divine through the ages? And why particularly in Russia? Why in those dead years between the two great wars? Perhaps the Russians have managed to keep deeper, purer, more basic emotions than the West towards the primitive arts. In those years when Dadaism and other "isms" were influencing European art, the Russian world was changing from top to bottom. Together with the Russian aristocracy, many of the country's best artists had emigrated. The West suddenly became aware to what dizzy heights Russian ballet had advanced.

So when the Ballets Russes of Boris Alexandre Lermontov booked Covent Garden for a season, the first two weeks were sold out for each of the eight weekly performances; and there were several more weeks to go.

Two

OUTSIDE THE GALLERY DOORS, THREE young music students—two men and a woman—stood, leaned, and supported one another, almost at the head of the gallery queue. Almost but not quite. By reaching out, Julian Craster (Composition and Conducting), Terry Tyler (Cello), and Ike Tanner (Piano and Percussion), were just able to touch the massive doors, soon to open on endless stone stairs leading to the highest balcony—the Gods. Two balletomanes, one male and bearded, the other female and cloaked, stood guarding the door like two characters from *Alice in Wonderland*, ready to resist, by force if necessary, any encroachment by the Rams. For the three students were advanced pupils of the Royal Academy of Music—RAM for short and ram by nature, as Julian remarked, when raising

Terry to the honorary degree of female Ram, or Ramess—and were all prepared to butt their way through the flimsy opposition to the three best seats in the front row of the gallery, where they could see the conductor and his orchestra, although their view of the stage would be restricted to the front part.

"My dear Craster," Professor Palmer had observed to his favorite pupil in his Master Class, "I had seen *The Valkyrie* fourteen times from the gallery before I could afford a seat down in the pit; and although my ears had told me what to expect I could hardly believe my eyes when, to Wagner's sensuous music, the doors of the courtyard burst open, the lovers escaped into the forest, and I saw an enchanted paradise, the foliage glistening with raindrops after the storm. I was ravished by the sight, Craster, and yet there was something missing to my ears. Trust your ears, Craster! Trust your ears! Wooden benches are hard on the bottom, but good for acoustics. Even now, with my stalls tickets in my hand, I have to restrain the urge to dash up any visible stairs leading to what is so justly called 'the Gods.' "

Good old Palmer! thought Julian. All his pupils would be here tonight. What a turnout! Not only ex-pupils and pupils-to-be, but friends, enemies, critics. The crowd was building up outside the gallery doors. The orderly, patient, British queue was in danger of relapsing into a dogfight. Taxis, arriving with leading dancers of the Lermontov company, were being mobbed by the fans. Four members of the orchestra, sharing a taxi with their instruments, were not allowed to get out. They found the taxi door slammed in their faces by the police, who obviously considered the chaos of vehicles inching their way along the street preferable to a lynching by the mob.

As it was a first night, the curtain was to rise half an

hour earlier than usual, at eight o'clock. At half past six, Julian—maintaining his place in the mob by a deadly use of elbows and knees—said, "Shush!"

"What d'you mean, 'shush'?" gasped Ike, the end link of the chain of which the middle link was Terry. A head popped under his arm, with the intention of breaking through. Ike placed a large fat hand on the face and pushed. It vanished and the gap closed. "What do you mean, 'shush'?"

"Voices," reported Julian from his listening post near the doors.

Beardie and Weirdie, the two *Alice in Wonderland* characters, had their ears pressed to the panels. They shook their heads. "You imagined it," snapped Weirdie.

Terry retorted, "You're talking about the two most sensitive tympanic membranes North of the Thames."

A battered china pot was thrust under her nose and a voice said, "Thank you!"

"My father will pay," said Terry, indicating Ike.

The trio of buskers—accordion, clarinet, and vocalist—that had been entertaining the queue had suddenly broken off their act, split into separate coin-collecting units, and were doing the rounds, with a chant of "Thank you! Thank you!"—which was not an expression of gratitude but meant, "Put something in the pot!"

Weirdie and Beardie appeared to have gone suddenly deaf, but Ike dropped in sixpence, asking, "What's your hurry, Archie?"

"The coppers have got their hands full," confided the vocalist. "They've asked the management to open the gallery doors ahead of time." With a wink at the three Rams and a glare at the Arty-Crafty duo, he resumed his progress.

With a sudden effort Julian hauled his two friends out of the ruck and up to the doors, where they were

Eleven

jammed nose-to-nose to the balletomanes. Julian and Beardie, four inches apart, eyed one another like two athletes about to compete in the 440.

Beardie jerked his head in the direction of the pot-clinking vocalist. "You know him?"

"Socially?"

"I mean, what does he do?"

"He's a busker. He busks."

"I mean in the daytime."

"Who knows where a busker goes in the daytime? Probably folds his wings and hangs himself up by his little claws to the rafters."

"Where do you know him from, then?"

"From here."

"Are you a busker?"

"No. I'm a mountaineer."

"A what?"

"A mountain-climber." He nodded toward Ike and Terry. "He's a mountaineer, too. She's a mountaineeress."

"You're kidding."

"She's the granddaughter of Edward Whymper, conqueror of the Matterhorn."

"Great-granddaughter," gasped Ike, hauling Terry closer to him.

"You're having me on. What mountains have *you* climbed?"

"These ones. The unconquered heights of Covent Garden. The South Corridor leading to the Gallery Cornice. The icy stones of the Staircase, swept daily by avalanches of dirty water from the buckets of char ladies—"

Suddenly, bolts grated on the other side of the door. The waiting queue writhed like a sea-serpent. The gallery-slaves cursed and roared. Each one held the exact amount of money for his ticket in his clenched hand.

Julian shouted: "We climb them five times a week!"

"We're opera-goers!" Ike put in.

Terry, realizing she would never be closer to a balletomane's eardrum, added, fortissimo, "Not balletomaniacs! That's why we've never seen each other!"

The assistant administrator, standing courageously on the stone staircase, had signaled to the uniformed toughs holding the door to let the mob in. Emergency rails to provide a zigzag run for the box office window had been fitted for the occasion.

With a shout from Julian—"Down with the tyrants! Remember the Bastille!"—the doors crashed open, flattening Gog and Magog against the sweating walls. The Rams, turned into battering-rams, burst between Beardie and Weirdie, reached the zigzag trail first. With a crisp slalom movement Julian arrived at the window, slapped down his money, grabbed his ticket, set the turnstile clicking. With a nimble sidestep that would have put a famous bullfighter to shame, the assistant administrator saved his skin. Julian was halfway up the first flight of stairs, Terry clinging to his hand, Ike clinging to Terry, before the field got going. Shrieking with rage, the balletomaniacs came leaping, half a step behind them— Weirdie's beads, scarves, and cloak flying, Beardie's beard bristling in the wind of his passage. Shrewdly using Terry to fend off against the walls, Julian skidded around landing after landing, higher and yet higher, gasping out encouraging slogans for the Rams, lugging Terry upwards as if he were Saint Peter bent on saving a sinner from a rout of demons; Ike pounding in their wake, the ample displacement of his comfortable body effectually blocking any attempt to pass.

In this order they burst out at the top of the stairs into the empty, echoing amphitheatre. Like the steps of some huge dry waterfall, the tiers of seats, bare, ungarnished, unnumbered, fell away at a steep angle to where the curving brass guardrail gleamed ready to prevent overenthusiastic patrons from plummeting sixty feet into the seats below. Casting off Terry's hand as an airplane parts company from a glider, leaving it to find its own way down through the upper air, Julian shouted, "Into the Valley of Death!" and, scorning the gangways, reached the front row one-fiftieth of a second sooner than anybody else, just stopped himself from taking a header into the auditorium, and flung himself down at full length in the middle of the front row, thereby reserving three places.

In an incredibly short time the gallery was teeming with devotees scrambling for seats. A cloak floated through the air and settled on the seats beside Julian, half-smothering him in its folds. It belonged to Weirdie, who had launched it, screaming, "My cloak! My cloak!" A moment later she and Beardie came rushing in on that side, while Terry and Ike fell into Julian's arms, gasping, "Into the jaws of Death, Into the mouth of Hell, Rode the six hundred!" Simultaneously the balletomanes sat down on their cloak, Weirdie leaning across to shout, "You have no right to keep two extra places! First come, first served!" Julian smiled seraphically and kissed two fingers to her.

Before folding his raincoat and placing it on his lap, Ike produced two objects: something he called opera glasses (they were actually naval binoculars) and a program. Terry opened it to a studio photograph of Professor Palmer, wearing white tie, a flower in his buttonhole and a self-conscious expression. On the opposite page the Ballets Lermontov presented the new work *Heart of Fire* with music by Andrew Palmer. Terry at once found fault with the photograph. The Prof was letting the team down. A composer should not look like a tailor's dummy. A composer should not be photographed in white tie and tails. A composer should be photographed in a cardigan, or in his shirtsleeves, at work.

"Like Schaunard," corroborated Ike, "In *La Bohème*."

"Yes," said Julian. "But when my opera is put on at Covent Garden, I shall be conducting it. And I shall be photographed in white tie and tails."

"A conductor's different. He and the soloists. It's expected of them."

Terry rose to look down over the rail into the auditorium, a privilege only front-seaters can avail themselves of. Julian hung over beside her.

"Filling up?" asked Ike, opening a box of hard-centered chocolates.

"Not one tiara," reported Terry.

"Not a muttonchop," said Julian.

"Which would you prefer?" Terry asked Ike.

"Muttonchops."

For the next half-hour the Gods applauded everything that moved under the huge glass dome. The front row's view was restricted to about two-thirds of the stalls, one side of the circle and boxes, the orchestra pit, and a few yards of the stage, but those behind took their cue from them and applauded anyway. They clapped for the first living soul in the stalls. They clapped for an usherette; and then for a second usherette. They clapped for a meeting between the two usherettes. They clapped when a program, dropped by Beardie, parachuted lazily down into the orchestra pit; and they gave a special ovation to the fire curtain going up. They cheered the first dinner jacket to show its satin facings in a box and succeeded in driving its owner back into the shadows when he realized that he was the object of the Gods' admiration. His disappearance was, in turn, greeted with a regretful "Aaaah!"

By now Ike's chocolate box was empty and there

Fifteen

were twelve minutes to go. The orchestra members were filing into the pit with their provoking air of not knowing they were in a theatre: they were friends who had stopped on a bus tour to give a little concert by the roadside, quite unconscious that they were being watched by three thousand eyes that had nothing else to look at. A member of another flock of Rams in the gallery called: "What's the form, Ike?"

"Quite a turnout," yelled back Ike.

For once Terry agreed with her fat friend. "Old Palmer's stuff had better be good."

This threat was too much for their two neighbors. Weirdie cleared her throat menacingly, in order to give weight to every syllable: "Boronskaya would hardly be creating the principal role if it were not!"

"If what were not?" Terry had lost the thread.

Julian said silkily: "Boro—who?"

If it was meant to be a goad it served its purpose.

Beardie said, with what he hoped was biting irony: "Since you have stood in a queue all day to see her dance—"

Julian cut him short: "Not to see. To hear."

Terry pushed her program into his long, bony face. "Have *you* ever heard of Professor Palmer?"

"Never."

"You will—after tonight," prophesied Ike. He tapped the program. "See? Music composed by Andrew Palmer."

"We're all in his Master Class at the Academy," Terry explained.

"So Boro—whatsername—" Ike took the program back from Terry and searched for the great ballerina's name. "Boronskaya had better be good!"

At these impious words Beardie drew a deep breath, and the Ancient Curse of the Balletomanes was about to descend upon the Rams when Weirdie created a diversion. Far below, two figures in white ties and tailcoats had entered the box: one of them, burly in figure, bland in manner, obviously unaccustomed to the fierce light of public interest that shines upon occupants of the Royal Box; the other, tall and slim, gesturing him to a front seat. Weirdie shot halfway over the rail, and screamed: "Lermontov! Boris Lermontov! Bravo!"

Not to be outdone, the two Rams and their Ramess bellowed: "Palmer! Palmer! Bravo, Palmer!"

Their immediate neighbors took it up. Palmer, hearing himself identified by a chorus of Gods, fingered his beautiful white butterfly of a tie, half in embarrassment, half in delight, and glanced in a deprecating manner at his host, who had at once seated himself in the opposite corner, in the shadow of the red curtains, where he could see without being seen. Palmer, uncertain whether to acknowledge the welcome or not, gave half a glance up to the gallery, the other half at the brilliant house, then sat down.

The wave of enthusiasm in the gallery, receding, gathered new impetus from the arrival of Eustace Livingstone on the podium. The famous conductor, with his autocratic manner and notorious eccentricities, was dear to the public and regarded highly by the Rams. When the balletomanes clapped and called "Livingstone! Bravo! Livingstone!" Julian led his fellow students in a *"One-Two-Three Livy! Livy!"* which raised a sardonic grin from the conductor. After which, Julian leant across Terry and Ike, to tell the balletomanes, with emphasis, "We know *him.*"

The first performance of a new work in the theatre is like a public execution. Once the moment has come, the routine is short, unemotional, irrevocable, bloodcurdling. The victim—in this case the score—lay before the executioner—in this case the case-hardened Livingstone. His short, dynamic figure commanded attention. The noise died down. A hush fell on the spectators. The air trembled with expectation. The conductor pressed a button. A light answered. The houselights faded. The executioner reached for the baton lying on the open score. He gave a hard look at the wind section and raised both arms. For the composer, for anyone connected with the new work, the moment was bloodcurdling.

Julian shivered. With exaggerated care, as a dog turns round and round in its basket before collapsing into the chosen position, he settled himself to listen. He froze, his eyes on the executioner.

There was no introduction to the first theme; three strands—clarinet, oboe, flute—were intertwined from the beginning. The texture thickened and was enriched by a piccolo, drifting in and out, like the ribbon in a woman's braided hair. An expression of bliss crept over Julian's face—he had been telling people it would be wonderful, and it was wonderful. He knew Palmer's style. This was it, from the first bar, the real McCoy. Terry nudged Ike; their friend was in a trance.

Suddenly the strings took over with a staccato passage, tearing the strands to pieces. This second theme startled Julian and broke his concentration. He looked at his friends. The music had gripped them too; jammed together, they seemed oblivious of their surroundings. Then Terry's head came up like a startled pony's.

Julian whispered, "D'you remember my string quartet?"

Ike, irritated by the interruption, grunted, "Forget it."

But Terry understood, her own suspicions confirmed. "Your quartet! That's it! That's the Allegro from it!"

People around them shushed. The Rams ceased bleating. The short introduction came to an end. During the applause they whispered:

"Must be an accident."

"Did you show him your quartet?"

"Of course. I show him all my stuff—"

Ike was blunt. "You don't think he lifted it?"

Julian said warmly, "Of course not!" He only hoped he could forget the interruption. The light glowed on Livy's rostrum. The conductor raised his arms again. The curtain rose in silence. The music began. It was his music. Even the orchestration was the same. His head hurt. His world was crashing about him. He watched Livy's arms as if they did, indeed, wield the executioner's axe. The whole orchestra swept into the main theme . . . *his* theme. . . . He buried his face in his arms and groaned.

Terry whispered to Ike, "Shall we get him out of here?"

"Better wait for the intermission—Here! Steady on, old boy!"

Julian had jumped to his feet and, paying no attention to his friends, was struggling his way out along the row, causing savage shushings from music-lovers and balletomanes alike. Terry loyally jumped up and followed Julian, hissing angrily at Ike, "What are you waiting for?"

The waves caused by Julian's passing, just subsiding, were stirred again by her ruthless passage, to be parted in turn by Ike, who had taken a second or two to make up his mind. It was a wonder that all three were not lynched. As Julian stumbled out onto the gangway, the music reached its climax amidst tremendous applause and cries of *"Boronskaya! Boronskaya!"*

Blind, mad, suffering tortures to which the jealousies of first love betrayed were nothing, Julian ran up the steep steps to the exit, through the swinging doors, which closed on his heels, and down the stone stairs, leaving his friends further and further behind him, while the music, like the Furies, still pursued him. Terry called, "Julian! Wait!" But he paid no heed. He needed no friends. Friends always want to calm you down, sympathize with you, restrain you, just when you feel like murdering some bastard. Now he was at street level, in a concrete cul-de-sac, the doors to the street closed. But he kicked at the safety bar, the doors crashed open, and he was in the street, in fresh air. Behind him he heard hurrying feet. He turned left into the awakening Market. The first heavy trucks, loaded with vegetables from the country, fruit from the docks, were arriving. Porters were wheeling their barrows, laden with boxes, the iron wheels striking sparks out of the cobbles. An avalanche of rotting fruit cascaded into a vast iron container under Julian's nose. The sign above read PERISHABLES. He stepped aside to avoid a backing truck. Perish Professor Palmer!

The next couple of hours were almost a blank in Julian's memory. His feet must have known where they were going and strayed on accustomed paths, because he found himself among the crowd leaving the Wigmore Concert Hall, graveyard and springboard of so many musical reputations. There were hardly more than forty people leaving, and most of them looked like relatives, plus a second-string critic or two each hurrying home to his Bloomsbury bed-sitter, or to Lyon's Corner House, to write his piece about the new genius. To avoid meeting anybody he knew, Julian crossed to the other side of Wigmore Street. What a night to choose for a début, he thought—the night the Ballets Lermontov presented the masterpiece of that monument of British music, the noted, or notorious, Professor Palmer. The name made him hot under the collar, as he pictured the laurel-crowned composer accepting the plaudits of Covent Garden.

THERE ARE ALWAYS PEOPLE WHO HAVE to leave early to run and catch their train, but you don't expect them to be in a box in the grand tier at Covent Garden, dressed by Molyneux and Schiaparelli. As the curtain fell, to thunderous applause, one of the two ladies, the elder of the two (though she wouldn't have thanked you for pointing it out), appeared to be in a great hurry to go, while her young niece, madly clapping, was desperately hoping to catch a few curtain calls.

Lady Neston touched her ward's arm, "Come along, Vicky!"

But Vicky was deaf, dumb, and blind. It was doubtful whether she heard her aunt.

Lady Neston rose. Even that majestic movement made no impression.

"Vicky! We must go!" She had an obligation. She was Lady Ottoline Neston, famous hostess, who was giving a party tonight in honor of her protégé, Professor Palmer. He, in turn, had promised to bring the great Boris Lermontov, the supreme prize for any hostess in London. She had to be there to receive them. "Vicky!"

Vicky rose, but not to follow her aunt. She was ruining her gloves, as she beat her hands together and joined in the chant: "Boronskaya! Bravo! Boronskaya!"

The curtains remained obstinately closed, while the waves of applause beat against them. Vicky knew that the ballerina was surrounded by ministering slaves, carrying towels, combs, brushes, powder, like seconds around a prizefighter, working frantically to send their man up fresh for the next round. In another moment one of the gorgeous footmen would hold open the curtain in a caressing curve around the immaculate figure of the dancer,

Twenty-one

not a hair out of place, not a bead of perspiration visible, smiling sweetly, when a moment before she had been gasping air in in great gulps and streaming with sweat. It was all part of the game. Curtain calls are part of the performance.

Vicky wanted to study every nuance of Boronskaya's technique in completing the part: the startled glance of recognition that there *was* an audience; the realization that all that shouting and noise was not for the composer or conductor or choreographer, but for Little Me; the deprecating look of gratitude, the humble figure sinking in a curtsey to the floor, the bowed head; and then the glorious eyes raised to flash her humble thanks to her millions of fans: all this Vicky wanted to savor and treasure. And then the flowers! Nobody could receive flowers like Boronskaya: the open lips, the greedy hands, the little yelps of appreciation as bouquet after bouquet was borne on out of the darkness of the wings by smiling footmen to be piled in a sacrificial heap around her shining legs; the open arms and repeated curtseys to the boxes, to the grand circle, to the loges, to the stalls, with perhaps a momentary pause and a blown kiss to one particular figure in a box to whom all eyes turned in curiosity or amusement; then, the gracious turn toward her dancing partner, who had been grinding his teeth in obscurity waiting for his call, the generous gesture of a white arm which brought him on to share the storm of applause, the milking of that applause until it became a frenzy—"BORONSKAYA! *Bo-ron-skaya!* BOLESLAVSKY! *Boleslavsky! Bo-ron-skaya!*"—the gracious presentation of one wilting flower to her partner from the blossoms in her arms: all this had to be seen, analyzed, and stored away by Vicky.

"Please, Auntie Ottoline! Please! Just one curtain call! Just one—!"

"You have gone mad, Vicky! Come along at once!"

Lady Neston weighed in at 162 pounds, and countless murderous games of croquet in country houses had developed her muscles. She dragged her niece, still applauding, out into the corridor and started off at a great pace in the wrong direction, so that Vicky, brought to her senses and starting to giggle, had to run after her aunt and grab her.

"Not that way, Auntie! You're going backstage. This way!"

Hand in hand they dashed down the curving corridor, where doors to private boxes were starting to open, like a corridor in a nightmare, stumbled hysterically down the grand staircase, ran across the lobby, and came out into the waiting arms of the doorman, who hurried them to where Ram Singh and the white Lagonda were waiting with steam up. The doorman held the door open; Vicky helped her aunt in, picking up dropped opera glasses and stuffing in yards of satin and acres of chinchilla, stepping in nimbly herself with a grin to the doorman, who slammed the car door and stood at the salute, while the car drew away, before he hurried back to the crowds of people that were starting to appear. With a smooth, oily rush of power, the Lagonda overtook and passed a dawdling taxi and swept round into Long Acre, where the way lay clear, lined with trucks of flowers and vegetables, to St. Martin's Lane, the Mall, and Belgravia.

BY MIDNIGHT THE ROOSTING PIGEONS in Belgrave Square and Eaton Place looked down on a packed mass of Rolls-Royces, Bentleys, Hispano-Suizas, and Daimlers. Taxis were still rolling up, dropping their chattering passengers, and joining the rank at the cabmen's shelter, where they could eat sausage and mash and drink endless cups of tea until the party broke up.

A hired car deposited Professor Palmer and Lermontov on the red carpet that stretched from the mouth of the canopy, across the sidewalk, and up the steps to the blaze of light spilling from wide-open doors, where the deafening sound could be heard of the uninhibited English upper classes enjoying a reunion with their fellows, after having been subjected to a dose of culture.

Lermontov realized he had been deceived: "I thought you said a few people."

"This is Lady Neston's idea of a few people." As they climbed the steps, Palmer added: "It's her last party of the season. Next week she's off to Jamaica. And I believe Australia."

They went in, gave their trappings to the servant in the cloakroom, glanced in the mirrors, mounted the stairs, and were received by Lady Neston at the top. Not only was she as cool as a great London hostess can be—cucumbers took lessons from Lady Neston—but she had also had time to change her dress and was sporting the Neston emeralds.

She was greeting a famous actor manager as they arrived: "You wicked merciless man, Sir Gerald, I love you as much as I hate you. I hear from everybody that you've been counting my opening gambits to my guests. Are there really sixty-two in my repertoire?"

"Sixty-three after tonight, dear Lady Neston." He bent and negligently kissed her hand as if she were the only woman he'd ever loved, then passed on toward the buffet.

She opened arms and eyes to Palmer and his companion. "Welcome to the guest of the evening! Professor Palmer, we're all proud of you!" She even went to the length of clapping her hands gently together before giving an exaggerated start and screaming out, "But good heavens! Who is this? Don't tell me! The great man himself!"

Lermontov bowed formally over her hand.

"I never imagined I would get you here tonight. I must be a very clever woman."

He gave an enigmatic smile: "*Enchanté,* madame."

IN VICKY'S ROOM, HER IRISH MAID Maureen came running in. She had been leaning over the wall of the staircase. "He's come!"

Vicky, too, had changed: she was now an exquisite powder-blue ballerina, from flaming top to padded toe. She carefully tied the laces of her shoes, reflected full length in the wall-to-wall mirror that covered one end of the room. A practice bar ran the length of the other wall. At Maureen's words she glanced at a table where a caricature of Boris Lermontov was framed among signed photographs of Anna Pavlova, Tamara Karsavina, and her famous and beloved teacher and patron, Marie Rambert. The artist had caught Lermontov rather well. Vicky had hardly dared to hope he would turn up. Now that he was there, she felt composed, sure of herself.

"He looks very distingué, Miss Vicky."

"And d'you know why, Maureen? Because he *is* very distinguished. He's the most important man I shall ever meet in my life."

"To think of that! It would scare the living daylights out of me, meeting a man like that. I couldn't utter a word."

Vicky put her foot down and stood on her points, trying out and breaking in the shoes. She looked at herself in the mirror—tall, pale, composed—and swept back her red hair in a way she had: "I must be good tonight. I must!"

The color of her flaming hair in the mirror seemed paler than the genuine article, full of life and glitter, that set off her transparent skin. Maureen gave it a final touch

Twenty-five

of the brush. "Good, is it? Sure, didn't we all see you on the stage of the Mercury Theatre, moving and gliding, more beautiful than any real swan? We was all talking about it belowstairs."

"You don't realize. This is the most important night of my life!"

"Tsk! Tsk! Tell that to the marines. He's just a man. He'll fall for you like a ton of bricks."

"Boris Lermontov is . . . well . . . he's the most important person in the world for a dancer to meet. If he takes me on, nothing can stop me. *Nothing!*"

"It's a long climb to the top of the hill. . . ."

"I'm not going to climb. I'm going to *dance* there!"

LADY NESTON WAS CIRCULATING ON the arm of Professor Palmer, introducing him as her gently roaring lion, at the same time keeping a sharp eye on Boris Lermontov, her real quarry. Earlier, she had presented him to a pride of bankers, a secrecy of diplomats, and a benevolence of patrons; she saw with satisfaction that he was enjoying himself.

He was the center of a small group and was being addressed by a tall young lady, so thin and elegant that she resembled nothing so much as a mop dripping with sequins. "But don't you get awfully *bored,* Mr. Lermontov, with this sort of gypsy existence, going from country to country, with never a home of your own?"

"A gypsy's never bored, Mrs. Saumerez. I must be a gypsy, because it suits me perfectly."

Her husband, puffing a cigar, put his oar in: "But a permanent 'ome, Mr. Lermontov. Somewhere nice, where you can keep your pictures, your books, your knickknacks, and share 'em with your pet friends."

"And your pet enemies," chimed in a very small gentleman with a very large red carnation in his button-hole.

"And with your pets!" cried the mop lady. "Are you a dog man or a cat man, Mr. Lermontov? Let me guess! You have an air of *mystery* about you. You have exotic tastes. I can imagine you relaxing among the screams of peacocks, or among the sympathetic silence of tropical fish!"

Lermontov smiled. "A man who runs a ballet company has no need of exotic animals. By the nature of my profession I never stay more than two months in any one place. There are things I would not care to be without— a grand piano for instance. But one can always get a tolerable instrument. As for books, pictures . . . when you are accustomed to tour the world with a ballet company, a dozen ballets, and one hundred forty-seven crates of properties and costumes, it is not very difficult to add one or two crates more to the grand total. As for friends . . . I have friends, as I have enemies, everywhere, and when I—"

"Talking of grand pianos, Lermontov," interrupted Red Carnation, "you seem to have brought yours with you."

Footmen were pushing a piano into a prominent place in the ballroom under the supervision of a harassed accompanist. Lermontov's face fell. His air of pleasant, leisurely ease vanished. Without apology he left the group and went to meet Palmer, who was approaching with an embarrassed air. "Professor, something unpleasant is about to happen. If some fat harridan is going to sing, I must go! I cannot endure the human voice."

Palmer hastened to reassure him: "Neither, as it happens, can Lady Neston." As Lermontov still looked at him with suspicion, he added mischievously, "She has,

I believe, a niece who dances. But here is Lady Neston, coming to tell you herself."

He fled, leaving, to face one another, a master and mistress of the art of asking favors while declining to grant them. Nervous for Vicky, Lady Neston handled the situation with less than her usual skill. "Are you prepared for a surprise, Mr. Lermontov?"

"Do you mean a surprise, Lady Neston, or a shock?"

She took the plunge: "I have asked my niece to dance for us. What would you call that?"

"A shock."

She had steered him toward the conservatory where, to some extent, they were isolated. She laughed, but her laugh had a hollow ring. "Well, that was certainly candid." She was trying to save something from the wreckage of the conversation. "You know, I wouldn't dream of boring you with the performance of an amateur. Victoria has been dancing professionally for some time."

"Where?" His tone was merciless.

She felt herself getting flustered. "Well, at the Mercury Theatre, for instance. With Madame Rambert. The critics have spoken very highly of her work." She was getting indignant. Why wouldn't this ogre stop glaring at her?

Only when her silence admitted that she had nothing more to say did he ask, "Lady Neston, how would you define ballet?"

Now what on earth was the man driving at? Hadn't he got an ounce of charity? She floundered: "I suppose . . . one might call it the poetry of motion . . . ?"

"One might. But for me it is a great deal more than that." His tone was austere. "For me it is a religion. And one does not really care to see one's religion practiced in such surroundings as this." His glacial tone consigned

Lady Neston, her niece, and all her friends to the bottom circle of the Inferno. "You understand, I'm sure."

LADY NESTON TOILED UP THE STAIRS from the ballroom with a heavy heart. Everything had been going so splendidly, and now she felt an old, useless woman. She found her niece limbering up at the bar in front of the mirror, looking a perfect picture, as Maureen exclaimed, proud of her own contribution to the evening's excitement. As she saw her aunt, Vicky cut short her exercises and turned in excitement: "Now?"

Lady Neston shook her head. She couldn't speak.

In a flash Vicky understood: "He doesn't want me to dance!"

Lady Neston made a despairing gesture. She struggled to find words: "No, dear. I'm afraid he doesn't. He said . . . he said . . . Oh! what does it matter what he said? The man's a complete brute. Now listen, Vicky. I want you to do something for me—not for yourself, but for me. You're to put on your prettiest dress and your mother's earrings that I had reset, and come down and join the party. I want him to have a good look at you. After all, that's why we're giving this party. Perhaps, if you could know one another—"

"I'd rather die!"

"Rubbish! Do as I say. That green dress from Chanel is just the thing. Your girl can be getting it ready while you do your hair. Ballerinas must be able to do a quick change. I won't have you staying up here brooding about it."

Ten years ago, when Vicky was eleven years old, and a pupil of Pavlova's, the news had come of her parents' death in the Sydney yacht race. When her aunt sent for her and told her there had been an accident, the child said little and seemed unable to take in the news. But two hours later she had been discovered at the practice bar, collapsed from exhaustion. She had worked and worked to banish the news from her mind. The episode had made a deep impression on Lady Neston. She didn't want a repetition of that occasion.

YOUNG LORD STOCKTON, ONE OF LADY Neston's circle and a member of the Royal Ocean Club, was the first to see her join the party. She wore her hair to her shoulders and looked radiant. Before his lordship's admiring eyes she passed through the crowd, with a word here, a wave there, smiling, laughing, chatting, but obviously looking for somebody, a definite object in mind. He followed her into the next room, where a cocktail bar had been set up. She had twice refused a glass of champagne from the trays proffered by footmen. Now she asked the barman for a champagne cocktail. Anyone who knew Vicky intimately could have told she was on the warpath. She hardly ever drank. The barman apologized: he was out of lemon peel. As Lord Stockton approached, another voice said "Barman! A champagne cocktail, please." It was Lermontov, who had sauntered in from the other room.

The young man stopped, disappointed, then strolled away to rejoin the others.

The barman started to repeat his apologies, but Lermontov brushed them aside with authority: "Use orange peel." Then, to Vicky: "I recommend it."

She made no reply, but her silence was accepted by the barman as consent. He set to work.

Meanwhile Lermontov's sharp eyes played over Vicky's serious face. He was disposed to be friendly. "You know, at parties you're supposed to enjoy yourself."

The barman, in his wisdom, placed the two glasses on the bar rather closer together than the relative positions of his two customers warranted. They contemplated his handiwork: the *coupes,* not too shallow, not too deep, ice-cold; the wine still bubbling; a crust of sugar around the rims; a dash of bitters . . . It could be a description of the man himself, Vicky thought, lifting her glass.

He lifted his, and said, "But perhaps, like myself, you don't like parties." He took a sip, giving her a quick but courteous acknowledgment before doing so, and went on: "Still, as parties go, this might have been a great deal worse. We were, it appears, to have been treated to a little dancing exhibition. But now I understand we are to be spared that horror."

She sounded very angry: "Mr. Lermontov!"

The sound of his own name checked him an instant, rather than her tone. Then he answered: "Mademoiselle?"

"I am that horror."

There was dead silence. The barman polished his glasses. Vicky was stony-faced. Lermontov found the faux pas more fascinating than awkward—probably the barman knew who she was and had seen disaster coming all the way. Lermontov gave him an apologetic smile. "On second thought, I prefer lemon peel. Would you get some?"

The barman took his cue and withdrew.

Lermontov turned and regarded Vicky's delicious profile with appreciation. "It's a little late for apologies."

"Much too late."

"All the same, I'm deeply sorry."

She looked him in the eye. She had green eyes. "But you're not sorry I didn't dance, are you?"

"No."

"Why?"

"Because, my dear Miss . . . ?"

"Victoria Page."

"Miss Page . . . if I accept an invitation to a party, I don't expect to find myself at an audition."

"In other words, I behaved rather commonly. I admit it. And I'd do it again!"

There was no doubt about the red hair: it positively bristled. Equally there was no doubt about the temperament of its owner. The artist in Lermontov was moved. He replied, "What has always interested me in people is not what they do, but why they do it. So I shall now ask you, Miss Page . . . Why do you want to dance?"

He shot the question at her, and she answered with equal directness: "Mr. Lermontov . . . Do you want to live?"

Her adroitness amused him: "Of course."

"Why?"

There was more to this girl than an assured place in society and personal beauty. Lermontov lowered his guard and said with sincerity, "You're a very intelligent girl."

But that wasn't what she wanted to hear. She looked straight back at him, as to an equal. "I'm a very good dancer, too."

Lermontov realized that, in spite of his expressed intention, he had been given a remarkable audition.

Three

WHEN YOU ARE BURSTING TO LET OFF
steam in the shape of a letter, it is a frustrating experience to find an open post office, tables, inkwells, pens—
and no notepaper. Julian had stormed into Wimpole
Street, which besides being memorable for Elizabeth
Barrett Browning, has a post office that stays open all
night: a refuge for those who have missed their last bus,
had a quarrel at home, or have no home to quarrel in. Julian looked around at his fellow night owls. In one respect they were all alike: they were writing. Writing
what? Letters, poems, last wills and testaments—who
knows? If they were caught loafing they had to leave. So
they wrote.

Julian emptied his pockets onto the table. A gray-
moustached postman, opening the letter box to collect

the mail, misunderstood the situation: "Got a letter to post?"

"I haven't written it yet."

"Plenty of time. There's a collection every hour on the hour."

"When will it be delivered?"

"Every letter posted before one A.M. catches the first delivery. If it's a London district."

"Thanks."

"Don't mention it."

But Julian hadn't finished yet. "Is there a slot machine for paper and envelopes?"

"Only for stamps. But they'll sell you a letter card at the counter."

Julian considered this, while the postman swept the last of the letters into his Royal Mail sack. Finally Julian shook his head. "A letter card isn't good enough."

The postman began to take an interest in this pale, sandy-haired young man, whose eyes burned as if he had a fever. Perhaps he was a poet. He'd never met a poet. He asked with gravity, "Is it important?"

With equal gravity, Julian answered that it was.

"Is it a girl?"

"It's a matter of life and death."

"Wait here!" In a minute or two he was back with a sheet of paper and an envelope. "Mind if I ask what you do?"

"I'm a conductor."

"Tram or bus?"

"Orchestra. I conduct orchestras. I'm a composer."

"You don't say! Listen, there's one thing I always wanted to know. Do you follow the orchestra, or do they follow you?"

Julian held up his pen like a baton: "They follow me."

There were about a dozen people standing in front of writing desks, writing away merrily. Julian got stuck after a single word. That word of course was "Dear." What nonsense! he thought. How can you address a person as dear, when you hate his guts? When all you want to write is:

You're a thief, a liar, and a phony. Good day!

And why wish a man a good day, when you hope he'll slip on a banana peel coming out of Covent Garden and break his neck? Why write to him at all? He had a better idea.

He dipped the nib of his pen in post-office ink, removed the inevitable piece of hair from the point, and wrote, "Dear Mr. Lermontov."

For the next few minutes he wrote steadily, pouring out his heart to this stranger:

> *I am a student at the Royal Academy of Music in my fourth year. I intend to be a composer and conductor. I am in Professor Palmer's Master Class. I show him all my work. We discuss everything I compose.*
>
> *Tonight your ballet company presented a new ballet,* Heart of Fire, *with music composed by Andrew Palmer. I had to leave the theatre soon after the curtain rose. The whole overture, or most of it, was lifted from my String Quartet, Opus 2. In Act One the two principal themes, the development that follows, and probably a lot more. Please forgive this muddled letter. I ought really to write to Professor Palmer. But I can't. Just as I couldn't talk to my mother about sex. But I had to write to somebody, or I would explode from sheer bitterness. I don't want you to*

do anything. I don't want anything from you, or from anybody else. I just want somebody who cares about this ballet to know the truth. Forgive me for choosing you.

Sincerely,
Julian Craster

Fortunately the old postman hadn't waited for the letter, because Julian had no intention of posting it; he was going to deliver it by hand.

The famous hotel where he knew Lermontov was staying was only a few minutes' walk away, in Mayfair. As he made his way across Oxford Street, he imagined a conversation with the haughty head porter. It went something like this:

"How did you know Mr. Lermontov is staying with us, sir? It's kept rather confidential."

Then he would reply, nonchalantly, "I know a friend of his. Professor Palmer."

"I see, sir. Of course that's different."

The reality was different, too. Julian had never been inside such a hotel in his life. Its elegance impressed him. The carpets were thick; a raised voice was unthinkable. He liked the open fire in the period grate in the lobby: its gentle warmth, after the chill outside, was reassuring. Julian waited, while the receptionist handed a key and some messages to a dinner jacket accompanied by a lady for whom two hundred mink had given up their skins. Perhaps the couple had been to Covent Garden and had supped afterwards. Julian suddenly realized he was very hungry. There is a limit to the nourishment obtainable from hard-centered chocolates.

The frock-coated receptionist answered the telephone, spoke in a respectful murmur, made a note on his pad, looked at Julian. "Sir?"

"I would like to leave a letter for Mr. Boris Lermontov."

He held out the letter, but it was declined. "Mr. Lermontov is not staying with us at present."

"He's moved out?"

"Yes, sir."

"Have you got his new address?"

"I'm afraid we haven't."

It was a polite refusal, but Julian's sensibilities were on hair-triggers: he was ready to take on the entire capitalist world that night—the wind in the streets against the comfortable glow in the fireplace! But in spite of his training, the receptionist was not much older than Julian. He read his thoughts and was sympathetic. Julian sensed this and almost pleaded. "It's very important to me."

The receptionist held out his hand for the letter. "Leave it with me. I'll see he gets it." He saw that Julian hesitated and hastened to silence his doubts. "Somebody will be calling for Mr. Lermontov's letters in the morning." From a lower shelf he produced a tray with a number of letters and telegrams. "Even if we had the address, I couldn't let you have it. Drop your letter in here. I promise you he'll get it."

Now that his letter had joined the others on Lermontov's tray, Julian realized how tired he was. The thought of the streets and of the long walk home made him reluctant to leave the fire. Perhaps this understanding bloke could find him a corner where he could curl up and sleep: in the unlit part of the lobby, in the darkest corner. . . . But a party of Americans rotated through the doors into the lobby, demanding in chorus to know where the bar was. It took the combined efforts of the night porter and the receptionist to convince them that the bar had closed at midnight and would remain closed until eleven o'clock next morning. There were loud protests. Finally, reassured that the floor waiter was on duty, they crowded into the lift and vanished skyward, singing "Bye Bye Blackbird."

In the street the outside porter asked the gentleman if he wanted a taxi. No, the gentleman didn't want a taxi. The gentleman volunteered the information that the night was lovely, perfect for walking, and strolled off in the direction of Grosvenor Square.

He had a long slog ahead of him. The buses wouldn't start running again until 5:00 A.M., if then. His digs were on Primrose Hill, on the far side of Regent's Park, the first of the low foothills rising to the heights of Hampstead. He had gone there, on his arrival in London from the country, attracted by the name. He had stayed there because it was cheap. It was certainly not convenient, unless you were one of those early-to-bed-and-early-to-rise students.

It was not the first time that Julian had faced the long walk home through Regent's Park. But usually he was accompanied by friends, male and female, students like himself, talking, laughing, disputing, seeing him on his way, say, to the gates of the park, where, at an all-night coffee stall, they could get thick mugs of tea and hot bangers, with mustard on the sausages so strong it brought tears to your eyes. Still arguing, they would turn back down Baker Street and he would turn back with them, seeing *them* on their way, sometimes as far as Hyde Park Corner, where there was another coffee stall; and so on, to and fro, until they'd talked the dawn into the sky and it wasn't worth going home and there would be a pooling of the cash in their pockets to pay for breakfast at the Corner House. But now he faced the hour's walk home alone and at the nadir of body and spirit.

He crossed Oxford Street, just another weary student trudging back to his digs. The sign ORCHARD

STREET, up there on the tall facade of Selfridge's store, made him think of Covent Garden . . . "Cherries so red! Strawberries ripe!" He remembered the buskers in the queue. A burst of music—his music—filled his ears. How glorious that music had sounded with a full orchestra and Livy conducting! How much better it would sound with himself conducting! How about a symphonic poem? *Late Night Walk to Primrose Hill.* How should it start? Well, obviously at Covent Garden! Where else? With a young couple watching *The Marriage of Figaro.* He would quote from the opera, one of its loveliest melodies, young Cherubino's breathless aria. What would old Palmer say to that? Come to that, what would Mozart say? Julian giggled. He whistled the tune as he marched up Baker Street. Baker Street! 221B! Sherlock Holmes and Professor Moriarty . . . a change of mood, mysterious, a bit sinister. . . . Still composing, he passed Baker Street Underground Station. The tall iron gates of Regent's Park yawned before him. A sign read TO THE ZOO, where the lions were roaring. Steady on, Craster! Don't let your artistic imagination run away with you! Lions roar at night in Africa, because they're out hunting. In the zoo they put their heads down at night like anyone else. All right, we'll soon fix that! See the dark shape of that boat on the lake? Holmes and Watson have found the body of an ex–Cabinet Minister! Ting-a-ling! An ambulance is arriving, followed by the fire brigade and searchlights. Hark! A roar from the zoo. The noise and the lights have woken up the bloody lions! Bassoons and trombones! Muted.

Now the young lovers are crossing the canal into Prince Albert Road. The roaring dies away behind them as they climb the slopes of Primrose Hill. Alpine music . . . cowbells . . . a distant yodel. . . . Julian chuckled: if only that ballet-crazy couple, Beardie and Weirdie, could see him now! He, Julian Craster, mountaineer and

Thirty-nine

conqueror of the Gallery Steps of Covent Garden, panting up Primrose Hill, which rises, stern and forbidding, 220 feet above sea level! He's at the top.

Julian stopped composing. He had arrived home. *Late Night Walk to Primrose Hill* was roughed out and felt quite fresh. An hour ago, life had seemed impossible. An idea had come and, suddenly, all worry was forgotten. Inspiration took over; he started to work and everything seemed possible.

He opened the front door with his latchkey, pressed the automatic switch, and ran up to his second-floor room where, for thirty shillings a week, Mrs. Tuckwell provided bed and breakfast. The switch gave him exactly ninety seconds to reach his room and turn on the light. He won hands down. He closed the door. There was a message on the floor (it had been pushed under the door), and there was a sealed letter on the table. He read the message first: it was in two different handwritings, both familiar to Julian. Ike had scribbled:

> *I lost a bet with Terry. Thought you'd go straight home. She didn't. Give us a ring when you come in. Doesn't matter how late.*
>
> *Ike*

Terry's contribution was mostly exclamation points:

> *Darling! I won a bet on you! Five quid! You know I'm a fatalist! Mark my words it all happened for a good reason! Let's you and I spend his money together! Just you and me!!*
>
> *X Terry X*

What pals! They'd been here looking for him. Still, Ike had a car, a venerable Model-T Ford. They didn't have to walk. Much.

He almost didn't open the letter on the table. He recognized the official envelope. Anyone who borrowed a book or a score from the library of the Royal Academy and failed to return it within two weeks got these official chasers. Julian always had several at any given moment. He sat on the bed, and tore it open. It was a handwritten note from Professor Palmer:

> *Dear Craster,*
>   *At long last I've spoken to Lermontov about you. Give him a day or two to get settled in his apartment, then telephone him at Mayfair 5462 for an appointment. Good luck.*
>
>> *Yours ever,*
>> *A. Palmer*

Julian sat staring at the letter. His Innocence A. Palmer wrote as if he hadn't the slightest idea of what he had done.

Well, what had he done?

When discussing phrasing, harmonics, tonality, modulation, and a thousand other fundamentals in music, students and teachers exchange themes and ideas. Who can tell, several months later, who contributed what? "Dear Craster"? Or "Yours ever, A. Palmer" . . .? The more he thought about it, the bigger fool he felt. Tomorrow he'd go through his notebooks and diary. He might find confirmation of his doubts. Anyway, what's a string quartet? Brahms wrote dozens of them before he thought one worth publishing.

God! What a fool! His letter to Lermontov! What a fool's fool! He could do something about that. But he'd have to be pretty nippy. Not much sleep for him tonight. Let's see! Whoever collected Lermontov's mail wouldn't do so before seven or seven-thirty, if for no other reason than to include the morning's post. He ought to go right back to the hotel while his friend the receptionist was still on duty. Coaxing his letter out of a stranger couldn't be done. He stretched out on the bed and read the brief letter again. "Yours ever, A. Palmer." He had about twenty-five bob he'd saved up to pay the fare for one of his rare visits home. If he could find a cab, he could ask the driver to wait at the hotel. He could be back in half an hour and sleep till Mrs. Tuckwell brought the breakfast tray . . . He languidly read the letter again. . . . It dropped from Dear Craster's hand.

Four

THERE WAS A KNOCK AT THE DOOR.

Mrs. Tuckwell's peculiar booming whisper inquired, "Mr. Craster! Are you all right?"

No answer. She opened the door with great care, averting her eyes in case her lodger was improperly dressed. Julian lay fully dressed on the bed: the fact that he had more clothes on than usual shocked her as much as if he were naked. She whisperboomed, "Mr. Craster! Haven't you taken your clothes off all night?"

It was broad daylight. The alarm clock said seven-thirty. Julian was furious—with himself and with the world.

The fact that he had no time to talk to her added fervor to her whispered indictment: "I heard you come in—thundering upstairs like a herd of elephants. It was after two o'clock! There's your dear father making all sorts of sacrifices to have you taught your music, and what do you do?"

He had flung off his coat, lathered his face and was scraping away for dear life. "Well, what do I do?"

His landlady, who had a soft spot for Julian, approached him, still carrying the breakfast tray, still booming softly like a warning bell in a thick fog.

"Your two friends were here asking for you last night. They wanted to wait in your room. Students! No better than they should be! They know my rules. Aren't you going to eat your nice egg? Where are you off to now?"

"Mind your own business, old Tucker-Upper!"

He seized her, tray and all, whirled her around, sat her down on the bed, and ran downstairs, leaving her speechless. Eons ago, she had been a smart parlormaid in a famous country mansion, not far from the village where Julian was born. There she had been trained never to raise her voice above a whisper, yet still to make herself audible. It suited the housekeeper at the Hall, but left her at a disadvantage in a shouting match with Julian. She sighed, then ate his egg.

THE TAXI WAS A NEEDLESS LUXURY. IT was almost as old as its driver, who seemed to be wearing four overcoats. A bus would have got him there quicker.

He asked the cabby, "How much?"

"Seven and six."

Julian protested: "Your meter says five and three!"

"Why ask, then?"

In the hotel lobby, the fire had been freshly made up, a pillar of smoke rising from its heart beneath the heap of black coal. Was this the kind of fire that burned inside every creative person? Even in Professor Palmer? A fire, sometimes smoldering, sometimes smoking, occasionally bursting into a glorious blaze?

Julian told an abridged version of his story to a group consisting of hotel guests, two pages, and two new receptionists, one of whom wore glasses and answered, "Someone fetched Mr. Lermontov's letters already."

"Do you know when?"

"Before I came on this morning."

A squeaky page boy, festooned with morning papers, volunteered, "Mr. Dmitri took them at quarter past seven."

He got a glance reprimanding him—and conspiratorial smiles from Julian's sympathizers. The receptionists went over to the majority, and Julian took advantage of the prevailing good-will: "Perhaps you could let me have his new address?"

"We haven't got it." Of course they wouldn't give it to him.

Julian played his ace: "May I use the telephone?" He fumbled for Palmer's letter.

The receptionist said, "The page will show you the telephone for outside calls."

Julian grinned at the little rascal, who grinned back, seeing half a crown in Julian's eye.

But the receptionist put his foot down: "Not you! You!" He beckoned a still smaller page, who, as Mark Twain remarked, was not so much a page as a paragraph. The page escorted Julian to the phone booth, where, consulting his letter, he called Mayfair 5462. The page heard him say, before he closed the door, "Mr. Dmitri? My name is Craster. I have an important favor to ask you—"

When Julian finished the call, he couldn't resist stopping at the desk on his way out and handing the receptionist a piece of paper. "Thanks for your help. Here is Mr. Lermontov's address. In case you may need it."

The receptionist looked blankly after the departing man, holding the address in his hand. His colleague pushed over a large volume. It contained guests' forwarding addresses, including Lermontov's. They compared the two. They tallied.

FROM THE HOTEL TO CURZON STREET was only a few minutes' walk. Julian crossed through Berkeley Square, the haunt of ghosts and nightingales. A baby was yelling its head off, its nanny was pushing the perambulator along the gravel walks beneath the giant plane trees. The square reminded him of his first visit to London, with his father, a reward for winning some prize or other at school.

First there had been the exciting journey by train to Liverpool Street Station in the City. His father took him across the bridge to a platform where dozens of post-office vans were drawn up, waiting for the Royal Mail, their teams of horses munching their breakfast, noses deep in their nosebags. His father had spoken with the supervisor who, if not God himself, was at least his visible presence. Craster senior was postmaster of Debenbridge, as his father and grandfather had been before him. Crasters had been the backbone of the post office ever since Rowland Hill introduced the penny post.

While the two men gossiped, Julian patted the horses. He had already set his heart on being the church organist. When he was eight and a half, he had confided this ambition, not to his father, but to the teacher at the village school, who had warned him that the vicar's son already had his eye on the job. Julian had bided his time and studied the piano. . . . He helped the horse he was patting to forage deep in his nosebag for a precious piece of salt that had sunk to the very bottom.

His father called him and announced they were going to Piccadilly Circus by bus; the open top of a bus was the finest way to see the sights. Julian had set his heart on traveling by the Underground Railway more than anything else. But bus it was! Somehow or other they ended up at Berkeley Square, feeding the pigeons with crumbs from their sandwiches. Julian looked through the railings at the tall trees in the garden in the center of the square.

"Can we go inside, Dad?"

"Whatever for?"

"To measure the trees."

"What with?"

"My arms."

"Some of those trees must be twenty feet round."

"You can stand on one side and I can stand on the other and see if we can touch fingers."

They tried the iron gate. It was locked.

"It's private, see?"

"What about those nannies?"

"They've got keys."

"We could ask them to let us in."

"They wouldn't do it. They're worse than the nobs who live here."

THAT WAS BEFORE THE GREAT WAR. There were still nobs living in Mayfair, although horses had given way to motorcars. He turned out of the square and ran down the steps into Curzon Street. He found the house, which had been converted into a few extremely elegant and expensive furnished apartments. He was in luck: the door was open and a delivery truck from a piano firm was blocking the entrance. A uniformed porter was trying to decide whether to use his carpet sweeper now or wait until the men took themselves off. He allowed Julian to use the house telephone and, when nobody answered it, to go upstairs by himself. Dmitri's regal ways had undermined his confidence.

The trail blazed by the piano was clearly visible. Julian arrived at another open door. Through an elegant vestibule he could see a number of men in the flat: piano-movers, floor waiters, a valet—and Dmitri, supreme.

"The piano always by the window!" he directed. "No! No! The other way! Turn it so that the daylight falls on the left side. The desk, over here! No pictures on the walls!" While the men moved the furniture, Dmitri started himself to strip the walls of pictures. "The telephone, here! Not there! You must get a longer cord. . . . The breakfast table out of the sunlight. . . . So! I alone serve him! You! Invisible! He cannot bear strange faces."

The other men rushed about executing his orders. Suddenly Dmitri clapped his hands. "Attention! I hear him coming! Go! And close the outer door behind you!" He tipped the piano-movers and shooed the lot of them out. They scurried about like startled sheep chased by a lone sheepdog, each of them bigger than his pursuer, but none of them certain what he should do next.

In the hall Dmitri met Julian head on. "What do you want?"

"I spoke to you on the telephone. About a letter—"

"Mr. Lermontov never sees anyone in the morning. You go now!"

"Who is it, Dmitri?" said a voice from the inner room.

Dmitri hesitated, in two minds. "You stay now!" He went to report to his master. The intruder could hear every word. "A young man, Boris Lermontov. He telephoned from the hotel. I told him you were sleeping, but he did not believe me."

"Then you must be a poor liar, Dmitri, or he's a clever young man. Show him in."

The education of Dmitri was never-ending. His first lesson should have been never to be surprised. Life with Lermontov was full of surprises, yet Dmitri, somehow, never got used to them. He came back for Julian, introduced him, then busied himself with serving his master's breakfast.

Julian was conscious of the expensive furniture, the central heating, the scent of eau-de-cologne on freshly shaven skin, the man himself, in a Tartar robe (probably designed by the painter Sergei Ratov, chief designer of the company), his hands full of letters, newspapers, telegrams, his voice neither tenor nor bass—a warm baritone: "What can I do for you, Mr. Craster?"

He seemed neither friendly nor unfriendly. He sat down, without asking his visitor to follow suit, and said, "Serve breakfast, Dmitri."

Embarrassed, Julian hesitated.

Lermontov glanced at the young man. "Well?"

"Forgive me, Mr. Lermontov, but it's a matter of great importance to me." He stopped again. His throat felt dry. He needed a word of encouragement. He didn't get it. Whatever he had to do and say, he would have to do and say on his own. He forced himself to speak. "I'll come to the point."

"Yes?"

"Last night I wrote you a letter. It was a stupid letter and I should like it back before you read it, please."

"I see."

Lermontov reached for the pile of letters and began going through them. As he came to one near the bottom of the pile, Julian said, stretching out his hand, "That's the one!"

After a slight pause Lermontov picked it up. "Un-fortunately, Mr. Craster, I have already read this letter."

He showed that it had been slit open. Julian's response was a very slow "O-o-oh!" Only now did the two men size each other up. Dmitri started serving breakfast for one. Out of the corner of his slanting eyes he watched the other two. His master, after a searching glance at Julian, took the letter out of the envelope, propped it up, and reread it, while his hands went automatically through the breakfast ritual. Dmitri, as acolyte, served deftly, one move ahead.

When he had finished reading, Lermontov spoke, always continuing to breakfast: "It is worth remembering that it is more disheartening to have to steal than to be stolen from. Take Professor Palmer. Even if he were a second-rate composer, he's an intelligent man. He knows all about plagiarism. He knows that neither he nor anybody else could get away with such a thing as this. You have been master and pupil together for so long, it is perfectly possible that you have learned things from him—techniques, tricks—that you believe now were your own. . . ."

Julian nodded. It made sense. His one thought was to get away as soon as possible.

But Lermontov was pointing to the letter with the butter knife. "You say here you have composed a string quartet, among other things. Would you care to play me something?"

Julian was past being surprised by this amazing man. He said, "If you wish," and sat down at the piano.

"You can also tell me if the piano needs tuning," Lermontov said.

Julian ran his fingers over the keys. It was quite unintentional, but anyone who knew it well would have recognized in his arpeggios the first theme of *Heart of Fire*.

Lermontov certainly did and shook his head, speaking with his mouth full: "Something indisputably your own, Mr. Craster."

Julian paused. Lermontov, behind his back, threw him a keen glance. Then Julian started to play and Lermontov went on with breakfast. Melody filled the room, the sort of melody which worshippers of the gods made in the dawn of the world. Lermontov opened a letter. Gradually a tune made itself heard, vanished, returned, became stronger, ravished the ear. Dmitri brought scrambled eggs and bacon. Julian, his back turned to his listeners, started to speak through the music. "It's an opera. *Cupid and Psyche.* It was submitted to them at Covent Garden before Christmas. . . . They called me in a couple of months ago. They're really interested. . . . They've kept it, anyway. A good sign, I suppose. . . . This is the passacaglia."

A great landscape was being unveiled to his listener's ears. The music changed to a processional march. "The people are taking Psyche in procession up the mountain to be sacrificed. . . . Bassoons. . . . This is where the first violins come in. . . . Now the harp. . . ."

He glanced over his shoulder. Lermontov was reading a letter. Dmitri was pouring more coffee. He stopped playing, staring at the keys in silence.

Lermontov looked up. "Is that all? That was very interesting."

Julian stood abruptly. He felt cheated; even worse, he felt like a child cheated by a grownup. He *was* childish, when he said, "For a moment I thought you were really interested."

He turned and made for the door; Lermontov let him open it before he said, "By the way, Mr. Craster, I need an extra coach for the orchestra, to help out my conductor. Would you be interested?"

The answer came like a shot: "Yes. I would."

Fifty-one

"I'm glad you're not one of those masterminds who want to think everything over. I can't give you very much money to begin with. Eight pounds a week? And expenses?"

Julian stuttered his acceptance.

"Good. Get yourself some breakfast and come to the theatre. We are rehearsing on stage this morning."

His world reeling, Julian was about to obey.

"Your letter, Mr. Craster!" Lermontov was holding it up between finger and thumb. Julian took it from him. "If you take my advice, you will destroy it."

"I shall!" He was about to go, but Lermontov stopped him.

"One more thing, Mr. Craster! You haven't told me—"

Julian was beginning to understand his new boss: "If the piano needs tuning? It doesn't."

The next moment he was gone. A pity—he missed the faint smile on Lermontov's face.

Five

WHAT A NIGHT! AND WHAT A DAY! Julian found himself in the street. He must have got there by levitation. What a perfectly marvelous, absolutely stupendous, totally incredible day! And it was still going on! Some people were just getting up! Some people were still in bed! Where was the nearest telephone booth? Shepherd's Market. He levitated down Curzon Street. He'd been to a first night. He'd been plagiarized. (It sounded painful. It was!) He'd denounced the thief—to *Boris Lermontov!* He turned under the archway into the market. He'd met the great man—and he really was a great man! He'd asked him—Julian Craster—to play some of his stuff! He'd given him a job! And it wasn't half past nine yet! He lifted the telephone and dialed Ike's number.

Fifty-three

It rang and rang: *Brr-brr! Brr-brr!* Julian was piti-less. If old Ike thought he would hang up, he had another guess coming. *Brr-brr! Brr-click!* Aha!

A sleepy voice said "Who is it?"

"It is I," said a voice with a heavy Russian accent. "I am being the hoosband of the great Russian ballerina La Boronskaya, no? You have made the corny joke about my wife, yes? I am coming up to see you! We fight a duel!"

"Julian!" Ike shouted, now thoroughly awake. "How are you? Where are you? Am I glad to hear your bathtub tenor!"

"No duel?" persisted the outraged husband.

"You're the worst actor in the world! Where are you?"

"Mayfair! I've just left the great Boris Lermontov." Julian spoke in his natural voice. "I'm on my way to Covent Garden. He's invited me to join his company and I've accepted." Now that he was speaking the exact truth, it sounded a bigger lie than ever.

"Stop fooling!"

"Cross my heart! Hope to die!"

"Are you home? I'll come and get you. We'll pick up Terry and have lunch at a pub—"

"I can't. Let's make it dinner. At the Corner House. It's on me! If one of you lends me the money."

"Julian! You are all right, are you?" Ike sounded quite worried.

"Yes, tovarich, I'm in the pink. See you seven o'clock."

"Well, I hope so. And try and think up a better story. We're not going to swallow that one!"

Outside the phone booth, there was a litter bin. Julian took the libelous letter out of his pocket and was about to drop it in, when he thought better of it.

Watched dispassionately by two errand boys, he tore the letter across and across, made a little pile in the gutter, lit an expiatory bonfire, and fanned the flames with his hat until it was totally consumed. This sacrifice performed, he dismissed *Heart of Fire* from his mind, put on his hat, bought two doughnuts at the baker's under the archway, and, munching them out of the bag, set his course down Piccadilly to Covent Garden.

THE MORNING RUSH HOUR IN THE streets was over, but not at Covent Garden. The big trucks rumbling back to their farms and market gardens had been replaced by the vans of restaurants and the barrows of barrow-boys, lining each side of Long Acre and leaving for the traffic only a narrow canyon carpeted with rotting vegetables. Garbage trucks and their crews were shoveling and sweeping the streets; under the great glass roofs of the market, porters were hosing down the flagstones as Julian picked his way, not without difficulty, to Floral Street. Only thirty-six hours ago he and Ike, Terry, Beardie, and Weirdie, had started to queue at the gallery door. He looked back condescendingly, from the height of a member of the Lermontov Company, to that time, ages ago, when he had been a simple student, a Ram.

Musing thus, he slipped on a banana skin and was nearly run over by an opulent limousine, which beat him to the stage door by a yard of saffron paint and chromium steel, surmounted by a silver replica of a Degas ballerina. Julian decided he would have the same make, after the success of his *Cupid and Psyche* opera, only with a coupé body and with a live ballerina astride the bonnet. The shining door of the car swung open and a tall gentleman got out. He looked like a Guardsman.

Two slender hands passed a diminutive white poodle to his care. He accepted the trust with gravity. Two shining silk legs, shod with high-heeled shoes, ornamented with extravagant bows, now swung into Julian's view, followed by the rest of a sleek and elegant female. The poodle shivered, while a discussion began in the French language about his immediate destiny. Was he to go with his mistress, or stay in the Mercedes-Benz with his master? His name appeared to be Jo-Jo.

Ju-Julian went inside and found Jerry in one of his moods. In answer to Julian's confident good-morning, he merely grunted. In answer to Julian's statement that he was a member of the ballet company, Jerry reached for his list.

"Name?"

"Julian Craster. C-R-A—"

"Not on the list."

The lovely poodle-fancier came in, sans poodle, just in time to hear an irritated Julian say, "As Mr. Lermontov only engaged me this morning, it isn't likely that my name would be on the list, is it?"

She looked with approval at this interesting young man: he was young and sympathetic and therefore worthy of attention. She said, in delightfully accented English, "Good morning, Jerree-ee-e!"

The answer came in fractured French: "Bonjour, madame. They are cherchaying après vous! Got the search parties out. Compris?" He handed her a bunch of letters along with the warning, and awaited her answer which was dismissively Parisian.

"Ah! Flute!"

Julian stepped forward, determined not to be put down in front of this enchanting person. "Please don't keep me waiting any longer."

"What is your name, young man?" inquired the

lady. She was at least three years older than Julian, and a Parisienne, which entitled her to address him as if there were forty years between them. Julian told her. "Well, Jerree, if Monsieur Lermontov 'ave asked Mr. Craster to come this morning, I am sure it is all right."

"Okay by me, Madame! Okay by me." In the same fatalistic tone, Jerry would have agreed to hand over his precious keys to Monsieur Dmitri. He disclaimed responsibility for Julian and shoved the list out of sight.

The lady addressed Julian over her shoulder, as she swung away: "Follow me, young man."

He thanked her as he hurried to catch up. She walked delicately but swiftly. They passed through swinging doors and down a lit corridor, her long heels clicking on the concrete. He panted, "Are you a dancer?"

"Sometimes. Not very much in the morning."

She stopped at a door marked STAGE and gave him the full charge of her eyes. "Who is it you want to see?"

He hesitated. "I—I'm not sure. I suppose—"

She interrupted him. "They are all in there. So you can take your pick!"

The little colloquial phrase had great charm on her lips and was accompanied by a smile as genuine as it was unexpected. Julian realized that, under her Parisian haughtiness, there was a simple heart. He smiled back and almost forgot to thank her. She went on her way and he went on his, through the door marked STAGE.

He had never before stood on a stage.

Its size surprised him, its bareness, its lack of any glamour: the scenery of the night before had been struck and stacked against the huge brick walls and was lost in the shadows. Overhead, high up, there was one stark lightbulb, illuminating the boards and putting years on the faces of the young dancers, who were whispering together in groups. Gradually pygmy Julian, like Gulliver among the giants, discovered an enormous cavern, a Fingal's Cave covered in dust sheets, which arched up to somewhere out of sight, but where the sound of carpet sweepers and of dustpans and brushes betrayed cleaners at work. It was the auditorium. Up there, somewhere, some young fool had broken his heart, or thought he had.

His vision readjusted itself to the gloom of the theatre. He could see now that there were several men and women in the stalls, clustered around what looked like a table with a light shining down on it. Here and there, in the sheet-covered seats, there were dancers waiting. These must be the principals. The corps de ballet was on-stage. Class was over and they were practicing steps, lifts, fouettés, pirouettes. All the dancers were in practice costume: the girls in woolen tights, worn under gauzy tarlatan skirts, their breasts restrained and flattened, their hair tied up in scarves, prepared to look more like crayon sketches of women than the real thing. The men, also austerely clad, were either practicing leaps or working with their partners, experienced hands supporting hips with the severity of an acolyte. Now Julian could identify technicians and stage staff: stagehands, electricians, property men, not more than half a dozen, a wardrobe mistress showing a costume on a dancer to an elderly gentleman who was reacting with a look of deep depression; two dressers, with trays of makeup and towels, chatting together; and a group of women, sitting against the backstage wall, darning tights.

He addressed one of these but before he finished his question, she answered without looking up from her darning, "It's no good asking me, young man. I'm just somebody's mother—and that doesn't mean much around here, I can tell you!"

A man in overalls passed by. Everybody trusts a

man in overalls. Julian was no exception. "Could you please tell me who's in charge here?"

"No idea, mate. There's half a dozen of 'em thinks 'e is."

He tried a male dancer, who was contemplating his own navel with admiration, and who answered smartly, "In charge of what?" continuing at the same time to vibrate his relaxed muscles until it seemed he was trying to shake off any possible contact with the intruder.

Julian looked around in despair and caught a pretty girl's eye. He smiled. She smiled.

"I'm new," he said. "Who's in charge?"

To his astonishment she pointed to a dancer who was making the most astounding jumps and spins, alone in the middle of the stage, and who seemed prepared to continue indefinitely. "He is! Grisha Ljubov."

"Bless you!" He made a beeline for the whirling figure. She felt sorry for him.

Even Rams had heard of Ljubov, the Moscow actor-dancer who had been chosen by Diaghilev to replace the great Nijinsky as choreographer and premier danseur; the friend of Karsavina, of Pavlova; the creator of the Miller, the Shopman, the Blue Danube Hussar; the most-feared, the most-hated, and the most-loved of the triumvirate of geniuses who, inspired by Boris Lermontov, not only created a string of masterpieces year after year, but sometimes achieved perfection.

Even seen from the back of the stalls or the height of the gallery, Ljubov's stage personality and muscular control could galvanize an audience; in his tireless body he represented the physical ideal of ballet. Seen from close he was a volcanic center of grace and beauty. When he turned to speak to you, as he now turned to Julian, you felt a physical shock, as the dark eyes in the sallow face, over the poised muscular body, met your eyes.

Julian felt confronted by a human whirlwind, a dark sandstorm, as those eyes met his and waited, motionless, hostile.

"Mr. Lermontov asked me to come here this morning."

"Why?" The mask did not change. Only the mouth uttered the monosyllable.

"He's engaged me."

Like a cat, Ljubov drew away to survey this intruder from top to toe. "Not as a dancer, I hope?"

"No."

With a lightning change of manner, Ljubov turned and summoned his dancers from the shadows: "Allons, mes enfants!" He had lost all interest in Julian. In a few seconds the whole group were whirling like dervishes.

Julian felt he had had enough of the stage and everybody on it. He decided to join those shadowy characters in the auditorium: if nothing else, he could learn to darn ballet shoes. He had already discovered two important facts. One was practical: there was a bridge over the orchestra pit, connecting the stage with the stalls. The other was psychological: if you wandered about asking questions, you aroused the suspicion of the natives, if you looked as if you knew what you were doing, however crazy, they accepted you. Accordingly he marched across the bridge with all the assurance in the world.

Behind him, a languid voice announced, "Here comes the great Boronskaya!" It was Ivan. Ivan Boleslavsky was premier danseur and principal commentator on the private and public lives of the troupe. His honeyed fangs dripped venom in the friendliest possible way. On joining the troupe he had brushed aside all conventional information with the quote, "You can tell me all that later, darling. What I want to know is, who is sleeping with whom?" And the first time he partnered Boronskaya, he had upstaged her for the whole of the Second Act of *Swan Lake.* But not the Third.

Julian couldn't resist a peep at the world-famous prima ballerina, even though he considered ballet an inferior form of musical art. To his astonishment, the girl walking toward the speaker wearing sweat-stained practice tights, with hair tied up in a duster, was none other than the friend in need, whom he had asked, "Are you a dancer?"

She was now being assailed by Ljubov with a calculated burst of fury: "And today she's only forty-three minutes late! Am I supposed to congratulate myself on that?"

Ljubov seemed prepared to work himself up into a big scene. She, on the contrary, continued to walk toward him with great calmness, while the grinning faces of the company showed that they were familiar with such outbursts.

Ljubov shouted: "I tell you, Irina, my patience is at an end. I shall go to Lermontov and tell him that no theatre is big enough to hold both you and me!"

She stopped in her tracks. "Then I go."

This startled Ljubov, "Go? Where?"

"To start packing."

He looked searchingly at her. She didn't mean it! Or did she? He compromised: "Oh! there's no hurry. He may choose to dispense with my services. He's quite crazy enough."

She put her lovely arms around his neck. "You don't imagine I would stay a single day without you, Grisha?"

He smiled. Who wouldn't? She kissed him. He sighed.

Julian sighed too. And smiled . . . when suddenly a sound came from beneath his feet, a reassuring sound in the circumstances, the single note of an oboe. It meant as much to Julian as the melancholy cry of the rare hoopoe does to an ornithologist. Find that oboe and you are among your own tribe! The members of the orchestra were assembling in the pit, which was littered with their instruments. They had evidently had a tea break, a useful thing at Covent Garden, where the pubs open early for thirsty porters—and orchestras.

Julian leaned over the richly gilded railing and inquired of a fiddler among the second violins, "Is Livy here yet?"

The young man took his violin from its case and shoved the case under his chair. "He's coming."

A flutist had it straight from the conductor's mouth: "He's finishing his eggs and bacon in the canteen."

"How do I get into the pit?"

"The short way." A chair was passed up and placed on the conductor's rostrum. "Hurry! Before he gets back."

Julian scrambled over. He stood for a moment on that hallowed spot, where every budding conductor dreams of standing, then jumped down from the chair. He was home.

On stage, Ljubov was making mincemeat of another newcomer: he had turned from a furious altercation with one of the assistant stage managers to find himself confronted by an assured young woman who, like Boronskaya the Great, had tied up her hair, which was flaming red, and had donned practice costume. He snapped, "Who are you?"

"Victoria Page."

The name meant nothing to him, and he was at pains to show it.

She went on, calmly, "I expect Mr. Lermontov has spoken to you about me. He invited me to—"

He cut her short. " 'Invited.' Is this a tea party?"

"No, M. Ljubov."

"Are you sure?"

"I don't dress like this for a tea party."

Her tone was mild, even reverent, but her eyes snapped sparks. Ljubov recognized temperament. "Do you see those five young ladies over there?"

"Yes."

"They have also been in-*vai*-ted." He drawled the word out with infinite distaste. "Please to join them until Mr. Lermontov arrives to welcome his—guests!"

"Yes, M. Ljubov."

She turned and walked to join the forlorn little group of aspirants. He watched her. She might or might not be a dancer, but she walked like one.

The only chair on the stage was occupied by Sergei Ratov, painter and designer, who was admitted by all who knew the Ballets Lermontov to be the only sane member of the company and a master craftsman. He was old; and even Lermontov treated him with respect and consideration, almost with love. His towering, bony frame, his cavernous eyes, his long, powerful arms and fingers, made it seem impossible that such delicate sketches and working designs should flow from his brush and pencil; but one glimpse of his eyes, with the dancing light of charm and sensuality that belied his eighty years, dispelled such doubts. He sat now on the little chair, a large portfolio propped againt his knees, while he looked gloomily at a foreground piece of scenery against which Grisha Ljubov had declared eternal war. A voice from the orchestra pit hailed him, above the din of the tuning orchestra. "Sergei Sergeivitch!"

It was Livy, whose upper half was visible. He rapped for less noise as Ratov answered, "Yes?"

"Are you acquainted with either the works or the person of Julian Craster, composer and conductor?"

"No."

"Nor I. Which proves, my dear Sergei, how very

much we lag behind the times. For here he is in our midst. Lermontov has engaged him this morning. He'll probably sack him this evening. Meanwhile, what shall we do with him?"

Ratov's gentle soul always reacted with some discomfort to Livy's sharp tongue. He was glad the object of the conductor's sarcasm was invisible to him. He murmured before opening his portfolio and taking out some sketches, "You must make his short stay with us a pleasant one, Livy."

A gloomy Julian stood at the back of the pit, between whispering woodwinds and refreshed double basses. The orchestra was still reassembling. Livy had time to frolic a little with Lermontov's protégé.

"I presume you know the instruments of the orchestra, Mr. Craster? What is the name of that one, on the chair beside you?"

"This one?"

"Yes. That one."

Livy looked around the smiling players to make sure he had an attentive audience. Without replying to his question, Julian picked up the little monster and inspected it. He pulled a handkerchief from his pocket and wiped the mouthpiece. By now everybody was watching and repressing a giggle. Julian set his lips, and the next moment an exquisite rendition of a rather rare work by Mozart astounded Livy's ears. There was a stir in the cello section; the leading cellist recognized the piece, and from memory he began to play the cello part of it.

The little impromptu was appreciated. Several members of the orchestra applauded. Julian stopped in midbar and replaced the instrument, handling it with loving care. "It's a bassoon."

Livy snapped, "What is this? A conspiracy?"

The cellist answered with due reverence, "It's

Mozart's Sonata in B Flat Major for Bassoon and Cello."

"Köchel Number 292," said Julian, completing the identification with professional accuracy.

Before Livy could recover, a voice they all knew called out from the stalls, "I want to rehearse Act One of *Heart of Fire*. Will everybody not concerned leave the stage, please."

Lermontov had arrived. As when Jove, King of the Gods, descends to earth, there were mortals everywhere, waiting to have their problems solved: Ratov had his foreground piece and the sketches for the new costumes to be inspected; Ljubov had six stagestruck young ladies to dispose of; the assistant stage manager hoped to dispose of Ljubov; and Vicky Page imagined that the coming of Lermontov would put her where she belonged, up near, if not next to, Boronskaya. As she put her foot on the bridge to the stalls Ratov stopped her, with a tap of his cane on the boards and a twinkle in his naughty old eyes.

"Where are you going, my dear?"

"I'm going to talk to Mr. Lermontov."

"Don't you think it would be better to wait until after the rehearsal?"

"You see, I know Mr. Lermontov personally."

The wrinkles in his face deepened and the irony in his voice sharpened as he answered; "Oh, well, that makes all the difference, of course."

At that instant Lermontov called up, "Sergei! No! Stay where you are. I'll come up."

He ran up the steps to the bridge and halfway across he passed Vicky. She smiled and was about to speak, but, in the fleeting, indifferent glance he gave her, there was not the slightest hint of recognition. He went on to the stage and she heard him say: "Now look here, Ratov, somehow or other we've got to have more room here. In the finale last night, the corps de ballet had scarcely room to turn. Ljubov was right after all."

"Ljubov is always right." He had joined the group.

"Ah! Grisha! Now about these new girls who arrived this morning . . ."

Ratov saw the disappointment on Vicky's face as she crossed back to the stage. He gave her a word of comfort: "Well, you see, my dear, Mr. Lermontov is a very busy man. Now why don't you go over and wait there with the others?"

She acknowledged with a smile the wise old man's advice and wished she had followed it in the first place. She joined the others not a moment too soon.

Ljubov crossed, swiftly and suddenly, to them and, stopping at a certain distance, examined them one by one. He circled them, as impersonally as if he were buying a horse, viewing them from front, rear, and sides. Then he spoke: "Attitude!"

The six, some quicker than others, took up the classic first position.

"Arabesque!"

The six rose on their points, executed the movement, poised on one leg. But how infinite are the variations of six bodies and twelve legs! Still, one or two, including Vicky, impressed him as not too hopeless.

"Rest!"

He beckoned Vicky out from the mob, as much with his eyes as with his fingers. She came forward uncertainly; stood in front of him in the correct attitude. The two exchanged looks. Commanding her with his magnetic eyes, Ljubov made a precise series of movements with his two hands, in the sign language of ballet. Vicky followed the movements without difficulty and executed a brisé, a pirouette, and an assemblé. Ljubov, poker-faced, executed another, more intricate, movement. Vicky obeyed the silent instructions. Once more Ljubov's hands flickered; once more, Vicky executed the movements flawlessly.

"Encore!"

She did it again. If she had known Ljubov better she would have known that the fact that he had not yelled at her was already high praise.

He marched them off with a command.

"Come! All of you! We go to the rehearsal room!" They had to trot to keep up with him.

Seeing Ljubov quit the stage, the assistant stage manager gave silent thanks to heaven.

THE REHEARSAL FINISHED AT TWELVE sharp. Orchestras are expensive things to keep on tap, especially when they are augmented to sixty performers to fill Covent Garden's regal pit and satisfy Livy. That martinet had gone off, with a brusque "Back at two! Craster!" Saddled with an assistant conductor by Lermontov, Livy had no more idea what to do with him than Julian had of his duties. But, by the time he returned from the Garrick Club, he had thought up some grisly labors for the young Ram: all the orchestral parts for all the ballets in the repertoire (there were seven) needed classifying and, in many cases, recopying. Sections of the permanent orchestra badly needed a brushup from their newly appointed coach; the brass had been all over the place on the first night. Julian was not, however, required to be present at the evening performances. In fact, Livy gave him to understand that a pale and anxious face peering at the conductor during the second performance of *Heart of Fire* would definitely be unwelcome. They parted that afternoon without the usual civilities: Livy to an audition, Julian home.

Although a wind, apparently straight off the North

Pole, had started to blow with British persistence, Julian opened the sashes of his window to their fullest extent, otherwise he would never hear the opening bars of Beethoven's Fifth, which was Ike's signature tune. By leaning dangerously out, Julian could see the street, in winter; but, in summer, a grimy laburnum, pride of Mrs. Tuckwell's heart, took up all the available space. Fortunately Ike had a piercing whistle, and his performance was augmented by a most extraordinary moaning sound—like a seasick cow, as Julian had often described it—that Terry produced from a gadget she had mounted on the dashboard of the Ford. She claimed to be reproducing the same phrase by Ludwig van, that Ike was whistling.

But hark! There was Ike's whistle! And hark again! There was Terry's contraption singing its little heart out. Julian put his fingers in his mouth, gave his cabman's whistle, and ran downstairs.

"Where's the wedding?" Julian remarked, on seeing both his bosom friends in their Sunday best. Terry's cello occupied the back seat of the jalopy. "I brought my harp to the party," quoted Julian, "But nobody asked me to play!"

"That's where you're dead wrong. I've just had an audition," Terry shouted.

Julian squeezed into the front seat, putting her in jeopardy from Ike's hand on the gear-lever. Nobody seemed to want to ask Julian questions; it was he who was expected to ask them. "Where?"

"At the Academy."

"What time?"

"Six o'clock."

"What for?"

"For the Hallé! Isn't it marvelous?"

"Oh, *Man*chester!" Julian's dismissal of the midland capital was full of the worldweariness of a cosmopolite. After all, *he* was a member of the Ballets Lermontov.

Ike roared, "Yes, Manchester! What's wrong with that?"

"Oh, nothing! But why the glad rags? The flashy necktie? The dark blue suit? You look like a pimp, not a drummer."

"Percussionist, do you mind? The dressing up was Terry's idea."

Julian kissed her ear. "Yours?"

"M'm! I figured we had a good chance because the Hallé would have come to the Academy first. They'd be sure of finding a good academic standard. Then I thought, why is it a matter of honor with students to come to auditions looking like tramp jugglers? A secretary wouldn't come for an interview in old shoes and crooked hem lines. She'd wear sheer silk stockings and a tight-fitting jumper. I got Ike to change his shirt."

"Who were the judges?"

She hesitated, looked at Ike, then said, "Livy . . . a bloke from the Hallé . . . and . . ."

Julian completed it for her: "—and old Palmer?"

They both looked at him. The car swerved. It was the first time that the name of the archvillain had been pronounced. Terry had led up to her disclosure with care; and now here was Julian dismissing the culprit as "old Palmer."

Ignoring her unspoken questions, Julian asked, "How many auditioned?"

Ike answered. "Three for the cello. *Fourteen* for the percussion."

"Did you hear the other thirteen?"

"Of course I heard them. The whole of Marylebone heard us."

"Well, were they any good, the others?"

"Marvelous!"

"And you?"

"In a class of my own."

Julian clapped him on the back. He loved this guy. "You think you got it?"

"I know I got it."

"How do you know?"

Terry leaned against him. "Aren't you going to ask me if *I* got it?"

Julian's arm was around her shoulders. His grip tightened a little. "Of course you got it. Nobody could resist you, darling."

"You can," she said.

They had a bang-up meal to celebrate their triple triumph, at Lyon's Corner House, the one on the corner of Oxford Street and Tottenham Court Road. There were not only white starched tablecloths, but efficient waitresses—"nippy's," they were called—whose smiles were white and starched as well. They didn't openly expect you to wolf your food and make room for the next customer and had also been instructed—like Mrs. Tuckwell—in the art of whisperboom which, if nothing else, proved the class of the establishment. Here in these marble halls, tilting their chairs back against inlaid walls depicting fountains and exotic trees on panels of Carrara marble, on the days that an aunt, or a godfather, came through with a check, they would order a double mixed grill between three (price: six shillings, fruit salad and black coffee to follow, included.) This day was such a day. Terry traded her black coffee for a telephone call and Julian swapped his fruit salad for the cheapest cigar. As their faces grew flushed and their belts tightened, as their eyes grew moist and they interrupted each other more often, as they ordered another big glass pitcher of continental beer (cheaper than British) and, barbarians that they were, insisted on it being topped up with ice cubes (they liked their beer cold), as each one told his tale and boasted of future triumphs, as the pauses grew longer and the affection for each other grew deeper, as the air grew mellower and the phrases more incoherent, as they finally left the restaurant, with Terry arm-in-arm between Ike and Julian, a vague, bittersweet sentiment crept into their feeling of accomplishment. They had won something, they had lost something: with their first jobs, their little circle of friendship was breaking up.

Six

WHEN A STUDENT FINISHES SCHOOL, HE usually leaves the classroom behind him. Life is just beginning. For a ballet dancer, the classroom is the beginning and the end of life.

Vicky attended her first class with Ljubov at 9:30 A.M. sharp! If, on stage, Grisha was the uncrowned king of choreography, in the classroom he was God.

One side of the long room was all mirror. On the opposite wall was the practice bar. At the bar stood a long line of dancers in practice clothes, sweaty, unglamorous, hardworking, sexless—principals, corps de ballet, pupils, all the same, with no distinction, except those under direct instruction from Ljubov, or his assistant ballet master.

There were trays of rosin on the floor to rub ballet

shoes in, to keep them from slipping. There was an old piano, thumped by a young pianist. Daylight streamed in from the high windows. An air of high seriousness prevailed. Every muscle, every tendon, every nerve was being brought into play. Sharp eyes noticed and pointed out the slightest error in an attitude, the carriage of a head, the straightness of an arm, the angle of a knee. On and on thumped the piano. On and on went the tireless ballet master. On and on went the arms and legs and lungs of the little soldiers at the bar. No faltering! Even though some of them were ready to drop. . . .

"Class! Rest!" Ljubov adjusted a half-net over his black shock of hair. "Irina! Avec moi! . . . Class! Attention!"

Everybody watched with admiration as he executed a beautiful series of movements with Boronskaya, ending with a grand jeté. Selecting one of the new girls, he beckoned her out and repeated the movement with her. Dissatisfied, he beckoned to another one. Vicky was longing to be asked. She wasn't. But someone else had his eye on her. She found Boleslavsky standing by her, holding out his hand. "Try with me."

He led her out of the line. Vicky spun through the movements and took off like a firebird, caught dexterously by her partner in the spectacular dive of the grand jeté. Ivan bowed in formal homage and returned Vicky to her place in the line, with a sidelong look at Ljubov who, since God sees everything, had made a mental note of the dazzling technique of Lermontov's society girl. This was one of the effects intended by Ivan. The other was not long in coming. Boronskaya went back to the bar and started working—hard.

"Class! Ronds de jambe!"

Ljubov nodded to the pianist. The next moment, the whole line had kicked off as before.

About noon, Lermontov and his old colleague

Ratov were coming along the corridor after the dancers were finally dismissed. Last to leave the classroom was, of course, Ljubov. They stood waiting for him as the dancers trailed by, too exhausted to talk, hardly noticing where they put their feet, their eyes staring straight ahead, without objective or hope.

Ratov shook his head in fatherly disapproval. "Look at those youngsters, Boris. They are dog-tired. He is too hard on them."

Lermontov shrugged it off. "They love it. They boast about it. They're young and their bodies are there to be used. When Grisha has finished with them they are as tired as if they had been making love all night. And that evening we have a good performance."

Ratov looked unconvinced. He was no fanatic. No painter is.

As Livy joined them, Lermontov asked, more to change the subject than out of curiosity, "What's that incredible noise, Livy? Coming from your rehearsal room?"

"Trombones. Six of them. Your protégé, Boris, is rehearsing the trombones."

"What's his name?" asked Ratov.

Lermontov shrugged. "I forget. I must say he makes up in enthusiasm what he lacks in experience."

Livy went into the rehearsal room. Vicky plodded by, like the others, too tired to care who she was, or where she was, a towel saturated with sweat around her neck, her glorious hair plastered in damp ringlets on her forehead. Lermontov gave her a glance devoid of any recognition. Ratov's eyes twinkled; like Renoir at eighty, he couldn't resist a pretty girl. "You see! Not even that infernal racket makes any impression on her. She's dead to the world!"

In the rehearsal room, Livy tapped Julian on the shoulder. The sound of elephants rutting stopped. "That will do, Craster. The rest of the orchestra can do with your attention. Tomorrow."

He little knew what his incautious words had started.

ON THE FOLLOWING SATURDAY, JULIAN stepped onto the conductor's rostrum in the orchestra pit at Covent Garden and addressed the assembled members of the orchestra, all sixty-one of them. It was nine-thirty in the morning.

"I'm sorry, ladies and gentlemen, to ask you to come in so early but having conducted you piecemeal, so to speak, I'm burning to conduct you as an orchestra."

So far he had prepared his speech. Now, he launched into improvisation: "You are not only the finest orchestra I have conducted, but the first." He got a few friendly giggles and opened the score of *Heart of Fire,* which lay on the desk in front of him. *"Heart of Fire.* I have been in front on two occasions for this particular ballet, and there are one or two things that I . . . that we . . . that I really must put right. From the beginning, please!"

Now or never! A few bars and he would know if he had told the truth to the old postman: whether he followed the orchestra, or they followed him.

They had hardly played twenty seconds before he rapped with his baton and brought them to a halt: "Horns! Have you got an E flat there?"

"No. I've got an E sharp."

"Ah! that makes all the difference, doesn't it?" The remark was copied from Livy and raised a titter. "It should be E flat. From the beginning again, please."

That's it! He was conducting and they were following him! It was his music, his alone: he was getting what he wanted and they were trying to give it to him. He smiled with pleasure and said out loud, "Very nice!"

Another voice cut through the music. "Mr. Craster! Have you taken leave of your senses?"

The voice came from behind him. Livy, cold and straight as an icicle, was standing in the stalls, hands in the pockets of the black overcoat with the velvet collar, black Homburg hat rammed down over his eyebrows, folded copy of the *Times* under his arm, a look of fury on his face. Julian rapped with his stick; the orchestra stopped playing.

Livy continued: "Do you realize that, in calling the orchestra an hour earlier, we shall have to pay them?"

His awful eyes rolled towards the brass, where a *sotto voce* remark, "You bet!" showed that his point had been appreciated.

Julian could only stammer, "I'm sorry."

He saw Lermontov and Ratov in the shadows of the auditorium, while Livy raised his voice in an icy, impersonal tirade: "And why are you rehearsing *Heart of Fire?* Have I ever asked you to do that? Tell me! I'm interested. I'm sure Mr. Lermontov will be interested, too."

Julian could only bleat, "I like it."

The simplicity of his explanation seemed to outrage Livy even more than the crime itself. "You *like* it! You may break, ladies and gentlemen." Over the scramble to get to the canteen, he continued to take it out on his young assistant: "I have no doubt you also like the National Anthem and the 'Marseillaise,' but I hope you are not thinking of summoning the full orchestra at dawn to practice these noble melodies! Well, Lermontov! I leave this young man to you. After all, he is your discovery, not mine. Coming, Sergei?"

But Ratov shook his wise old head. With a bony, raised finger he indicated that he wanted to witness Lermontov's handling of the culprit. It was not long in coming.

"Mr.—er—You have heard what Mr. Livingstone has said. I must ask you to exercise a little more control over your natural ambitions. And why you should have selected *Heart of Fire* for this expensive early-morning escapade is a mystery that I cannot ever hope to solve. May I see that wrong note in the score, please?"

Once more Livy made an effort to drag Ratov away, but he wouldn't go just yet. Julian silently indicated the passage to Lermontov's keen eye.

"Thank you! I can at least commend your taste. There are passages in *Heart of Fire* of which no one need feel ashamed, Mr. Craster."

A very moved Julian murmured, "Thank you, Mr. Lermontov."

Only now was Ratov satisfied. As they went to the canteen he whispered in Livy's ear, "He couldn't remember the boy's name the other day."

THE MEMBERS OF THE BALLETS LER-montov came to work in different ways and at different times, but at lunchtime they streamed out as if the factory whistle had sounded. Dancers, musicians, electricians, bosses, all out en masse.

Floral Street was flooded in sunlight. Near the stage door, a shiny limousine was parked, the chauffeur standing on the alert, the windows open to admit the balmy air, the owner hidden behind the *Financial Times.* As Vicky walked briskly past the car, fully conscious of her new spring coat, the chauffeur saluted her. "Good morning, Miss Page."

"Good morning, Evans. Is Sir George with you?"

"Yes, Miss."

She gave the *Times* a little knock.

George Tarlyon peeped around it, then gave a broad

smile when he saw who it was. "Mornin', Vicky. Small world, what?"

"What are you doing so far from your club and cronies? Don't tell me you've come to Covent Garden to read your paper in peace!"

George uncoiled himself with enthusiasm and stepped out of the car. If you are six foot three you might as well show it. He grinned down at Vicky. "I'm havin' lunch with Boris Lermontov. You know, the johnnie who runs the ballet. Your aunt's idea."

"Oh . . ."

Already she could hear Lermontov talking to Ljubov. A moment later he came out and greeted Tarlyon with a "Hullo, George! I hope I haven't kept you waiting."

"How are you, Boris? I want you to meet a charming friend of mine, Victoria Page."

Again there was no hint of recognition in his eye. He bowed slightly over her hand, murmured his inevitable "Enchanted," and, with a conventional smile, got into the waiting limousine.

Before following his guest, Tarlyon paused, hopefully. "Can we give you a lift anywhere, Vicky?"

"No thank you, George."

With an apologetic smile to her, the chauffeur closed the door and took his place at the wheel. The car slid away.

"Bye-bye, Vicky! Remember me to your aunt!"

"Good-bye, George!" She was left on the pavement, stunned. The man was really outrageous.

The same evening Ljubov addressed three words to her. This was a pleasant surprise. Since their first memorable encounter he had spoken to her only collectively as one of the Six Foolish Virgins sent by Lermontov to plague him. But now he asked, "What's your name?"

Seventy-nine

She told him. He repeated it—"Victoria Page" —then instantly forgot it. He never remembered anybody's name; she knew that. But she would bet her life against a perforated brass farthing that he remembered how many pirouettes she had done in class that morning.

"I need another swan for *Lac des Cygnes*," he said. "Well?"

She blushed easily and could feel she was blushing now. Should she tell him that she had danced the principal part, the Swan Queen, many times? And that she was dancing it again this coming Saturday (if she could get permission) at her beloved teacher's Mercury Theatre.

Ljubov misunderstood her hesitation. "Don't be afraid. You can do it." He added, by way of warning, "The London season ends on Saturday. Or is it Sunday?"

"Saturday week, Mr. Ljubov." She dreaded the day.

"It would be your last chance."

"I'd love to do it, Mr. Ljubov."

"It is not a promise, mind!"

HE NEVER ASKED HER.

The company gave two evening performances of *Swan Lake* and two matinees, but either Ljubov had forgotten her or regretted his first thought. In any case he never referred to it again.

It was the only time her courage faltered. If the imminent departure of the company for Paris next week had not prepared her for the natural end of her dreams, she might have left then and there. Lermontov's treatment had humiliated her; but Lermontov was complex, intricate, sphinxlike; there was no guessing what went on in his mind.

Ljubov, on the other hand, was honest, simple, singleminded. Like a goldminer who only cares about gold,

Ljubov spent his life waiting for the exceptional dancer to walk into his classroom and perform miracles. Often he had been deceived. When he recognized that his swan was a goose, he could be brutally short about it. So it was in very low spirits that she arrived at the Mercury Theatre on Saturday, to find stickers on the *Swan Lake* posters announcing that she was dancing by permission of the Ballets Lermontov.

No detail, however insignificant, relating to his company could escape Boris Lermontov. When Dmitri had placed a list on his desk for approval, the request by Victoria Page for permission to dance for Madame Rambert had been among them. For a moment his fountain pen hovered over the item with consideration. Then he ticked it. "Yes. She may dance."

It was in this shoebox of a theatre (as Agnes de Mille has since described it) that Vicky reached the turning point of her life. Once a church hall, the Mercury seats 150. The Mercury was forever Madame Rambert; and Marie Rambert, once a member of the original Diaghilev Company and closest woman friend of Vaslav Nijinsky, was forever the Mercury Theatre. She ran it in the great tradition. It was not listed among London's forty-eight theatres, and its Notting Hill address was far from the West End, but the Mercury had its own public and those who loved the arts knew it well. The posters outside announced:

LAC DES CYGNES
(Swan Lake)

choreography by
Marius Petipa
music by
Peter Ilyich Tchaikovsky

THE LONDON SYMPHONY ORCHESTRA

What matter that the whole LSO was accommodated on a kitchen table in the wings, where two record players were supervised by two dancers to make the change-overs? What matter that the stage was fifteen feet deep, while the Maryinsky, where *Swan Lake* was created, has a stage 120 feet deep and seats 3,000? There was as much dedication, as much religion, in that one-time church hall as there ever was in the Imperial Russian Ballet. For Lermontov was right when he read the lesson to Lady Neston in her own house: ballet is a religion, to those who practice it. And when Vicky was dancing Odette-Odile for Madame Rambert, she was dancing for a critic who was second only to Lermontov himself.

And there he was! In the fourth seat of the third row of the stalls!

Vicky couldn't believe her eyes. A moment before, she had pirouetted across the stage, lights, dancers, and audience an indistinguishable blur. She stopped at the footlights. Lermontov sat watching her, his large, handsome eyes motionless and attentive. His hands were clasped in support of his chin and he looked as if he had been watching her from the beginning of time, although she could have sworn that he was not there before. The music swept her on. She could feel the emotion being returned by the audience and knew that she could do what she liked with them. She ran off to a roar of applause. When she returned she dared to look again at Lermontov. He was gone! His seat was empty; and a fat, genial individual was pushing his way along the row to take his place.

Had he ever been there at all? The man was beginning to haunt her! And yet she had seen him and knew that he had seen her dance!

A turmoil of emotions seized hold of her and she danced *Swan Lake* as she had never danced it before.

Seven

ON THE SATURDAY WHEN VICKY
danced at the Mercury Theatre, Julian was discovering
that the business of running a touring ballet company
was as crazy as its reputation. The first warning came
from Jerry at the stage door of Covent Garden.

"Message for you from Livy. You're to wait for 'im
in Lermontov's office. Compris?"

"Okay, Toots!" Julian ran upstairs. Why in the
Holy of Holies? he asked himself. Why not in Livy's office? It looked bad. There was nobody there, and he had
a quick look round. On the desk lay a copy of the score
of *Aurora's Wedding,* Lermontov's shortened version
of *The Sleeping Beauty.* Tchaikovsky! Julian wrinkled
his nose; he was a disciple of the revolutionary Igor
Stravinsky. He looked at all the photographs in their sil-

ver frames, all inscribed to "Dear Boris." He examined the books, mostly Russian and French. He nearly knocked over a plaster cast of Anna Pavlova's foot that stood, with arched instep, on a pedestal near the window. And as the hours passed he became aware that there must be a mistake somewhere. . . .

There was a rap on the door and Colin, the assistant stage manager, put his head in. "Where've you been? We've been paging you everywhere. Livy wants you!"

"Yes, but where?"

"He'll be at Kentner's Restaurant in Soho for lunch. You're to take the score of *Aurora's Wedding* to him."

"This one?"

"Suppose so. Grab it and take a cab."

If Julian expected Livy to bear him malice for kidnapping his orchestra, he didn't know his boss. It was never referred to again. Livy's authoritarian manner was all put on. His sarcastic speeches veiled an idealist who adored youth and the companionship of fellow artists. Discipline had required him to scold Julian's presumption; secretly he admired his cheek. He hailed him cheerfully from Kentner's bar, where he was buying drinks for a bunch of musical types, all of whom Julian knew by sight, ordered him a brandy and soda, swept aside his apologies, and invited him to join their table. After a lunch which started with smoked salmon and finished with Hungarian pancakes, he gave him his marching orders, while lighting a Double Corona: "Lermontov"—*puff-puff!*—"wants to do *Aurora* in the Paris Opéra season"—*puff-puff!*—"We've got to get a corrected score to them at once"—*puff!*—"so that they can rehearse it. You've got Lermontov's?"—*puff-puff!*—"Good! Here's mine. Collate the two of them over the weekend and get a copy off to Paris on Monday. It'll be there Wednesday at the latest. What's the matter?"

Julian explained that he had intended to go home for

the weekend. His father was meeting him at Ipswich station.

"Hasn't he got a telephone?"

"He's the postmaster."

"That's all right then. A man of power and authority. He'll understand."

Julian reflected that his dear, gentle, dithering father, postmaster of Debenbridge, population 768, purveyor of sweets and stationery and owner of the only hired car in the neighborhood, was the last person to understand the change of a plan that had already been broadcast to all his customers; but he said, "Of course."

"Take another day off instead. How about Thursday?"

"Fine."

The proprietor of Kentner's, making his courtesy-round of the tables, reached Livy's. "I trust you have found everything to your liking, gentlemen?"

"Excellent!" Livy's cigar was going nicely.

The proprietor bowed. "Thank you very much." He continued his round, putting the same question and receiving the same stereotyped answers. Julian sipped his Bisquit Dubouché. This was the life! Debenbridge could wait.

THEY GOT THE SCORE OFF TO PARIS BY the late mail on Sunday night. Monday morning, notices in French, English, and Russian greeted the company on arrival at the theatre:

BALLETS LERMONTOV

FINAL PERFORMANCE SATURDAY APRIL 21ST:

MATINEE: 3:00 P.M.—EVENING: 8:00 P.M.

GRAND GALA RECEPTION: 5:30 P.M.—6:15 P.M.

THE COMPANY WILL ENTRAIN FOR PARIS ON

GOD! WHAT A LOT OF IDIOTS WE MUST look! Vicky was inwardly fuming. But in spite of her brave attitude she felt as sick as the rest of them. The Six Foolish Virgins were lined up at the side of the stage, as so often before, but this time they were in street clothes. They had been advised not to change into practice garments, to stress the point that they were only visitors, whose visit was at an end. They saw Lermontov and Ljubov approaching, the former all charm and polish, the latter scowling. The six stood petrified.

"Good morning, my dear young ladies," Lermontov began.

The girls smiled sheepishly, Vicky included. Lermontov continued. It was a speech he had often delivered and in several languages.

"Now, there are just one or two things I would like to say to you. As you know, the Ballet is leaving on Sunday for Paris. I can't imagine anything more delightful than to take you, all of you, with us, but alas! that is impossible. Don't be discouraged. Being left behind does not mean you are bad dancers. It means simply that this year we haven't got room for you all. Now, Miss Fane, will you step out here please. And you, Miss Baines."

The two happy girls stepped forward, their faces flooded with intense relief.

"And you, Miss Hardiman."

Almighty God, make him choose me, too! prayed Vicky.

"And you, Miss Lovat!" Vicky heard Lermontov say. She put her strength, faith, hope, into a single sigh! *Merciful God, make him call my name!*

But her prayer remained unheard; or at least ungranted.

Suddenly, the world turned upside down. *Lermontov isn't . . . he can't be . . . calling the names of those chosen to go with the company! He's already called 4 out of 6! Oh, God! Don't let him call me! I've been praying for the wrong thing all the time!*

His voice seemed to drawl . . . "And you, Miss Crawley!" Victoria Page was never mentioned. Instead, he addressed the five: "Well, dear young ladies, I want to thank you very much for the hard work you've done with us. And I'm sure my gratitude is shared by Mr. Ljubov here . . ."

Ljubov, who had been listening in an attitude of sulky gloom, now emitted a kind of groan which could have meant anything.

Lermontov concluded: "So I wish you all the greatest happiness and success; and next year, I hope we may have the pleasure of working with you again."

He treated them to a dazzling smile and left the stage abruptly, followed by Ljubov.

Vicky stood still.

Ratov lumbered up. He misread the tears rolling down her cheeks. "Now, now, my dear . . . it's not the end of the world. . . ." Then he saw the unlucky five retreating and changed his tune: "Or are these the tears of joy?"

She nodded several times.

"That's quite another matter. In that case you may have a little cry. In fact, you should. . . ."

JULIAN, THE OTHER NEWCOMER TO THE realm of topsy-turvydom that was the Ballets Lermontov, had arrived in Ipswich on his Thursday off. His father always met him on Platform Three, and Julian was leaning out, looking ahead, as the London train clattered out of the tunnel. No Craster Senior was to be seen, but a big chap called Simon Manning, a railroad engineer and ex-schoolmate, was looking out for Julian and rushed him along to the exit where a chalked announcement board summoned Mr. Julian Craster urgently to the stationmaster's office.

Postmaster Craster came galloping to meet him. "It's a message for you. From London!"

He made it sound as if it were distant as China and that every second was costing a small fortune. Turning about, he led the way, still at a gallop, followed by Simon, Julian bringing up the rear.

"They're hanging on. It's something to do with soup!"

"Soup?"

"Yes. I think so. It's not a very good line."

"Who's calling?"

"Someone called Libby. He's in soup."

Julian grabbed the receiver, tendered by the stationmaster himself. It was Livy. "Craster? We're in the soup!"

The score had never arrived in Paris: he was to take another one himself to Paris tonight. In eleven minutes Julian was waving good-bye to the devoted group of postmaster, stationmaster, two porters, and railroad engineer.

As the up-train vanished into the tunnel, the reception committee, which had so suddenly been turned into a farewell committee, looked at one another and shook their heads. Postmaster Craster stoutly declared, "Whoever's to blame that the package didn't get to Paris, it couldn't have been anyone on our side."

"They seem a lot of maniacs, these Russians your son is working for, Ned," said the stationmaster.

"What did Julian tell you about the ballerinas?" asked Simon.

The two porters said nothing. They were only supers in the drama.

At Liverpool Street Station, Julian was ambushed by a young man he had never seen before. "I'm Mr. Trigorin's assistant. We're arranging your trip to Paris. Have you got a passport?"

Julian nodded. "In my digs."

"Thank God. Come on. I've got a car."

After they drove to Primrose Hill to pick up Julian's things, they went to Covent Garden, where Livy was waiting. He seemed to be taking a humorous view of the whole thing. He handed Julian a typewritten page of names and telephone numbers.

"Jean-Pierre Baron—he's about your age—will meet you. He's your opposite number at the Opéra. I'll phone him later and tell him you're coming. You phone me as soon as you've delivered this." He pointed to a posh briefcase, tan leather, saddle-stitched. "Everything's in there. I've checked it, but we'll check it again. Open it!"

Julian opened it. It was full to bursting.

"If you lose it, I'll kill you."

"If I lost a single page, I'd kill myself."

"I mean the briefcase. It's mine."

He would probably have accompanied Julian to Victoria Station, if for no other reason than to watch over his briefcase, but he was conducting *The Nutcracker* that evening. Ike and Terry couldn't be contacted, so it was left to the company's secretary, Mr. Trigorin, to see him off. For Julian it was a number of firsts: his first visit to Paris, his first boat-train, his first sleeping car, his first appearance as an emissary of the Ballets Lermontov, to name only a few.

People who had dealings with Mr. Trigorin knew him as a kind, obliging little man, except in money matters. With mock apology he handed Julian the tickets. "I am afraid there are no more second-class tickets. You'll have to make do with first class." That was not all. He had to fork out twenty pounds' worth of French francs. You could see it hurt him. (He was known behind his back as "willadollado"—on the American tour that had always been his reply when asked for an advance: "Will a dollar do?" It had stuck.)

The attendant took Julian's tickets and passport, told him the time of arrival at Calais, and at the Gare du Nord in Paris next morning. "What time do you wish to be called?"

"I don't think I shall sleep at all," confessed Julian. "First-night fever!"

But he did. He woke up once: his carriage was moving gently, there was a jangle of steel against steel. Probably they were coupling up. Men were talking under his window, talking in French. . . .

Paris

AT THE GARE DU NORD ON FRIDAY morning, a young Frenchman met him, yawning and bleary-eyed. "M. Julian Crastaire?"

"Oui. M. Baron?"

"You spick French?"

"You parlay English?"

"Leetle."

They smiled at one another. Julian opened his briefcase. "Here's the score! *Aurora's Wedding.*"

Jean-Pierre showed what he carried in a very similar briefcase. "Look 'ere, Julian!"

It was another score. The one that Livy and he had sent. Julian stared. "When did it arrive?"

"Dees mornin'. Like you!"

They burst out laughing and went for breakfast to the Café de la Paix.

An orchestral rehearsal had been called for ten-thirty. They only had to cross the Place de l'Opéra; and, miracle of miracles, Julian succeeded in reaching Livy on the antique instrument called a telephone by the Administration of the Opéra.

"How's it going?" yelled Livy.

"They seem awfully young," reported Julian doubtfully. "And they write down an awful lot of notes." Livy, for some reason, seemed to find this amusing. Julian said hastily, "See you tomorrow. I'm catching the boat train back tonight."

"Are you mad? Stay where you are! The whole company is crossing on Sunday. Are you a member of this company or not?"

"Am I?" Julian wondered.

"Of course you are!"

"Oh!" Julian digested this information slowly. "But I've got an important appointment in London! A lunch-date!"

"Is she pretty?"

"Not my type. It's Professor Palmer."

"Where are you meeting him? . . . Kentner's? Leave it to me!"

WHEN LIVY GOT TO THE RESTAURANT it was after two. He found a sour Professor Palmer sitting alone at a table for four.

"Hullo! Palmer. All alone? Mind if I join you?"

"Provided you like duck. I ordered two ducks for my party, and they've stood me up."

Livy sat down. "Do I know them?"

"All three are my students. The two you auditioned for the Hallé. And Julian Craster."

He poured out a glass of wine for Livy. He had already emptied one bottle. Under the wine basket Livy's sharp eyes spied orange envelopes. He picked them up. "Telegrams! For you!"

"Telegrams! I never noticed them!" He tore them open. He was a changed man. He beamed. "This one's from Manchester. They had to report at once. They didn't have time to say good-bye. And this one's from Craster. From Paris!"

Livy tasted his wine, smiling. "Little bastard! He didn't trust me."

"What's he doing in Paris?"

"I sent him there. What's that?"

The waiter was reverently unwrapping a napkin around thick slices of hot toast. "Pâté maison, m'sieur." He served it. Livy was about to take a bite when Palmer grabbed his arm.

"Don't eat it! It's off!"

"Off?"

"It's bad! Terrible! Wait till I tell old Léon. Here he comes now, with his eternal bleat: 'Is everything satisfactory, gentlemen? Thank you, gentlemen!' We'll give him a big surprise."

The manager had just started to gather his opinion poll about the lunch. The professor waited until he arrived at the next table. "Now, listen to this," warned Palmer—as if Livy needed any warning. A moment later the manager stood before their table: "I trust you are finding everything satisfactory, gentlemen?" Without raising his voice the professor replied, "What we had was atrocious. It couldn't be worse." The manager bowed, said "Thank you very much," and passed on.

Livy burst out laughing; Palmer joined him. They finished the second bottle as the ducks arrived.

*   *   *

A Telegram From Manchester

JULIAN CRASTER BALLETS LERMONTOV
OPÉRA DE PARIS PLACE DE L'OPÉRA PARIS

Julian read this much through three times. How
could the text ever match the beauty of the address?
Then he read on:

SORRY MISS YOUR EXODUS STOP OUR FIRST
APPEARANCE TCHAIKOVSKY'S FIFTH AND
SIXTH UNQUALIFIED SUCCESS STOP REQUEST
DETAILS PRIVATE LIFE JULIAN CRASTER LOVE
BOTH TERRY IKE.

Julian replied on the backs of a series of picture post-
cards.

PICTURE POSTCARD No. 1

*Is your Tchaikovsky the same Tchaikovsky
who composed ballets* Swan Lake *and*
Sleeping Beauty? *If so, shut up! Am sitting
pavement of Fouquet's café, Champs
Elysées, sipping café crème and watching
girls' legs. Or rather I was watching them
until a waiter loomed up. What is French
for "Go away, old man! You're spoiling the
view"? He counters in Franglais: "You wish
café more, m'sieu?" I summon up all my
resources and answer "No. Merci!"*

PICTURE POSTCARD No. 2

*Am watching gendarme conduct traffic.
Hope to get tips for conducting French*

orchestra. Gendarme stops truck carrying sand. Unloading device starts to deposit tons of sand unknown to driver. Tiny sports Amilcar behind him disappearing in sand hoots furiously. Innocent truckdriver knows it can't be him. He goes, leaving mountain of sand on top of Amilcar. My waiter blocks view of gendarme's reaction. "Another café crème m'sieu?" How do you say in French, "You asked me that three times already"?

PICTURE POSTCARD No. 3

Algerian brush vendor offers genuine Algerian brushes for sale to large party aperitif-sippers. Nobody takes notice him or his brushes. He starts demonstration brushing everybody. They let him brush, still take no notice. Now big fellow stands up menacingly. My waiter again! He takes my empty cup, wipes the bottom of it, wipes the saucer, bangs down my freshly wiped cup in saucer. How do you say in French, "You're making me miss the best part of the brushing drama, old man"? Ah! Here's Jean-Pierre! He orders a vermouth cassis. Gets rid of the waiter. Now I can see. The big fellow just wanted his back brushed as well. Nobody buys a brush and the Algerian moves on.

PICTURE POSTCARD No. 4

Jean-Pierre explains that waiters in top cafés don't get paid. They live on tourist tips. That's why they pester the customers.

*"Garçon! Another café crème!" J-P is to
Paris Opéra what Julian C is to Ballets
Lermontov—Assistant Conductor. He's sad
because his beloved dachshund, Wolfgang
Amadeus, has tangled with the Theatre cat
and got the worst of it. We open tonight
with Rossini's* Boutique Fantasque,
Schumann's Carnaval *and Adam's* Giselle.

To everyone's astonishment, Lermontov had ordered a dress rehearsal of *Giselle* Act One for that afternoon. It was to be held in the Hall of Mirrors at the
Opéra and was to finish at 6:00 P.M., only three hours before the curtain would rise on the opening performance.
Lermontov never did anything without a reason, but
this time nobody could guess it. Not even Ratov. It was
a full company call.

Rumors connected it with Boronskaya. She had not
made the crossing with the company on Sunday; she had
arrived on Monday afternoon, and here she was, in magnificent form. Wherever she might have spent the weekend, she was a young girl in love for the first time: to
Boleslavsky it seemed that he held the real Giselle, radiant and adoring, in his arms. Lermontov sat by the piano
and never took his eyes off her. If he had looked at the
faces of his company he would have seen for himself how
brilliant her performance was. He never did. He hovered
over the performance as a hawk hovers over a dove.

One other person never took her eyes off the prima
ballerina: Vicky. A member of the corps de ballet, she admired and she feared her. Could she ever achieve such
perfection? Of all the classical roles, Giselle is the greatest, the Hamlet of ballet. What could she bring to it of her
own? Could she ever create a leading part, if she were
lucky enough to have one written for her some day?

Irina was dancing the Mad Scene. For the last time

she pressed Albrecht's hand to her heart. For the last time she dashed it aside. She seized the sword and stabbed herself. A mad, frenzied dance . . . a few faltering steps . . . arms outstretched to her lover . . . she has fallen dead in the arms of her girlhood friends. The piano stopped. Everything stopped.

But only for a moment. A murmur of love and admiration was heard from the whole company. Kisses were showered upon her. Ljubov rushed to embrace her. She opened her arms to her friends as if she wanted to take them all into one big hug.

"Thank you! Thank you, all of you! Merci, cher maître!"

The hubbub grew. She felt Lermontov's eyes on her. She cried out, "Listen! my friends whom I love and who love me! Listen!"

Suddenly, everyone felt that they were going to hear something of importance—that they would learn the secret of this unheard-of rehearsal, that the two things were connected. Silence fell. Applause, compliments, died away. Breathless, they stood like statues in their brilliant costumes, waiting for the next words, knowing, and yet not knowing, that it would affect all their lives.

She spoke quietly, the tears glistening in her eyes. "I have something to tell you. Something very important. Until this moment I have not dared to say it. I have not dared even to decide it. Now, with you all around me, I dare! I am fiancée! I get married!"

The silence of consternation greeted her words.

Ratov was the first to move. But Ljubov was the first to speak: "Irina! But to whom? But when?"

"But to Charles, Grisha! My tall Englishman. And soon, soon, soon!"

Ratov took both her outstretched hands in his. "My dear child, all my love and best wishes for your future happiness."

She burst into tears. They embraced. It broke the spell. All was laughter, tears, cheers, and congratulations.

Ivan kissed her hand to the elbow. "Little horror! I wish you many performances with your new partner."

"Don't be jealous, darling. Grisha! Where is Grisha?"

He broke through the circle that surrounded her. "I'm here!"

"Grisha, darling—Do you hate me?"

His great eyes answered her. "I could never hate you, Irina. But how can I ever forgive you?"

"Kookooshka," she whispered in his ear. "You forgive me a thousand times! That I know."

Livy's face appeared smiling over Ljubov's shoulder. "Are you going to quarrel with your husband as often as with your conductor?"

She was radiant once more. "It will be my best role! Tu vas voir! Charles will conduct and I shall follow...."

"That will be the day!"

"... But I set the tempo. That is normal."

"Normal! I seem to have heard that before!"

She was not listening. She had realized that one voice, an important one, was missing.

"But where is Boris Lermontov? Boris? Has he nothing to say to me?" The pitch of her voice had risen as she spoke.

She burst out of the circle and took a step toward the piano. But he had left one second after Ratov's words of congratulation.

Two

AN HOUR BEFORE THE PERFORMANCE,
Julian was in the orchestra pit, checking the parts already laid out on the music stands.

Jean-Pierre poked his head through the pit entrance.
"Have you seen Lermontov?" he asked. "He wants you
in his office."

"What for?"

"No idea."

"Perhaps he thinks we've mislaid the orchestra."

"Come and meet them. They're all there."

The orchestra waiting room was full of strangers.
Julian was presented to the leader, a distinguished-
looking, bearded gentleman, whom he'd never seen in
his life; then to other equally distinguished performers—Maître Ceci, M. le Professeur Cela, etcetera

etcetera—until his brain reeled; but the most alarming thing was that, although he had attended two full rehearsals of the Opéra orchestra, he didn't recognize any of them. As soon as he could, he whispered a question to Jean-Pierre.

"Of course you have never met them, mon cher," he replied with a chuckle. "This is a performance. The members of the Orchestre de l'Opéra are much too important to come to rehearsals. They send their pupils. To take notes."

Julian caught Lermontov on the way out. He was told to sit down and wait. He waited. The books in the glass-fronted bookcase were French, the pile of the carpet was deeper, the curtains heavier, the uncomfortable Second Empire furniture richer than that at Covent Garden. But at Covent Garden, members of the theatre orchestra came to rehearsals in the flesh. . . .

He recognized certain authentic Lermontov props: the powerful reading lamp, the leather-bound diary, the photographs in their silver frames, a grand piano. He could imagine Dmitri unpacking these special objects— even the piano—from special cases, on arrival. Voices sounded from the corridor. Hoping to learn where Lermontov had gone, he jumped to the door, opened it, and bumped into him. He had changed into evening dress and wore the button of Chevalier de la Légion d'Honneur. He took Julian's presence in his stride.

"Ah! There you are, Mr. Craster!" From the pile of scores on his desk he fished out a thick handwritten one. "I have a job for you."

"Good!"

His emphatic tone caught Lermontov's attention. "Am I to understand that you have not been altogether happy with us so far?"

Perhaps his whole career would depend on his

answer to the question. He said, cheerfully, "Coaching an orchestra isn't exactly a young composer's dream, is it?" He had rated his answer at five out of ten, but raised it to six when he saw a faint smile on his boss's lips.

"The job I have for you may not be exactly your idea of a young composer's dream, either, but I hope you will not consider it entirely unworthy of your talents."

He handed him the score. In bold letters across the cover was written *The Red Shoes.*

"The ballet of *The Red Shoes* is from a fairy tale by Hans Christian Andersen," Lermontov said. "It is the story of a young girl who is devoured with an ambition to attend a dance in a pair of red shoes. She gets the shoes and goes to the ball. For a time, all goes well and she is happy. At the end of the evening she is tired and wants to go home. But the red shoes are not tired. The red shoes are never tired. They dance her out into the street; they dance her over the mountains and valleys, through fields and forests, through night and day. Time rushes by, love rushes by, life rushes by. But the red shoes dance on!"

He was standing by the cast of Pavlova's foot on its pedestal, and on the last words he caressed her marvelous instep as if he held a living woman's foot in his hand.

Julian said dreamily, "What happens in the end?"

"In the end she dies. The music was composed for us last year on our South American tour by Felipe Beltrán. You will see there are some passages marked with a blue pencil—passages I do not like. I should like to see what you can do, Mr. Craster, in the way of a little rewriting."

Julian nodded.

"Take your time. There's no need to hurry."

Julian thanked him.

There was a knock at the door: the callboy. "L'Ouverture a commencé!"

Lermontov moved toward the door. Julian opened it for him as a matter of course. He murmured, "Thank you, Mr. Lermontov."

The great man lightly touched his arm. In the circumstances it amounted to a friendly pat.

Julian remained in the doorway. From the moment that he heard the title *The Red Shoes,* a theme had come into his brain. He had hardly heard Lermontov's outline of the plot. Now the theme returned. . . . What if he treated it more like a machine? A sort of perpetual motion? He went back to Lermontov's desk to jot down the theme.

When he had finished, something odd caught his attention. Were the framed photos the ones he had seen in London? The frames were. Not the photos. The English faces with their affectionate, or admiring, dedications to "Dear Boris" had vanished. Cocteau, Matisse, Poulenc, Pierre Monteux, Coco Chanel, smiled out of their frames, with long and indecipherable apostrophes to "le cher Boris" in French. Would you believe it? he thought. Dmitri switches celebrity photos in every country visited by the Ballets Lermontov. In Peru he presumably puts up Felipe Beltrán, composer of *The Red Shoes.* In Covent Garden he might one day put up Julian Craster.

"To the one and only Boris Lermontov." He savored it, then added "From Julian."

VICKY, TOO, HAD SOMETHING TO LEARN about Lermontov that night. As she waited for the music cue for the entrance of the corps de ballet, one of two dozen ghostly maidens standing in a row, she heard voices. Ljubov and Lermontov were talking as only theatre people dare to do, knowing instinctively the dead spots on stage from which, across the desert of boards and the chasm of the orchestra pit, no sound can reach the audience.

Ljubov was still in his costume of the Can-Can Dancer from *La Boutique Fantasque:* tight-fitting cutaway coat and trousers of black velvet, checked vest, and patent-leather shoes; his hair crimped in glossy curls, his sideburns and moustache shining with pomade. He still had time to seize hold of Vicky's tarlatan skirt and primp it up, like a girl with her dolly, as he exclaimed to his companion: "Ah! Look at our Boronskaya! She's in wonderful form tonight!"

Lermontov almost snarled as he answered, "I can take no further interest in the form of any prima ballerina who is imbecile enough to get married."

Vicky's eyes were on the stage, but she soaked up every word. Perhaps she made a slight movement with her head. It almost seemed as if Lermontov's next words were addressed to her alone.

"You cannot have it both ways. The dancer who relies upon the doubtful and uncertain comforts of human love is not and never will be a great dancer!"

Ljubov turned his eyes on his friend. There was a note in his voice that transcended the mascara on his lashes and the red splashes of doll makeup on his cheeks. "That is all very fine, Boris, very pure and fine, but you can't alter human nature."

The answer came, crisp and final: "I think you can do better than that. You can ignore it."

The cue arrived for the corps de ballet; with a serious and dedicated face Vicky floated with the others onstage. Their heavily madeup faces, like clowns, or dolls, close up, were transformed by distance into visions of exquisite beauty. But as she danced, it was not the music that rang in her ears, but the words of her fellow perfectionist, Boris Lermontov.

"Tell me one thing, Boris, just one thing." Ljubov had a loyal and loving heart. "Has Irina ever given a better performance before she decided to get married? I don't think so."

"You don't think so? Would she have been better or would she have been worse if she went straight onstage after a weekend in the arms of her fiancé?"

The contempt that he got into the word "fiancé" startled even Ljubov, who knew something about his friend's possessive jealousy of the artists he "created." He ignored the tone and answered gaily, "You'll never know, Boris! You'll never know!"

"Won't I? Why else do you suppose that I called a dress rehearsal this evening before the performance? Rather an expensive warming-up, wouldn't you think? But necessary."

Ljubov's eyes were big as saucers. "You couldn't have known. . . ."

"I know everything. Everything I need to know."

THE WORD WENT OUT: BORONSKAYA was considered persona non grata. Of course, the news of her impending marriage would be in the society rags, but there was to be no story of her leaving the Ballets Lermontov. She was dancing every performance of the Paris season, and that was enough. Whether she stayed in Paris, returned to London, or went with the company to Monte Carlo was to be left in the air. Lermontov needed time for suitable countermeasures and it was also necessary that M. Boudin, Director General of the

Théâtre de Monte Carlo, should learn nothing from the papers. The scheme almost succeeded: almost but not quite. As the company boarded the Blue Train at the Gare de Lyon, accompanied by the press, the fans, the admirers, the legendary 147 crates of costumes, properties, and other knickknacks, not to mention the freightcars loaded with scenery, Boronskaya swept onto the platform. She looked radiant, was wonderfully turned out (by Callot Soeurs), and sparkled with gold and diamonds. Strictly speaking she was outrageously overdressed. But then, even more strictly speaking, nobody spoke. They just gaped. Not because of her clothes. Because of what she was.

She had come to say good-bye to everybody! Charles was with her, taller and more English than ever. He carried her little dog.

She ran full tilt against Lermontov's dark glasses, which he invariably wore when traveling. He stood rigid, impeccable, one hand resting on his cane, the other holding an evening paper. She took a step forward. "Boris!"

Nothing. Only the blank, impenetrable lenses. "Adieu!"

And he was gone.

Charles frowned. It had been more than rudeness. It was like a blow in the face. He looked at his lovely fiancée and his face softened. She had taken the rebuff like a child.

Above them, at the train window, one of the girls saw Vicky watching the little drama. "I'd like to be in her shoes," said the girl.

"Would you?"

"Fifty thousand pounds a year. Anytime!"

"Will that make up for it?"

"For everything!"

Vicky was still watching Irina and Charles. The girl

stuck to her guns: "If it doesn't, then some people don't know when they're lucky."

They watched the milling crowd. Ljubov, Ratov, Livy, and Boleslavsky crowded around Irina. Doors were banging. Conductors shouted, "En voiture!"

Vicky said slowly, "To leave all the wonderful people who have shared your triumphs and failures, who have bullied you and praised you and loved you and made you what you are. . . . And then suddenly to wake up one day and find it's all over. . . . It must be like dying . . . for fifty-thousand a year."

On the platform Boronskaya and Ljubov were holding hands.

"Charles says if I'm late for my wedding like I'm always late for you, he won't marry me! Then I shall come straight back to you, my little pumpkin. That would give you a terrible shock, wouldn't it?"

He made a disastrous effort to be flippant: "Now you'll be able to sleep as long as you like . . . eat sweets every day . . . go to parties all night. . . ."

She joined him in the same forced, despairing note of gaiety: "And you! Class will start punctually . . . no more shouting at rehearsals . . . no more hysterics two minutes before the curtain goes up . . . no more . . ."

He took it up: "No more Irina!"

It was too much. He flung away his gold-topped cane, he opened his arms, she rushed into them, and they broke down completely.

"My little Grisha!"

"Irina! Irina!"

"Kookooshka!"

Tears were pouring down their cheeks, while the last doors were banged, whistles were blown, and the train started to move. A hundred voices from the windows screamed: "Ljubov! Ljubov! Grisha!"

He sprang from her arms, leapt after the train, was

hauled on board. Boronskaya picked up his cane and came bounding after the train like an antelope. She hurled it up to him. He caught it with a magnificent gesture.

The train gathered speed.

Monte Carlo

THE BLUE TRAIN . . . LE TRAIN BLEU . . . *One*
the initials PLM! Paris–Lyons–Méditerranée. What visions of spendthrift luxury and romance on wheels those names conjure up to the traveler between the Wars. Do you remember (have you ever heard of) Maurice Dekobra's throbbing romance *The Madonna of the Sleeping Cars?* You have! Then you must be over fifty-five. Still . . . what a title! What an obvious best-seller! What an experience it was, in the twenties, to roll with dignity out of the Gare de Lyon in the late afternoon, dine and wine lavishly, tête-à-tête, in the pink glow of the lamps of the dining car, fall into your bunk, or someone else's, as you trundled southward down the opulent breast of France, half-waking to hear a long-drawn-out, nasal voice, call from a great distance *"Av-ign-on!"* half-consciously

hearing at Marseille a great rattling and banging, as the new engine was coupled on and the order of the train reversed. What a theatrical experience to fumble with the heavy blind until it rolled up with a snap to reveal the bluest sea in the world, running and laughing within a few yards of the wheels of the train, while at the landward window olives, yuccas, and giant agave plants lined the railroad tracks, brown little villages hung like swallows' nests from the hills, white-walled and red-roofed towns, framed in flowers and decked with palaces, awaited the condescension of your visit.

At Cannes starts the real Riviera, with bunches of yellow mimosa and armsful of long-stemmed carnations thrust through the carriage windows into your arms for a few francs. After Cannes, Golfe Juan, where Napoleon landed from Elba; Cagnes-sur-Mer on its rock, crowned by the square tower of the Grimaldi; Nice, nestling under the mountains, with its three rivers in their wide, stony beds, and then, by the most romantic, burrowing, tunneling railroad track in the world, carved out of colored rocks that have run with the blood of massacred villages and echoed the sirens' song, Monte Carlo! Hanging on the steep slopes of the Alpes-Maritimes, Monte Carlo, a fief of the principality of Monaco; Monte Carlo, synonym throughout the world for gambling and extravagance, wealth and destitution, joy and despair; Monte Carlo, the home—where else for such a gambler?—of the Ballets Lermontov.

If the Paris Opéra, on its opulent site in the Place de l'Opéra, is considered to be the chef d'oeuvre of Charles Garnier, its architect, then the Opéra of Monte Carlo can be nominated as his dessert. Its exterior merges into the façade of the Casino, the triumph of sugar-plum architecture of which it is a component, but the interior of the theatre is a jeweled workbox. The auditorium, which seats not more than three hundred, is exquisite, a dream of white, gold, and crimson, of looped curtains, shining chandeliers, glittering ornamentation. The stage is professional, wide and deep, with plenty of space at back and sides, and with a roomy orchestra pit for its famous orchestra. As for the lobbies, they are unique. One can stroll from the lobby into the gaming rooms, and from the gaming rooms back into the lobby of the theatre, having become a few thousand dollars richer, or poorer, during the entr'acte. (They say that it is in the contract of the lessees with the Casino authorities that there should be a minimum of two entr'actes. Lermontov always had three.) Behind the stage are adequate dressing rooms and offices and, what is more essential for a ballet company, spacious rehearsal rooms.

The Casino stands among formal gardens on a rocky headland, facing the Rock of Monaco and the prince's palace across the deep-water harbor full of yachts. Inland, when you stand on the steps of the Casino, the Café de Paris, with its broad terrace, is on your right, the Hôtel de Paris on your left, while in front of you the palm trees and blazing flowerbeds climb the hill to the upper town. All the architecture is irresponsible and light as a soap bubble. The terraced slopes of the town merge into the gray slopes of the mountain, without a visible frontier, just as the Principality of Monaco merges into France. A knowing eye can spot on the cliffs, two thousand meters above the glittering town, the zigzags of the Grand Corniche, the military road along which Caesar marched into Gaul and Napoleon to Marengo. But here in the toy town, drenched with sunshine, opening our morning papers, there is only one topic of conversation: Who won and who lost, last night? And how much? For without M. Blanc and his Casino there would be no Monte Carlo, no principality, and, probably no sunshine.

Here, to this sugar-coated paradise, beloved by the

Russian Grand Dukes in the days of the Tsars, Lermontov had come, when the collapse of the Imperial régime forced him to find backers for the ideal ballet company he intended to create. Here he had found a refuge for himself and his associates after grueling world tours. Here were luxury hotels to tempt writers, painters, and composers to come and create new works for him. Here was a theatre, small but exquisite, with a very special audience who would ensure that anything created there, for their exclusive enjoyment, would be heard of within a few weeks in all the capitals of the world. He moved in. The Casino financed him. The prince patronized him. Riviera society idolized him. The Ballets Lermontov became a vogue. He was encouraged to experiment, to innovate. He dared greatly and was repaid with sensation, scandal, and applause. He repaid the Casino with the worldwide publicity resulting from his creations there. In a few seasons, Monte Carlo became known, not only as the playground of the rich, but as the home of the arts, with Lermontov as adjudicator.

The Blue Train arrived at the station of Monte Carlo at the civilized hour of twelve-thirteen precisely every morning. Of course, 12:13 P.M. was considered afternoon in the rest of the world. But not in Monte Carlo, where the Société des Bains de Mer owned not only the famous Casino but the Hôtel de Paris and the Café de Paris as well. Fun-loving members of fashionable Society liked to translate the name as The Mixed Bathing Society. In doing so, they were not only recalling the charming relic of Edwardian ogling, but also censuring the stuffiness of the Corporation. By arrangement the locomotive steamed almost into the Casino, in order that no time might elapse between the visitors' arrival and the placing of their chips on the green baize. The train rumbled out of the thirteenth tunnel since Nice onto a charming flower-decked terrace, directly below the grand terrace of the Casino and its theatre, and directly above the circular platform where the crack shots of Europe exhibited their skill in shooting live pigeons released from traps. Like everything in Monte Carlo, the railway station was unreal, theatrical. The rocky wall of the cutting was draped with bougainvillea and studded with flowering cacti. The platforms were half-smothered in gorgeous blooms. Baskets of flowers hung from every post and projection. The buildings were in the rococo Second Empire style, and an elevator, like an enormous birdcage, and shaking like an old man with the palsy, conveyed eight people, at most, from the level of the tracks to the level of the Casino terrace, whence a step took them into the gaming rooms.

While awaiting the arrival of the ballet company, M. Boudin—already mentioned as director general of the theatre, a fanatical admirer of Lermontov and all things Lermontovian—was seated at his usual table on the terrace of the Café de Paris, drinking his café au lait, and keeping his elegant shoes on the bars of his table, while the porter sloshed water from a hose over the red and white tiles around him. His complacency was disturbed by the interruption of Mme. Monique, his secretary, with the news of Boronskaya's defection: she had just had a call from the *Éclaireur de Nice*. Its editor had seen a news-agency release, datelined Paris, reporting that the famous ballerina had quit the Ballets Lermontov and would not be on the train arriving this morning! As if on cue they both saw, across the square, M. Rideault, resident producer of the Opéra, hurrying down the wide steps of the Hôtel de Paris, and coming their way as fast as his rather ample frame could carry him. He too had been telephoned and had gone straight to the hotel to learn as a fact that the booking for Mme. Boronskaya's suite had been canceled by Trigorin, ever watchful of Lermontov's purse.

M. Boudin looked grave. It wasn't like Lermontov to let the papers get ahead of him. What was the truth of the matter? There must have been a row. There had been rows before, many of them, but never a row of these historic dimensions. But what was this? Mme. Monique, returning all smiles, with a telegram dispatched from Dijon, first stop for the Train Bleu, during the night!

> CHER M. BOUDIN BAD NEWS IS SOMETIMES
> UNAVOIDABLE WHEN CREATING GOOD
> NEWS MILLE AMITIÉS LERMONTOV.

That Lermontov! He was up to something. Still it sounded better, and M. Boudin ordered two anisettes to go with their coffee. Again an interruption! This time it was the reception clerk from the hotel—looking, in his black frockcoat and pearl tie pin, and backed by the tall palm trees, like a sober beetle that had wandered into a hothouse. He waved a telegram. It had been handed in at Marseille and restored the booking of the canceled apartment! At the same moment they heard the train whistle and hurried down the winding stairs to meet the company off the train.

Lermontov was in excellent form; to see him step off the train as elegant and unruffled as when he mounted the train in Paris—his dark blue-to-black lounge suit immaculate, his eyes under the brim of his black Homburg impenetrable behind dark glasses, his silver-mounted cane in his gloved hand—was to see a magician to whom the problems of mere mortals were no problem. Boronskaya? Yes, she had left the company. They no longer saw eye to eye. Yes, he believed there was talk of her marrying, but we have heard that before, haven't we? Who could possibly take her place? Pooh! Who ever heard of Boronskaya before she joined the Ballets

Lermontov? The discovery of new stars is not so difficult. He might have been the Astronomer Royal lecturing to a bunch of school boys. M. Boudin was only too ready to believe him. Boris Lermontov was his Prophet.

M. Rideault was more skeptical: "A star like Boronskaya?"

"Far brighter."

The fantastic brass birdcage had wavered to a halt, releasing onto the Casino Terrace a group of girls, travel-stained and crumpled, who were checking lists of hotels. He addressed one of them—at random, it seemed—with nothing to distinguish her from the girls about her but her glorious red hair: "Well, Miss Page, are you very tired?"

This totally unexpected solicitude so astonished Vicky that she stammered, conscious of her greasy face and lack of makeup, "Oh! Thank you! Yes—I am." Then she got herself in hand. "I mean—I'm not very tired."

Lermontov introduced her to his two companions: "Messieurs! Je vous présente Miss Victoria Page, qui vient de nous joindre . . . M. Boudin, Directeur-Général de l'Opéra . . . M. Rideault, le Regisseur."

The usual bows and kissing of hands ensued, while two pairs of observant and very experienced eyes looked Vicky over. A third pair of eyes, eyes that missed nothing, dark and cavernous, was watching from the sidelines. It might be a whim of Boris Lermontov's, or it might not; in any case it was as well for Grisha Ljubov to be prepared for it.

M. Boudin, airing his English, resorted to the stalest of all gambits: "You'ave already visited Monte Carlo, mademoiselle?"

When Vicky answered that she had come last season in her aunt's yacht, she noticed an unaccountable increase in the attention of the two gentlemen. Broad smiles, nods, and an interchange of glances, accompanied M. Rideault's question: "Then you already know the Hôtel de Paris, mademoiselle?"

"Yes. But I believe that I'm staying at the—"

Lermontov interrupted, taking her arm: "—At the Hôtel de Paris. You will be more comfortable there."

IT WAS TO BE A DAY OF MIRACLES.

At lunchtime five dozen yellow roses were sent up from the flower shop. There was no card.

At tea-time—"le five o'clock"—a cable arrived from Lady Neston:

ON BOARD YACHT OTTOLINE KINGSTON
JAMAICA WISHING YOU LUCK DARLING

At cocktail-time there was a handwritten note:

My dear Miss Page—
My car will call for you at eight.
        Boris Lermontov

It was already seven.

She read it several times. It was an imperious little note. She had ascertained that he was not staying in the hotel. He always rented a villa. "My car will call for you." If he were taking her out, he would have written "I will call for you." It must mean dinner at his villa. Perhaps he was giving a dinner party for friends on his arrival. Thank goodness she'd spent the afternoon at the hairdresser's! She opened her trunk.

When she had packed three simple frocks, Maureen had protested, "Aren't you taking one single evening dress, Miss Vicky?"

"When would I wear it?"

"Wear it, is it? Parties, suppers, galas . . ."

"You forget I'm a working girl. Early to bed and early to rise—"

"—Gets a girl nowhere!"

Then at the last moment, her selection made, Vicky said, "I'll take this one, too." Maureen gave a tiny scream of satisfied delight as Vicky added, "Just in case. . . ."

One of her aunt's dictums: "When in doubt what to wear, remember: it is embarrassing to make everyone else feel underdressed, but far more embarrassing to be underdressed yourself."

Vicky looked at the three honest little frocks. Then she looked at the dress. She took it to the light. The setting sun gilded the sea and turned the grim Rock of Monaco black. The slopes of the Tête de Chien shone in the low sunlight like steps to Paradise. How many apples did Eve have to choose from? Did she waver on which to pick?

She chose Jacques's grandest creation. The peacock blue of the gown rivaled the hue of the sea.

THE FRONT PORTER TOOK OFF HIS UNI-form cap and stepped into the territory sacred to the Hall Porter. He called out, "Mr. Boris Lermontov's car for Miss Victoria Page!"

The Hall Porter started, looked up, and beheld a vision descending in the crystal cage of the elevator. The glass door opened. The Lift Porter bowed. The Hall Porter bowed. The Front Porter bowed. Vicky crossed the wide marble floor, her skirt rustling over the glistening surface. On her head she wore a little gold crown. As she descended the outer staircase to the street, where Dmitri sat at the wheel of an open Rolls-Royce, she lifted the long dress, and close observers—there were many—got a glimpse of multi-colored layers of muslin petticoats and an ankle in a bronze stocking. A waiter in the Café de Paris, celebrated for having carried twenty-eight glasses of beer singlehanded without spilling a drop, pulled up so abruptly that the solitary bottle of Perrier water on his tray overturned. Gloomy losers, leaving the Casino, smiled; hopeful gamblers seeing an angel appear on the steps of the Hôtel de Paris, remembered the time-honored prescription: "When you see an angel in your dreams, rub the money in your pocket and make a fortune."

The Rolls mounted the Gardens and took the turning to the left, which climbs steeply to the Moyenne Corniche. They were soon out of the town and into the mountains.

Seated on the cushioned throne of the back seat, caressed by the soft evening air, the light blue sky above her and darkening sea below, Vicky was borne as by a magic carpet into the upper air. The immense panorama of the Alpes-Maritimes was unrolled for her: great cliffs tumbled down into the sea for her diversion; Cap Martin, Cap Ferrat, Cap d'Antibes, the coast's Three Graces, disputed the crown of Beauty for her judgment; far away, beyond Cannes, the rugged shapes of the Esterels pleaded for her admiration. Near at hand, the gray-green leaves of olive trees, whose fruit had dropped into Francesca's lap when Paolo laid his head in it, rippled and whispered as she passed by.

Great terraced villas, hanging gardens, princes' palaces, started from the stony soil. They were above Beaulieu. The car turned up into a steep, narrow road, between high walls, half-drowned in cataracts of geraniums, wisteria, bougainvillea; it stopped at a flight of Florentine steps, leading to a high, wrought-iron gate in the wall. Dmitri, like a genie from the *Arabian Nights*, his task accomplished, sat motionless at the wheel. The princess descended from her flying carpet and hesitated before mounting the steps. Over the wall she could see the tops of cypresses and hear the voice of an Italian gardener singing. A voice (was it Dmitri's?) said, "Montez, mademoiselle!" She climbed the steps and the car slid away.

The gate was ajar. She pushed it open and found herself at the foot of another stone stairway, which mounted into the sky. Tall cypresses marched up the mountain, lining her ascent like guardsmen. The garden was charmingly neglected. Weeds grew on the steps; the hem of her skirt flattened their tops as she climbed. She arrived at the top and found the villa waiting for her.

It was painted Pompeian red and was set around a small court where a fountain bubbled. More steps and a patio, lined with rose-colored marble columns, led to the front door. It was ajar. There were no locked doors in this castle. On a marble bench from a Sienese church, a number of coats, hats, and berets were thrown pell-mell. She recognized, with growing dismay, Ljubov's famous cane. She could hear his voice in the house, raised in the sort of throaty croak he used for arguments. She began to suspect she had misjudged Lermontov's invitation.

One of the long shadows thrown by the marble columns moved. A man detached himself from the column he had been leaning against and advanced toward her, against the backdrop of the setting sun. She could only see a silhouette and hear a voice which, without any preliminary, said, "Hello!"

Now she could make him out, although she didn't know the voice—sandy-haired, freckled, tall, slim, remarkable eyes . . . hadn't he something to do with the orchestra? She ventured, "Hello! You are English, aren't you?"

"As English as you are."

She passed that one. She was Scottish, but it didn't seem the time to insist on it. "Who's in there?" she asked.

Julian pointed out Ljubov's cane, Ratov's cape, Livy's unmistakable hat. "And someone who wears no hat, no overcoat, and never carries a cane." He indicated an empty space. "Boleslavsky."

She felt more and more embarrassed. "It sounds like a conference."

"It is a conference."

"Why are you here, then?"

"Why are you? You look a bit dressed up for an audition."

She gave him a blank stare. "I'm afraid I don't know what you do in ballet."

"I am under contract to Mr. Lermontov. I am a composer and conductor. He gave me the score of a new ballet and asked me to change certain passages in it—to be precise, seven. He had marked them himself in blue pencil."

She nodded, her ears attuned to the voices within.

"So I used my own blue pencil. I changed, not seven passages, but twenty-seven."

For a moment her attention was caught. "That was a bit cheeky, wasn't it?"

"D'you think he'll have noticed?"

"Did you use the same shade of blue pencil?"

He grinned. This dancer-girl seemed to have a brain, besides legs. He'd know her from the rest of the stable next time.

"He never notices anything you expect him to, so perhaps . . ." She switched back to her own worries. "I hate telling lies. Don't you?"

"I don't mind big ones. Real thumpers. Why?"

"Because I'm such a bad liar and you'll hear me telling one any moment now."

The front door opened wide, and Lermontov appeared. It was even worse than she had suspected. He was dressed in a loose jacket, trousers, and espadrilles, with a crimson scarf knotted around his neck. He said briskly, "Ah, there you are, Miss Page. Come in!"

She opened her mouth and uttered her thumping lie. "I was just going out, Mr. Lermontov, when I got your message."

She could have saved her breath. He had taken not the slightest notice of her elaborate toilette, and neither did any of the occupants of the room inside—except Ratov, who couldn't help nodding approvingly at any young lady who had tried to make the best of herself. They were seated around the dark Provençal salon and looked gloomily at her when Lermontov ushered her in.

All the shutters were closed to keep out the fierce, dying rays of the sun. Lermontov left her standing in the middle of the floor, while he leaned against the heavy oak table. It occurred to no one to offer her a chair.

"To be brief, Miss Page," Lermontov began, "I have asked you to come here because we are preparing a new ballet; and I have decided to give you the chance to create the principal part in it."

The world stopped. Vicky's eyes closed. She looked as if she were going to faint. She didn't.

"There is one thing, however, that I must tell you at once," he continued. "My belief in your talents is not shared by my colleagues."

What was he saying, this god, this genius, this instrument of providence? His colleagues . . . ? Pooh! Who cared about his colleagues? He, Boris Lermontov, was creating a ballet for her! In spite of herself, in spite of the sour looks she sensed on the faces of Ljubov, Ratov, Livy—Boleslavsky was poker-faced—a radiant smile began to break out on her face.

"But it is hardly necessary for me to add that whatever their personal opinions may be, they will all give you of their best. The rest is up to you." He walked towards her. "Well, Miss Page, that is all. We shall start

One hundred twenty-five

work in two day's time. On Thursday. I suggest you now go straight home to bed."

"Yes. I will." There seemed nothing else to say.

"And good luck!"

He shook her hand; she thanked him and went. Nobody saw her to the door. Outside, the sun had sunk behind the mountains. Julian waited in the afterglow.

"Well? What's up?"

She couldn't answer. Almost paralyzed with happiness, she only now began to realize her good fortune.

He persisted. "Is anything the matter?"

"I've been given a part. The principal part. In a new ballet. . . ."

"A new ballet? What ballet?" He almost shouted the question at her. But before she could confess that she had never thought to ask—how could she?—somebody started to play the piano inside the house. He recognized the first bars. *"The Red Shoes!"* Without ceremony, he pushed past her to the door and went inside without knocking.

In the salon nobody seemed particularly startled by his unconventional entrance. Lermontov turned on him as if they were in the middle of a discussion, pointing to the score on the piano, that Livy was playing. "Listen to this, Mr. Craster. It's disgraceful!"

Julian cheerfully agreed, adding provocatively, "I haven't worked on that bit. It wasn't blue-penciled."

"Horrors like that don't need to be blue-penciled! They speak for themselves."

"Oh! Well, in that case . . ." Livy made way for him and he sat down at the piano. "We'll throw away this old-fashioned hymn tune and go for a four-square chorale—like this—" He struck some chords and started to hum the tune. Livy nodded approval, Ratov beamed, Ljubov started to create some steps. The plainsong resounded through the room. Julian glanced up from the keyboard. "Shall I play 'The Dance of the Red Shoes'?"

The solemn music was replaced by a light, mocking tune, masterful, remorseless, diabolic, which set Ljubov's feet dancing, and made Livy, the sardonic Livy, clap Julian on the shoulder as if they were both students. The young man was only a little surprised when Lermontov unceremoniously broke up the session by collecting all the sheets of the score and dumping them into his arms.

"There you are, Mr. Craster! And this time change everything! I want a new score!"

"When?"

"Yesterday! Well ... ? You said you wanted to work, didn't you?"

"Oh! I do!"

"Then go home and start! Work day and night! I don't want to see your face anywhere until you've finished it!"

"You won't!"

Lermontov stopped him. "One moment, Mr. Craster! On second thought, I don't want you to look at that score again. Ever!"

He took the score from him and dropped it in the wastebasket. Poor Felipe Beltrán—dreaming of fame in Lima, Peru.

Two

THE CASINO OF MONTE CARLO OPENED every morning at ten and closed sixteen hours later at two the next morning. About midnight there was still considerable traffic in the square, dance music in the Café de Paris, drinking and chatting on its terrace.

The famous waiter who, in his youth, could carry twenty-eight glasses of beer in one hand, but nowadays could manage only twenty with two hands, was watching one of his tables with especial interest. He carried a wet sponge and a dry duster, in addition to the obligatory waiter's napkin. Around the marble-topped table sat the paramount chiefs of the Ballets Lermontov. Ratov, using colored chalk, was drawing sketches on the tabletop for discussion with the others, every now and then signaling to the waiter to come and rub them out.

Now, only a day or two ago, the waiter had glimpsed, in the best bookshop in town, a large and beautifully printed art book, *The Works of S. Ratov.* It was very expensive. Understandably our famous waiter harbored a design far more grandiose than earning just a few francs' tip. If these sketches had a value (and being done on marble could only enhance their attraction), they should not be wiped off and lost forever.

"Boris! Please . . ." It was Ratov, appealing to his friend. "Has it been decided whether we have four scenes or five?"

Ljubov answered: "Five, of course. And for the simple reason that it just can't be done in four!"

Full of nervous energy, he turned to Livy for support. But that worthy, reluctantly withdrawing his attention from a passing *poule,* disappointed him by murmuring into his balloon glass. "If there are five scenes, there will have to be an extra interlude . . . and I don't think that's a very good idea."

"Why?"

Livy had no real answer to this, so contented himself with murmuring a retort into the fragrant depths of his glass.

Lermontov looked from one to the other: "Are you still discussing *The Red Shoes?*"

Ljubov threw up his hands and collapsed back into his chair. "We have been discussing nothing else for the last half-hour!"

Of course Lermontov knew that. He had heard every word of their discussion. But it suited his tortuous method of control to ask, "What's the trouble?"

Ratov showed his four sketches on the table tops:

"Scene One, the Girl's house. . . . Scene Two, the Shoemaker's shop, where she buys the shoes. . . . Scene Three, the ballroom where the dance is held. . . . Scene Four, the street where she can't stop dancing. . . . And this possible fifth scene that Grisha shouts about would be the road to the church."

The waiter drew closer. Lermontov peered at the sketches. He always praised the work first, reserving his own opinion: "That all seems very nice."

His old friend beamed. "You like it? You shall have the drawings tomorrow. But you must decide for us. Four scenes or five?"

Lermontov smiled at him with great affection: not the filial affection of a son for a father, but the affection of a father for his child. "Perhaps it could be simplified a little, Sergei. For instance, the street where she cannot stop dancing could also be the road to the church. . . ."

"One less interlude." Livy appeared to be addressing the brandy.

Lermontov continued, "Do you remember how we saw them dancing in the village square at St. Jean? Perhaps we could have our dance in an open square. . . ."

Ljubov crowed, "Yes! Yes! I like it. Much better!"

Ratov looked from one to the other, pushed the table away—the waiter rushed in zealously—and started work on another tabletop. In a few broad lines he had the square, and asked as he worked, "Is there any reason why we shouldn't have the church on one side of this square?"

Lermontov replied, without emphasis, "I can't think of one. . . ."

Livy, who was of coarser fiber, exclaimed, "Who needs a street scene, anyway?"

Ratov explained, still drawing, "I had thought—I had planned—to have a donkey going along the street . . . drawing one of those charming Sicilian carts. A donkey would give something . . ."

Grisha brayed, "Anything a donkey might give would be most unwelcome!"

To the watching waiter's horror, Ratov started to

clean off the tabletop with his own sleeve. He rushed forward. "Not with your sleeve, M. Ratov!" He wheeled up another table on which Ratov roughed out the design in broad strokes.

"I have it! It's really very simple. . . . We just have this beautiful square in which the dance takes place. . . ." For a fleeting moment he pursued his pet idea: "The donkey would look charming in the square. . . ."

Ljubov made a vulgar noise.

Ratov sighed and continued drawing. "On one side of the square we have the church. . . . On the other side, we have the shop where she buys the shoes. . . ."

"What is on the third side?" Lermontov asked.

Ljubov supplied the answer. "The Girl's house, of course!"

Lermontov made a gesture of congratulation. "Perfect!"

"One set and no interlude music at all." Livy was happiest of all. "Boris! You're wonderful!"

Ljubov was quick to take offense. "Well! I certainly think I contributed my share!"

"Of course you did," said Lermontov. "And so did Livy. Not to mention Sergei, the creator of the whole design. In fact"—he sipped his coffee—"you are all children of remarkable talent."

From the dimly lit terrace in front of the Casino, the Café de Paris looked like an illuminated chessboard, but too far away to distinguish bishops and knights from pawns. Vicky had put on a sweater and slacks to take the air. She couldn't sleep. She stood with her back to the balustrade, bordering the deep cutting of the railway. Borne by the wind, the dance music came faintly to her ears.

All of a sudden, out of the darkness, making her

jump, a voice said, "Why aren't you in bed?" It was Julian.

"Goodness! You gave me a fright!"

"I meant to. Why aren't you in bed?"

"I was ordered to. But I was too wound up to sleep. So here I am."

"Are you? I haven't seen you."

"Thank you."

He knew she was smiling in the darkness. He added, "And you haven't seen me."

"Has he sent you to bed too?"

"No. I'm under orders to work night and day. It's going to be the masterpiece of the century."

"Is that my ballet?"

"Yes. Your ballet. Some people must work all night for it. Others must sleep."

Moved by the wonder of their good fortune, they gazed in silence toward the Café de Paris. They could just make out Lermontov's table. A gorgeously uniformed Monégasque policeman sauntered by, saluting them gravely and in silence. By now she could make out Julian's face in the darkness and could see he had heard something.

"What is it?"

"A train coming."

"I can't hear anything."

He shrugged his shoulders, looked back at the café. "They're all there, you know."

She nodded. "I saw them arriving."

"From here?"

"From my hotel window." She indicated the stately bulk of the Hôtel de Paris.

He whistled. "How many windows have you got?"

"Dozens. You?"

"One. But I've got a balcony. Have you?"

"No."

"Bad luck!"

Now she could hear the train as well. In fact she could hear nothing else. They leaned over the balustrade to see it pass below. A blast of hot steam struck their faces. It stopped in the station with a great fuss of steam and smoke. Still looking down into the cutting, he said: "In a few weeks we shall wake up and find ourselves famous. . . ."

"Not if we stay here talking much longer." She held out her hand. He took it. She had a firm grip. "Good luck!"

"Good luck! I'm glad we met."

"But we didn't!"

They both smiled, then parted, he one way, she the other, careful to avoid spotters in the Café de Paris. A newspaper blown by a sudden breeze off the sea came dancing toward her. She saw her own face and Julian's looking up at her from the pavement. It was the lead story.

Three

IF TOLSTOY HAD KNOWN LERMONTOV—
and it's quite possible that he did—the old master might
have written, "All ballet companies resemble each other,
but the Ballets Lermontov resembled only itself." And
as usual he would have been right. Something of the
princely largeness, of the generous vagueness, of the pa-
ternal indulgence, that characterized the imperial theatres
in the days and nights of their glory had brushed off on
Boris Lermontov. He—the modernist, the disciplinarian,
the perfectionist; the impresario who drew his share of
the box-office takings after every performance and knew
to a perforated centime the amount of the advance bookings; who watched from out front every night, and woe
betide anyone who fell below his standard of perfection!—he, Lermontov, feared, admired, hated, but

hardly loved, had allowed it to become a custom for the company, on arrival at Monte Carlo each year, to take two weeks off. More—before the official vacation started, two day's grace was allowed for settling in: the rank and file of the company were encouraged to unpack, collect personal belongings from storage, read nine months' mail, contact boy or girl friends, telephone parents, (reasonable calls were made at the company's expense) and within a radius of five hundred kilometers or so, to book journeys on the company! These were days of lunacy and license so far as Mr. Trigorin and his staff were concerned. But Lermontov persisted with it year after year. It was one of the things that made working for the Ballets Lermontov different. He said, carelessly, that he had snatched these children from the safety and discipline of their homes and he owed them some care and consideration. They were his family. It was good for them to relax: provided that they continued to attend Ljubov's class at nine-thirty every morning, bien entendu!

Otherwise Ljubov would have resigned. And as a matter of fact, very few of the company took advantage of their fortnight's freedom. A dancer who had achieved distinction in the profession to the point of being a member of the Ballets Lermontov was not likely to leave his or her particular rung in the ladder for too long: there were too many eager aspirants for the place. So much was happening in and around Monte Carlo every day, and the nights were even busier than the days. Scalpers circulated; tongues wagged; world-famous theatre directors, muttering dates and programs, appeared and disappeared, glamorously; newspaper columnists and critics infiltrated; talking, teletyping, mingling with the company, in the hope of picking up items strictly not for publication. Where else could you want to be? This was the hub of the universe!

The lives of the permanent staff, Ratov, Ljubov, and a few others—that was different. It was not a question of working or not working, for them. It was a way of life. It was in their blood, contract or no contract. They were experienced enough to have realized that, on their own level of achievement, they needed to work at full stretch. Nothing else could satisfy them. They looked to Lermontov, with complete trust, to provide the tasks and preside over their solution. He would look after their needs. They could work without the bother of personal, financial, and legal worries.

And who looked after Lermontov? There were three answers. In everyday matters, Dmitri. In his gambles with the gods, luck. In his dealings with human beings, Lermontov himself.

At ten o'clock on Thursday morning Lermontov stood at his big desk and looked at half a dozen sketches laid out on it: they were variations on the theme of the Girl's house in the ballet. Two constants were the green of the door and the red hair of the girl. In everything else, the sketches were different. He scribbled *No* on three of them, hesitated over the fourth, went on to the fifth, wrote *No*, came back to number four, scribbled *Yes*.

There was a discreet knock at the door. Dmitri announced: "Miss Page. . . ."

They were left alone. It was the first time they had seen each other since they had met at the villa. Vicky's long, pliant body was in practice clothes: a sweaty black maillot, a scrap of tarlatan, her hair tied with a shoelace. She carried two pairs of shoes in her hand. He was immaculate, as usual, fresh, spotless. He started to talk at once without asking her to sit down.

"My dear Miss Page, if you had been with us for a year, or longer, you would already know most of what I am going to say. In a week or two your collaborators will have contributed all they can to *The Red Shoes*.

Sergei his sets and costumes; Grisha his choreography; Craster his music . . ." He saw the question in her eyes and explained, "Julian Craster is the composer of the new score."

"And what do you contribute, Mr. Lermontov?"

"I contribute all three of them."

"And me as well," she remarked—not to provoke an honorable mention, only to give credit where credit was due. He began to understand her. She saw a joke well enough, but some matters were not to be joked about. Not all that different from the Lermontov philosophy. As if she guessed his thoughts, she made another unexpected statement, "I won't let you down."

"I know that. Otherwise what I am about to say would hardly make sense. By the way, won't you sit?" He indicated a leather armchair. "As I have said, my three friends can do no more than their job. Not in a creative sense. Ratov may repaint his door. Ljubov may change a few steps. Craster may take the overture a bit faster. But not the interpretation of the principal part: that is in your hands."

She smiled.

He was walking up and down, but he caught her point. "Perhaps 'hands' is not the most suitable way to describe it. But you know very well what I mean. They will of course explain their intentions. But a painter, a choreographer, a composer, each speaks the language of his art form and, being different from yours, some of it will be lost. Sometimes you won't understand what they are trying to say. It will be like an adult explaining to a child. You understand?"

She nodded, absorbed.

"You do? Good. Sometimes the artist must trust his instinct and leave the result to—not to luck, but in the lap of the gods. The greatest interpreters have had to do this when they got their first chance at the great roles—

Pavlova, Nijinsky, Bernhardt—all of them! All that Grisha, Sergei, and Craster can contribute has to filter through you. That's your contribution."

Nobody had ever talked to her like this before. It was like a god talking: Apollo through the mouth of one of his priests. He himself was possessed by the fire that he was creating. He was no longer giving a lecture; he was stating a creed.

"In this . . . possession . . . of you and your fellow dancers, is the whole meaning of performance: the difference that exists between the first night, the second night, and the fifty-second night. The process of creation, even when you have nothing but an inspired guess to go by, is intoxicating. In a sense you will feel like someone 'under the influence.' Your personality will split. Suddenly, there will be two of you. One is dancing, the other watching. The first will be quite satisfied with the job she is doing, the other will whisper, 'You can do better than that.' The first person is created by us, by Sergei, Grisha, Julian, me; the second is your very own. Technical accomplishment? Yes. It's important, once you're good enough to forget it, but at our level, in our company, there are a dozen with that sort of skill. The really great dancers are not those who are good every night, but those who never fall below a certain level of accomplishment and who are, on some nights, superb . . . and, once in a while, divine! These few have a bomb planted in their breasts, set to go off at the next performance, ticking away hour after hour, exploding at the right moment, shaking everybody—audiences, fellow dancers, you, yourself! Perhaps two critics, there in the audience, will exchange a conspiratorial glance, anxious to keep this unique moment for themselves. . . ."

A tattoo of knocks, drumming on the door with fists and feet, interrupted Lermontov. There were Russian shouts outside. The door flew open to reveal Dmitri

One hundred thirty-nine

trying to prevent a livid Ljubov from bursting into the room. Having waited half an hour for Vicky after class, he had found out that she was with Lermontov. Vicky jumped up, horrified. She had never doubted that Ljubov knew that Lermontov had sent for her. The one person in the world she didn't want to offend was Ljubov.

"All my fault, Grisha," pleaded Lermontov. "Don't blame her."

Ljubov's eyes were bloodshot and his voice crackled, sure signs that a fuse was about to blow. "It is not your fault, because you are free to do anything in this madhouse! But she is only free to be at rehearsal! Why do I go there? Only to occupy myself with Miss Victoria Page!"

"Grisha," Lermontov reminded him, "there is no music yet."

"I have enough music to start with." It was an unexpected declaration. Ljubov enjoyed his triumph. Forgetting his wrath and looking pleased with himself, he strutted about like a bantam cock. "I stole it."

"Stole what?"

"The score of Beltrán."

Vicky, who remembered her talk with Julian, understood what Ljubov meant, but Lermontov was completely in the dark.

"Beltrán? But Craster is writing a new score—"

Ljubov snapped his fingers under his nose. "Don't you remember, Boris? You blue-penciled seven passages for Craster to change. . . ."

"Well?"

"Well, he changed them! He played them to us at your place. You liked them. Don't say you didn't! Then you took the score from him and pitched it into the wastepaper basket. And I—I—when your back was turned, I fished it out! I have it! Here!" He showed the score under his arm.

"And here!" He tapped his head, that wonderful head!

Lermontov burst out laughing. "What about poor Craster? Doesn't he need it more than you?"

"He? That boy knows it all by heart. I watched him. He never turned a page. He doesn't need it. *I do!*"

He gestured to Vicky. "Come on!"

She went like a lamb. As they went down the stairs, they met Julian coming up. He gave them both a friendly "Hello!" Ljubov looked warningly at Vicky and led the way to the stage. As soon as they were out of hearing he did a little dance. "Seven little blue-penciled bits! Not so bad!"

"Not seven." She ventured to correct him. "Twenty-seven!"

Even Ljubov did not know what she meant.

WHEN HE WAS USHERED IN, JULIAN found Lermontov in an unprecedented good humor.

"Sit down, Mr. Craster. How is it going? How long will it take? And what can I do to get it done a week sooner?"

Julian sat down. At once he became conscious of a faint perfume: the smooth black leather transmitted a gentle warmth, the recent contact of a human body, distracting—even distasteful, if you had no feeling for the owner of the body; distracting but pleasant, if you had.

"I can promise it in four weeks, Mr. Lermontov."

"My dear Craster, God created the world in a week!"

Julian produced a packet of Gauloises. "May I?"

Lermontov pushed a lighter across the desk.

Julian lit up with a nod of thanks. "God left a lot of rough edges. Somehow I don't think that would satisfy you."

The flattery disarmed Lermontov. He also lit a cigarette, a long Russian one, and smiled.

"Working with me has certain advantages; but it also has certain limitations. Because of Boronskaya's retirement from the scene, I must rearrange the repertoire. It would suit us to present a new ballet. Your ballet."

This was a different kettle of fish! So the first night of *The Red Shoes* was already penciled in? Julian considered for a moment. "How much time can you give me?"

"Two weeks."

"Orchestration included?"

"No. Another week for orchestrations."

If Lermontov had simply been haggling, Julian would have refused and said it was impossible. As it was, he said simply, "I'll try." He stubbed out his cigarette and rose as if he hadn't a moment to lose.

"We are here to help you," Lermontov said. "If you need something—anything—ask me and I'll get it for you. The piano score for Ljubov is a priority, of course."

"He's got it already. Or some of it. While I was waiting to see you, I heard a rehearsal piano playing my *Red Shoes* theme."

Lermontov laughed and explained Ljubov's act of larceny. "Do you want it back?"

"No need. But I would like a conference. I'd like to play the main themes to you and the others. You could tell me your opinions. Better change things now rather than later."

"Very well. Telephone me when you are ready."

"Now!"

"What do you mean, now?"

"*Now* is now. I'm ready."

It was a rare occasion to see Lermontov perplexed. This was one.

"I have an appointment with M. Boudin. I'm late already. . . . Ratov is at the shoemaker's. If I stop Ljubov's rehearsal again . . ." He saw the grin on Julian's face and pressed the bell for Dmitri.

Julian nodded approvingly. "I'm sure God has a Dmitri."

Lermontov spoke as the door opened. "How long will it take to get Ratov here, Dmitri?"

"If you will telephone Nicolini's and tell him to be ready, I will fetch him with the car in three minutes, Boris Lermontov."

Lermontov was already on the telephone. "Get me Maestro Nicolini. Then M. Boudin." While he waited he said, "We need Ljubov and Livy."

Julian got to his feet; nothing seemed impossible to him today. "I'll get Mr. Ljubov."

Lermontov was amused. "Come back when you've failed and I'll see what I can do."

"That doesn't sound like God speaking," said Julian from the doorway.

Cheeky devil, thought Lermontov, but he said, "God created the world in six days, not seven. He rested the seventh day. I never rest."

The telephone buzzed. Nicolini was on the line. Lermontov burst into a flood of Italian. Julian hurried down to the rehearsal room.

IT WAS VICKY WHO SAW THE INTRUDER first, and her reaction gave the alarm to Ljubov. They both stopped working, and the bearded pianist broke off playing.

Julian went straight for the piano.

"What do you want?" Ljubov screamed. "We are rehearsing!"

"Only my score, M. Ljubov."

With an astounding leap, Ljubov got there first.

"How do you dare to interrupt my rehearsal? And this is not your score! It is Felipe Beltrán's score."

"I apologize to Felipe Beltrán. I only want my bits."

Ljubov realized that this young barbarian was in earnest. He resorted to the ultimate threat, "If you are not out of here in ten seconds I go to Boris Lermontov!" To add weight to his threats he shouted, "I resign!"

He snatched the score from the rack and marched out.

Julian grinned at Vicky. But she was far from returning his good humor. She was angry and dismayed. "Now look what you've done!"

"Don't worry. Lermontov is on my side."

"I don't believe it!"

"Fact. It was a trick to get him to Lermontov's office."

"You have no right to play such tricks. Ljubov is a great artist. Who do you think you are?" She exploded in three contemptuous syllables: "Bee-tho-ven?"

IN LERMONTOV'S OFFICE, WHILE HE talked to M. Boudin on the telephone, Livy said to Ljubov, who had burst in without knocking, "There you are. Good."

"What is good?"

"Good idea, this conference. With Craster."

"What conference?"

Julian walked in. "I've asked for a conference—to discuss the score. I intend to let you have a complete piano score by a fortnight today."

Ljubov, clutching his Beltrán score, croaked, "Who says so?"

Lermontov was still on the telephone. Julian sat down at the piano. "Mr. Lermontov says so. I say so, too. Provided you give me the green light today."

"Is there any reason why we shouldn't?" Livy wanted to know.

Ljubov still thought there was a catch somewhere. He said, suspiciously, "Why did you want the score back?"

"To get you to bring it to this conference, Grisha." It was Lermontov intervening with disarming charm.

Ljubov threw his arms wide. "Livy! You understand?"

"Certainly. What is there to understand? Boris got me. Craster got you."

Ljubov looked from one face to the other, then capitulated. "A conference! Very well. Let us have a conference. By all means." He sat down, then sprang up. "Sergei! Where is Sergei? He should be at the conference!"

"Dmitri has gone to get him," Lermontov said soothingly.

MAESTRO ROMEO NICOLINI, OF MILAN, was the most sought-after shoemaker in the ballet world. Boronskaya swore by him; Pavlova was never shod by anybody else. All the great dancers who appeared at La Scala made the pilgrimage to his little shop and waited humbly for his attention. Every year, accompanied by his wife and two assistants, the maestro came to Monte Carlo at Lermontov's expense and was treated as royalty was not treated. He had already nodded with approval over Vicky's strong, slender foot and beautifully arched instep. Now, he and Ratov were trying to decide on the exact shade of red of the Red Shoes. Strips of satin had been dyed in all conceivable shades, and Ratov lumbered up and down the chromatic scale, examining them through his eyeglass. Dissatisfied, he picked up a whole shoe, which had been dyed, and carried it to the window, watched hopefully by Nicolini. "This one isn't bad."

"Ecco!"

"What shade is this?"

"Crimson, naturalmente."

"But what shade of crimson?"

The dyemaster was sent for.

"Crimson lake."

"Ecco!"

"And this?"

"Burnt crimson."

Ratov became enthusiastic. "Burnt crimson lake! That's what we want. Dye me some shoes in shades of burnt crimson lake."

"How many?"

"As many as you have time! I'll be back in half an hour."

There were fifteen pairs of red shoes by the time Julian's conference ended. It had taken four hours, but all were in agreement. Everybody pledged to help Julian in every way possible. They trusted him. Livy and Ljubov swept him off, arm in arm, to have a drink at the Café de Paris.

When Ratov returned to Nicolini, he had Lermontov with him, who embraced the old man affectionately and kissed the hand of his wife. The fifteen pairs of red shoes were lined up for inspection, and he examined them attentively. The choice narrowed down to two or three pairs. Ratov and Nicolini exchanged conspiratorial glances. Finally Lermontov made his choice.

Ratov snatched it up and read out the shade written on the sole: "Burnt crimson lake!"

"Ecco!"

It made Ratov's day.

WHEN JULIAN ARRIVED AT MONTE Carlo he had been assigned a room in the Hôtel Méditerranée, a huge, old-fashioned, comfortable edifice where the company reserved dozens of rooms for the season. One of Trigorin's lively local assistants, Roberto Tomatis, known to everyone as Tommy, had asked Julian, "Okeydokey?"

"Okeydokey, what?"

"Room four-seventy-one." Tommy handed Julian a key tagged with his name and number. "Fourth floor. Okeydokey?"

"Anything higher?"

"Sure. Eighth floor. Okeydokey?"

He turned the key tab over. Sure enough, on the opposite side, it showed the number 871.

"L'hôtel est sur une pente—on a slope. Compris? From street side fourth floor. From sea side eighth floor. Okeydokey?"

"Okeydokey."

There had been a queue for the elevators, so Julian ran up the stairs. The lifts were something special. They were worked manually by ropes. The lift itself was an open cage with a rope running through it to the top and bottom of the shaft. You pulled the rope down, the lift rose. And vice versa. It was just a question of manpower. Or womanpower. The girls in the company started screaming as soon as they got in the cage and went on screaming until it bumped to a stop. Julian thought: "What a shame if all those lovely curves got straightened against the top of the lift shaft." Of course the lift was quite safe, the danger imaginary, and no more a cause for alarm than Frankenstein on the screen in a movie theatre.

He found it hard to break away from the Café de Paris and his newfound bosom friends without appearing impolite, but he was secretly in a frenzy to get to work. As soon as he could, he made a beeline for his hotel. He was going to have a shower, lock the door, take the telephone off the hook, and get started. He was all the more furious, on arrival, to find Tommy giving orders. All his things had been taken out of his room and dumped in the lobby.

Tommy was responsible. They had found just the place for him to live and work—the ballroom of the Riviera Palace. There was already a piano and they were moving a bed in there. The Riviera Palace didn't open until later in the season. He would be tranquil there.

"What are you talking about? Tranquil? I was tranquil here! I don't want to be moved."

Tommy scratched his head. "But your piano . . . your room 'ere 'as no space for a piano . . . the walls, they are thin, the floor it is weak to carry a piano."

"Who wants a piano?"

"Corpo di Bacco! You! You! You! Aren't you the composer Julian Craster, Mr. Craster? Yes or no? You write the new ballet *Les Chaussons Rouges* for M. Lermontov?"

Julian explained. Some composers composed on pianos. Some on paper. Some even managed it without a sense of hearing. He, Julian Craster, had everything he wanted except time.

"Please, Tommy, leave me alone. And put everything back where you found it. Okeydokey?"

When Julian returned from buying a few sheets of music paper, the hotel porter handed him a large parcel containing two hundred sheets sent with Livy's compliments. The porter had been on the point of sending it to the Riviera Palace. The reception clerk was surprised, too. He thought M. Craster had checked out! The femme de chambre was difficult to convince, too, that the new tenant was the old tenant. He got down to work at 4:00 P.M. and wrote Page One, Scene One.

The work went well, on cigarettes and coffee. When he stopped, it was eleven o'clock and dark outside.

He switched off the light and walked out on the balcony. The breeze off the sea was cool. The black mass of the Rock was broken with flickering yellow lights. Down on the harbor-front, men were playing *boule* under the flaring light of acetylene gas. He could hear the *chunk* of the balls hitting the sandy ground.

His legs cried out to be stretched. He walked up the hill, past the Sporting Club, where a line of chauffeured cars was waiting, and came to the terrace below the Casino, where he had met the great Miss Victoria Page. "What makes her tick?" he asked himself. "I hope she isn't going to ball up the part with her airs and graces." He told himself that she was the kind of girl he most disliked. He mimicked her: "Mr. Ljubov is a great artist. Who do you think you are? Beethoven?" What was that scent she used? Arpège? Or was it Coty? Her Mayfair accent made him tired. And what about turning up for an audition in a Paris gown and a crown on her head? I ask you! A bloody crown!

What he resented most of all was that she didn't sense he was here, fifty yards away, wishing he could tell it to her right in her face.

FOUR

FOR VICKY, TOO, IT HAD BEEN A FRUS-
trating day. She had ordered supper in her room, written a long letter to her aunt, and gone to bed early. But
she could not sleep. Every word of Lermontov's speech
was remembered, examined, turned over in her mind.
Every step and gesture imposed upon her body by
Ljubov was checked and checked again. She was in
greater awe of Lermontov than ever. Of Ljubov she was
terrified. She had supported the terrifying little maestro
against that conceited Beethoven, and what had it got
her? Four hours, hanging about the rehearsal room,
waiting for Ljubov to return, only to be told by the assistant stage manager to go to lunch. Then, when the
conference had broken up, she saw with her own eyes

Ljubov, Livy, and the pseudo-Beethoven strolling over to the Café de Paris!

Later in the day she heard Ljubov say to the rehearsal pianist, "This Julian Craster, our new composer, do you know him?"

The young pianist hesitated. What did he expect him to say? That Craster was a bit of an amateur, or that frankly he stank? The terrible little man continued, "A talent. An undoubted talent. He has a surprising amount of sense. For a musician."

Ljubov still had the Beltrán score under his arm. His anger with Julian seemed to have vanished. What was one to make of such a man?

THE NEXT DAY THEY REHEARSED ON the stage. Already Ljubov was roughing out the choreography. Vicky thrilled as she trod the boards of the famous little theatre. Here Karsavina had created Thamar. Here Massine had danced the Fandango in *Tricorne*, the Can-Can in *Boutique*. A solitary doorframe was clamped to the stage, Right Centre. Stage left, two flats indicated the Shoemaker's shop. That was all except for the pitiless overhead lights illuminating the stage, and Ivan Boleslavsky, seated astride a chair, making faces at himself in a mirror. The auditorium was dimly lit and dust sheets were draped over the seats, where one or two watchful figures could be felt rather than seen.

Vicky was dancing the homecoming scene to a running commentary from Ljubov, walking through his part of the Shoemaker. She was giving it all she had. Even the pianist was carried away by the diabolical theme of the Shoes.

"Now I am your mother!" Ljubov shouted. "She wants you to come home but she can't help you! The red shoes say No! No and No and No! It is I, the Shoemaker, who control the red shoes. You have paid for them. But they are mine!" He leaped across the stage. "I am here! Here! There is your fiancé!" He pointed at Ivan. "He loves you, but he only wants your body! . . . I want your soul!"

He beckoned. He grew in stature. His eyes were enormous. His hands were claws. The scene had suddenly come alive. She stopped, panting.

Boleslavsky's voice broke the spell. "She's putting too much into it. Tell her, Grisha!"

"Mind your own business!"

Ljubov's staccato retort (he used all languages impartially, speaking like a disembodied spinster) conveyed no offense and gave none to Ivan, who went on: "She's got the dance with me, and the dance at the Fair before this, and the big stuff still to come. She can't dance everything full out. She ought to know that."

A voice answered him from the darkened auditorium—Lermontov's: "How do you expect her to know it, Ivan Ivanovitch, if you never once dance full out yourself until the opening night?"

Ivan rose, placed his hand on his heart, and bowed to the dim figure in the stalls. It made no difference to Ljubov who was in front. He merely shouted "Encore!" But for Vicky, it was a painful experience. She felt self-conscious and clumsy, like a fledgling who tries to soar from the parental nest into a tree and finds itself fluttering over bumpy ground, rising, only to fall again.

It was fortunate for her that she could not hear the conversation between Lermontov and Ratov, who had come with designs for costumes in his hands. The old friends watched the stage in silence. "She'll be all right," said Lermontov, guessing the other's thoughts. "I hope so, Boris. . . ." He certainly didn't believe it, judging from the tone of his voice. "Will you look at these costumes, Boris?"

One hundred fifty-three

"One moment, please, Sergei...." Lermontov's eyes were on the stage. The piano was playing the same passage as before. Vicky was dancing.

Suddenly Ljubov erupted, "Enough! Enough! Assez! Basta!" The piano stopped. But not the merciless voice: "Miss Page, we are trying to create something of beauty. Might I suggest that while you continue to wave your arms like a scarecrow and bend your knees like an old carthorse, we are unlikely to succeed?"

He dashed his cane to the boards and stalked up stage to hold a long conversation with Boleslavsky in Russian.

Lermontov chuckled. "Grisha has set everything he can, and now he's run out of music and is taking it out on the girl."

They watched Vicky walk over to the piano and lean on it, watched with silent sympathy by the accompanist. Lermontov murmured, "You're still unconverted, Sergei?"

The old painter sighed. "She is, of course, a charming girl...."

"I know nothing about her charms and care less." Lermontov rose. "But I tell you this, Sergei. They won't wait until the end to applaud. They'll do it in the middle. Before the church scene."

"Ah! Come now, Boris ..."

"Sergei! Will you make a bet?"

"My donkey!" The old man's faded blue eyes gleamed. "If I am right, do you agree to reinstate my donkey?"

Lermontov hesitated. "You know, Sergei, there is something about donkeys ..."

Ratov crowed. "Is it a bet? Or not?"

"It's a bet. And now let me see those sketches."

* * *

OVER THE NEXT THIRTEEN DAYS, AT eight o'clock every morning, one of the three copyists called on Julian, delivered three copies plus the originals of yesterday's work, and collected the new pages. By Wednesday week it seemed pretty unlikely that Julian would deliver his piano score the next day, which was the promised deadline.

Julian, still in pajamas, yawned. "M. Dubouchet! Demain dernier morceau! The last bit!"

"Ah. Hah?" M. Dubouchet hadn't the slightest idea what Julian was trying to convey, but he was prepared to show polite enthusiasm.

Julian tried again: "Finito! Mañana! Tout fini!"

"Ah! Demain terminé. Bon! Bon!" He shrugged bravely. It wasn't good news. He had hoped for another week's well-paying work. "Dommage! Mais, enfin, à demain, M. Craster!"

Julian called after him, "Next week, orchestrations!"

He understood that all right, and cheered up.

Julian climbed into bed. He had worked all night in a final rush of inspiration and was exhausted. But as soon as his head touched the pillow he was wide awake. He was too wound up. Long-distance runners know the feeling: however much they may want to rest, they must press on to the finish line before collapsing. Julian got out of bed. He sat at his table and started to work. By lunchtime, with aching fingers, he had written the last note of the final chord.

And the word END.

He rose, closed the door to the balcony, sat down on his bed, picked up the telephone, and asked for the Hôtel de Paris.

He waited, an invisible halo of achievement around his head.

"Hôtel de Paris? Miss Victoria Page, please. . . . Not in? Tell her, please, that Ludwig van Beethoven called."

He had to tell somebody. He telephoned Lermontov's office. He was in Nice for the day.

Lermontov's secretary blundered, "He knows you won't make your deadline." Then she realized she had said too much and tried to cover up. "You know how he is. He has an instinct about things like that."

"Instinct my foot!" retorted Julian, and then instantly regretted saying even that much. He'd show Lermontov and his instinct! Everything now depended on finding Dubouchet and his fellow copyists, who were probably all over town. He asked the secretary if she had Dubouchet's address, or telephone number.

"Why not try the Music Department?" she suggested and added, "Pity. He was right here in this office this morning!"

So Dubouchet was reporting daily to Lermontov! Julian got hot under the collar. "Could you transfer me to Mr. Livingstone, please?"

Having twice boobed, the secretary was only too glad to oblige. But Livy was not in his office either. If he had been, Julian would have poured out his heart to him, how Lermontov didn't trust him, how he'd been working night and day for this monster, et cetera, et cetera, quite forgetting that the reason he was telephoning was to say, "I've finished!" But a strange young man answered, who was apparently Livy's new assistant. (Hm!) So Livy had a new assistant. The new assistant, addressing him as Sir (Hm! Hm!), said he would find Livy and get him to ring back.

"Is there anything else you want, Mr. Craster, sir?"

"No thanks." (Hm! Hm! Hm!) He rang off.

A moment ago he had been floating on air. Now he had hit the ground with a thud. Lermontov didn't trust him. Livy had a new assistant. And that stuck-up redhead was out with some millionaire or other. Then, as he sat on his bed, he thought how often he himself had marveled at the gullible credulity of publishers, theatrical producers, and impresarios, who pencil in dates of publication, engage actors, set opening nights, and advertise concerts, without having any more substantial security for their optimism than an author's pledge, an actor's signature, or an artist's promise to deliver by a certain date. The telephone buzzed.

It wasn't the Hôtel de Paris. It was Livy. "What's up?" he asked.

"I've finished."

"Overture as well?"

"Overture as well."

"Good God! You're a day ahead! Personally, I gave you till the weekend."

"Are you talking about delivering it?"

"Are you?"

"Not unless you can give me Dubouchet's phone number. Your polite new assistant couldn't help me."

"Marcello? He's not my assistant. He's yours. Lermontov's orders. And I haven't got Dubouchet's phone number."

"Who would have it?"

"Dubouchet would have it."

"Where is he?"

"There. I can see him paying the waiter for his aperitif."

"Don't let him go! If he and his gang copy my last fifteen pages I can save my good name and deliver tomorrow!"

"You sound like an unmarried mother-to-be. Hurry up! Bring your fifteen pages!"

"Where are you?"

"Café de Paris, of course."

"I'm still in my pajamas."

"Well, come in your pajamas. The girls do."

It took Julian less than ten minutes to get there.

One hundred fifty-seven

Fully dressed. And already Livy had mobilized his forces. A chasseur had hunted down Marcello, who arrived breathless. Livy introduced Marcello to his new boss, and waved Julian to a seat. "I ordered a magnum to go with your opus! Garcon! Servez Monsieur à boire!" He addressed Marcello: "Where is M. Ljubov?"

"Working. With Miss Page."

"Tell him to stop working and come over here."

Marcello shuddered and closed his eyes. Each season he managed to wangle a job with the company, and he had a widowed mother.

Livy eyed him over the rim of his coupe. "What's the matter?"

"He will kill me, M. Livy. He has been shouting at Miss Page all day."

"Listen! You go in and shout even louder than M. Ljubov, 'M. Craster has finished the piano score!' He will hug you and kiss you on both cheeks."

Marcello begged to doubt it.

"Then you say, 'M. Craster and M. Livy invite you to celebrate the occasion with a glass of bubbly!' "

"Of boobly . . . are you sure, M. Livy?"

"Well . . . perhaps he won't kiss you. But I'm sure about the hug. Allez! En route!"

By the time Julian was on his second glass, Ljubov was seen jauntily approaching, in a striped French sailor's jersey, a Spanish jacket, and a Basque beret, twirling his inevitable cane. He was just in time to see Dubouchet receiving the fabulous fifteen pages and to snatch them from him. With one hand he held out his glass to be filled, with the other he ran through the pages, watched by Julian. Not a shade of approval or of disapproval disturbed the mobility of that wonderful face. Only, as he read the last page, with its heartrending little tune, he muttered "Bueno!" Then he struck the top of the table with the flats of his hands, rubbed them together, beamed at everybody, and said, "I must have it by ten o'clock tomorrow. I've no more music to work with."

Livy signaled to Dubouchet, who collected the pages and vanished. Ratov was lumbering towards them from the theatre. Livy ordered another bottle. To Julian's amazement, these three, who had shared in the creation of so many masterpieces, were as excited as children about his ballet. He was enormously moved.

Ratov told them Lermontov had called from the Negresco at Nice; he had already been given the glad tidings via the grapevine. "If Julian will get the three copies of his piano score, we are to be at the villa for lunch tomorrow." Ratov's long arm encompassed a circle containing himself, Ljubov, and Livy. "Ivan, Mr. Craster and the young lady are to follow at three. He wants Mr. Craster to play us the whole score."

Livy asked Ratov, who knew more about Lermontov's ways than any living member of the human race, "What will be Julian's 'pot of caviar'? If his piano score is accepted as it stands, now, without any changes? What would his pot be then?"

Ratov explained. "Years ago, for 'accomplishments in the service of the Company' Lermontov used to award pots of Russian caviar for the fortunate winners."

"Small pots for small achievements," Livy corroborated, "bigger pots for more important wins."

Ratov nodded. "Later, Boris widened the scope of his awards. But we still call them pots of caviar."

Livy filled the glasses. "My baton with the golden end-piece was my 'pot' for conducting Stravinsky's *Rite of Spring* in the Colon without a single rehearsal."

"And Mr. Craster will have his 'pot,' that goes without saying," concluded Ratov. He doubted if Julian understood. He looked dead-tired. But suddenly he perked up.

"If I don't get lunch," he said with a yawn, "do I get a pot of black coffee?"

"Garçon!" cried Livy, now well away. "Du café noir!"

"Not now," Julian explained. "Tomorrow, at the villa. . . ." He rose and swayed a little. "And now I'm for bed."

JULIAN SLEPT, FOR SIXTEEN HOURS.

Around lunchtime a tramontana started to blow. The biting northeast wind came sweeping over the Maritime Alps to pounce down upon the terraces of the toy town. Parasols became airborne, pigeon shooters ran for cover. The blue Mediterranean turned dirty gray, as the wind whipped the waves over the coast road to Menton. The boats in the harbor started grinding together as the uneasy sea moved them in a slow dance. Anxious owners and their crews were on deck to fend each other off. Some of the bigger yachts slipped their moorings and steamed out to sea, meeting the fishermen running in for cover. It was not an afternoon for fancy dress. Crowns were not being worn.

As Dmitri drove up to the Hôtel de Paris at three, a sharp rainstorm chased Vicky down the steps and forced her to shelter under the porter's umbrella. She tumbled in, gasping an apology as she saw Julian already in the back seat, alone. Half to him, half to Dmitri, she said, "Where's Ivan?"

"Who cares?" Julian said.

Dmitri answered her from the front seat, "He has got his own transportation, Miss Page."

The partition window, between driver and occupants, was half wound down. There was a moment's silence, then she leaned forward. "Do you mind closing the partition window, Dmitri? There's a draft in here."

"If you would turn the handle, miss. ... It turns quite easily, and you'll find a lap robe on the seat."

Julian did the winding and found the small blanket. "Better?"

"Thanks." A moment later, looking straight ahead, she asked, "Was it you who left your name yesterday?"

Julian answered with his usual treble nod. A moment later he decided that nods were not enough. "The moment I'd finished, I had to tell somebody." He examined her profile. She had a delicious nose. She was smiling.

"You had Livy ... Ratov ... Ljubov. Even Lermontov. Why me?"

"Because you compared me with Beethoven. I'm a great admirer of his."

She turned and gave him a quizzical look. "I never compared you with Beethoven. I asked you whether you *thought* you were Beethoven. Are you conceited?"

He nodded. Only once this time. Then he asked, "Don't *you* ever think you'll be the greatest dancer that ever lived?"

She told a whopper: "Never." She sank back into her corner. He digested this for a while. Feeling his eyes on her, she felt an urge to be honest to this blunt young man. "But I dream of it some days. And every night."

By the time they arrived at the villa, the rain had stopped. This time Dmitri drove them up to the front gate and produced an umbrella against the dripping foliage. Each little olive leaf seemed to be shedding water. The tiled roofs were waterfalls. It rains so seldom on the Riviera that nobody ever installs gutters and rainspouts. There are no fireplaces to warm the marble villas, because the sun always shines. Today it hadn't, the villa was cold, and Julian was glad for his pot of coffee.

He had brought three copies and the original score, which he placed on the piano. Dubouchet had finished copying the last pages, and Dmitri had picked them up. Lermontov gave one copy of the score to Ljubov, one to Livy, and kept one himself. Ljubov at once started to riffle through his copy, without waiting for Julian to play. Dmitri had silently appeared, and Lermontov said, "No telephone calls. Absolutely no distraction of any kind!"

Boleslavsky and Ratov sat by Livy. Julian noticed that Vicky had settled down directly behind him. He wondered whether it was deliberate.

Without further delay, Lermontov nodded to Julian. "Let's hear it, Mr. Craster." He looked at his watch.

Julian ran his fingers over the keyboard, and, with a glance at Livy, announced, "The Overture."

OUT OF DOORS THE WEATHER PROVED its independence by disregarding altogether the moods of the score. When Julian stopped, the storm outside was over. The storm inside had just begun.

Ljubov danced up to Julian and embraced him. Ratov grabbed his hands and wouldn't let them go. Boleslavsky, who had bitten his nails to the quick before the performance wondering how to behave at the end, shouted, "Bravo! Bravo!" Livy puffed his cigar towards Lermontov, as if to say, "That's how the Music Department delivers the goods!" Lermontov smiled. He had an expressive smile. He even gave a semi-conspiratorial wink and nod to Julian, to indicate why Vicky was the only one of the little band to say nothing. Julian turned and looked, but he couldn't see her face. It was buried in her hands, to hide her tears.

Five

DURING THE NEXT WEEK, AN ACUTE
observer would have noticed signs of a new activity on
the Monte Carlo scene. Hotel doors revolved to spew
into the narrow streets hatless and coatless young men,
all in a desperate hurry.

Lermontov had allowed one more week for orchestration—for writing the full Orchestra Score. (This con-
tains the parts of all the instruments of the orchestra, and
the conductor conducts from it.) Copying out from it the
parts of the various instruments—the sheets placed on
music-stands for the members of the orchestra to play
from—was not Julian's responsibility. It was Livy's. For
some unknown reason, Livy, who did marvelous work
for the company, but was not exactly known for over-
doing things, had made up his mind to keep pace with

One hundred sixty-three

Julian. The orchestra needed six copies of the first violins' part, the same number of the second violins, four for the violas, three for the cellos and so on: double bass, woodwinds, the brass section, percussion—all required copies of their parts. Livy had scraped up copyists all over town but most of them were part-time workers and all of them worked at home. The ink was not yet dry on a finished sequence of Julian's orchestra score before Livy's henchmen seized it and made off with it. They tore up and down the steps leading from the Upper Town to the Lower. They dodged the yellow-and-white trams that groaned their way from sea-level to the cliff-hanging Jardin Exotique, from the prince's palace to Beausoleil. They leaped in and out of taxis, outpaced the sedate funicular tramway, and if our inquisitive observer had gasped, "Who are you?" as he trotted along beside each flying figure, he would be told "Clarinet," or maybe "Cello," or possibly "Double bass," although it was obvious that this last respondent couldn't be more than single of anything.

At the kiosks people were queuing up as usual to buy the green *Weekly*, which contained no news, no pictures, only mile long columns of figures: winning numbers from selected roulette tables—tables where the ball started rolling at ten in the morning and clicked into its last slot at two in the morning. At the booking office of the Theatre, the clerk still accepted, as good currency, ivory chips from the Casino. The sun still shone, the band still played in the gardens. Everything appeared as usual except for one thing: Julian Craster was writing for the Ballets Lermontov the orchestration of *The Red Shoes*.

For a composer, orchestrating must be like using oil paints after doing nothing but charcoal sketches. Now, at long last, the painter was painting. Although tempted to wallow in orchestral coloring, to out-Beethoven

Beethoven, Julian restrained himself. The spareness of Ljubov's choreography, its theatrical impact, had intrigued him. He toned down his colors, he underlined the dramatic movements, he added pathos to the end of the story. In all this he had the benefit of Livy's experience and enthusiasm.

On the last day of that hectic but unforgettable week, Julian got a typewritten message:

> *URGENT!!!*
> *Your pot of caviar awaits you*
> *37 Rue Grimaldi*
> *Livy*

Impressed by the combination of imperturbable Livy and triple exclamation points and curious to taste caviar for the first time, Julian took a cab at lunchtime and drove to the address, which proved to be a tailor's shop with the Russian name MENSCHIKOV over the window. Venturing in, he was greeted by a bearded gentleman: "Monsieur désire?" More and more puzzled and not wishing to withdraw without making a discreet inquiry, Julian murmured, "I've come for the caviar," then seeing the expression on the tailor's face, beat a hasty retreat.

He called at the theatre on the way back to clear up the mystery. It was the sacred hour: everyone had gone to lunch. He couldn't resist a peep into the theatre and went in, by the stage door. There was an enormous basket of flowers, blocking up the passage: carnations and roses, arranged against a background of mimosa and lilies. Curiously, he glanced at the card: MISS VICTORIA PAGE FROM NESTON SYDNEY. Whoever Neston Sydney was, he knew how to say it with flowers and, evidently, had a lot to say.

Three strange-looking elderly gentlemen, with big

One hundred sixty-five

padded bellies in gray cutaway coats and tophats, brushed by him and took the stairs to the dressing rooms three at a time. They were young character dancers of the company, minus their wigs, fresh from a wardrobe fitting. He went onto the stage.

The set was fully marked out, but there was no more scenery than a week ago. The piano stood in a different place; the score—his score—was open on the piano. He strolled over to see what they were rehearsing. He couldn't read the comment penciled in on the top of the page—it was in Cyrillic lettering—but a glance at the music told him it was the Fète, the scene where the Girl dances with all the men. He heard Vicky's mocking voice behind him.

"Nobody's pinched any of it. It's all there."

He turned, taking his tone from her. "Every quaver?"

She was wearing a tatty old robe over her leotard, and had a sweaty towel around her neck.

"Every demisemiquaver! I count them every morning. You haven't seen my dresser, have you? She went to get my lunch."

"Come and have lunch with me."

"Like this? No thanks."

"Okay. I'll sit on your sofa and—"

She interrupted him: "*I* shall be sitting on it myself."

"I'll stand, then. I'll whistle *The Red Shoes* while you eat."

"Whatever for?"

"Alibi."

Trying to find an excuse to stay longer in her company, he thought of Livy's message, and showed it to her. "It was a tailor's shop. It's not like Livy to play practical jokes."

She looked doubtful. "I don't know. There's a tale

that he once introduced a horse into Boleslavsky's dressing room."

"What did he do that for?"

"I expect it seemed a good idea at the time. One thing! Your message has nothing to do with roulette." He stared. She tapped the paper. "Number Thirty-seven. Roulette has nothing higher than thirty-six."

"By heavens, Holmes, this is marvelous! Beg pardon—Mrs. Holmes!"

"Miss!"

On the way to her dressing room they met Marcello, staggering under the basket of flowers. She stopped him. "I haven't got room for them, Marcello. But if you could send them over to the hotel . . ."

"Immediately, Miss Page."

She thanked him charmingly and ran upstairs, leaving Julian disappointed, Marcello gratified.

"Did you get Mr. Livy's message, Mr. Craster? I left it at your hotel."

Julian showed it. "What does it mean? Is it a hoax?"

"It's your tails."

"My what?"

"Your tails, Mr. Craster. Your dress suit. To wear on the first night. The tailor was waiting to fit you. Number Thirty-seven. Monsieur Menschikov."

Julian bellowed up the stairs: "Miss Holmes! Miss Sherlock Holmes!"

A distant voice answered, "Yes, Watson? What is it?"

"The mystery is solved. It's my tails!"

"Your tail?"

"My *tails*. For the first night. To conduct in!"

"You are going to conduct?"

"Yes!"

"*The Red Shoes?*"

"Yes!"

She sounded skeptical. "Have you ever conducted an orchestra?"

"Not in tails!"

He heard a giggle before a door banged.

ON THE DAY THAT THE PARTS FOR THE individual instruments of the orchestra were delivered, Livy called an orchestra rehearsal—not in the rehearsal room but in the theatre, during the dancers' lunch break. Nobody except Ljubov had been told, not even the principals. All morning they had been rehearsing the scene on the steps of the church to the sound of the piano, and now it was the same theme that the full orchestra started to play. At the unexpected sound, the theatre was invaded by the company: exhausted dancers stood in the wings, in the aisles, swarmed up ladders, lay on the floor, to hear the full effect of the music of their new ballet. They noticed a firmness in the handling of the orchestra, a tightening up of the tempo. The performance lasted perhaps a minute and a half, and the applause that greeted it was almost as long. Vicky clapped wildly with the rest and exclaimed to Boleslavsky, "Aren't you thrilled? Isn't Livy wonderful?"

To her astonishment, a voice in front of her said, in Livy's unmistakable tones, "Thank you, m'dear."

"The lunch break is for lunch," admonished Lermontov, who was sitting by Livy. "And for rest!"

The theatre emptied and she saw Julian, on the conductor's platform, turn and lean over to talk to Lermontov. She was leaving with the others when Lermontov called to her, "Miss Page!"

Ratov was hovering with a bundle of sketches, hoping to waylay him, but he took Vicky's arm. "In a moment, Sergei. I must have a word with Miss Page."

He steered Vicky up to the front of the house, where the administrative offices were. Dmitri opened a door and they passed through into an area of thick carpets and marble stairs. He answered her unspoken question: "We are going to my office, Miss Page."

"Have you been in front this morning, Mr. Lermontov?"

"Some of the time."

"Are you . . ." She changed her question. "Do you still think I can do it?"

He laughed, reassuringly. "With only one difference. When we open, in two weeks' time, you will, I hope, appear to be finding the whole thing supremely simple."

She said nothing. There was nothing to say. He still had hold of her arm. It was like two conspirators joined by a common ideal. He continued in the same tone. "Remember . . . an impression of great simplicity can be achieved only by a great agony of body and spirit."

He opened a door. It was his office. He held the door for her and she went in. A waiter was arranging a hot lunch on a side table.

"From today," Lermontov announced, "I have arranged that you shall take your lunch here."

"But my lunch is in my dressing room—"

"Was, Miss Page." He pressed a bell.

The door opposite opened and Julian appeared, carrying his piano score. He was grinning. He crossed the room and sat down at the piano.

"Mr. Craster is going to play the *Red Shoes* music at every lunch, tea, and supper you take until the opening night."

"I see." She sounded quite shattered.

"In this way you should become familiar with the music."

"Yes. I probably shall."

"Bon appétit!" He went to the door. She waited until he had gone. Then, one by one, she spied under the dish covers; helped herself, still ignoring Julian; heard him titter; and, unable any longer to keep a straight face, started to giggle herself.

"Well, I suppose you'd better start . . . in case he's listening at the keyhole!"

He shook his head. "He's gone. I heard him go."

"How can you hear all these things and I can't?"

He started playing the grand pas de deux. "You've got legs and I've got ears. That's the difference."

"I asked if you were conceited!"

"And I agreed with you!"

She changed the subject: "This bit you're playing, the pas de deux—what did you think about when you composed it?"

He went on playing, musing . . . inventing. . . . "The sea . . . white birds flying . . . cotton-wool clouds sailing. . . ."

"What's that got to do with the red shoes?"

"Nothing. . . . Everything. . . . Don't you ever think, 'I'm floating! I'm lighter than air'?"

"If you were a dancer you'd know it was hard enough to get off the ground without babbling about birds and clouds. . . . And speaking of being lighter than air . . ."

She was hesitating about taking a second helping of gnocchi. He encouraged her. "Dancers aren't like ordinary people. They convert food straight into dynamic energy. Or something. You're too thin, anyway."

"Ivan has to lift me and he doesn't think so. Still . . . let's give it the benefit of the doubt." Cheerfully she helped herself to a mound of calories. "Any other useful opinions?"

"Masses."

"I mean, on diet."

"Yes. It's known as Craster's Law. You feed a couple of pounds of pork to a pretty girl. Next day you find it converted into one pound of pretty girl."

She deadpanned that one. She went on eating, he went on playing. He started to glide from one theme into another. Presently he said, "Anything particular you'd like me to play?"

"Not especially."

But he was waiting, drifting, knowing it wasn't true.

Finally she came clean: "Play the girl's longing for the red shoes. . . ."

He played it. And he watched her face as he played.

THE NEW SEASON OF THE BALLETS LER-
montov at Monte Carlo opened on a Sunday with *Giselle*
and was followed during the week by two Tchaikovsky
classics. Three young ballerinas of the company were given
the chance to step into Boronskaya's shoes, but some of
her most famous roles were not in the repertoire ... yet.
Everyone knew that meant "Reserved for Victoria Page."
On Friday the Opéra remained closed to give *The Red
Shoes* the importance of a Saturday-night opening.

The printed program was an elaborate and glossy af-
fair, with the crown of His Highness the Prince of
Monaco on the cover, and with full page photographs of
Ljubov, Ratov, Boleslavsky, Livy, Victoria Page, and
Julian Craster. After all the blood, sweat, and tears, after
the threats of resignation, after the midnight hours spent

One hundred seventy-three

in composition, and the daylight hours in sublimation to Ljubov's demands and Lermontov's decrees, there was no doubt the program was a morale-builder. Julian saw it for the first time on Lermontov's desk at the last of their musical luncheons. Victoria had procured a copy already—she wouldn't say how, but she had a dig at him before letting him see it.

"You only want to see how you look."

"Of course I do!"

She opened it for him at the correct page: Musical Director Eustace Livingstone on the left, Composer Julian Craster on the right, both of them in tails, both brandishing batons.

"You're grinning like a Cheshire Cat," she teased him. "D'you want to keep it?"

"Do I?"

"That's what I'm asking."

"Well . . . yes. Thank you. I want to send it to a friend. It really does make us look important, doesn't it? There's no picture of Lermontov!"

"Yes. I'd noticed. Apparently there never is."

They looked at each other in silence, contemplating the extraordinary man who had picked them out of nowhere. Julian put the program in his music case. "I'll mail it tonight."

"Actually, conductors' faces should never be photographed." She was pulling his leg. "Your public only see you from the back."

"Ah! But this fellow Craster's the composer as well. Which reminds me—I have a present for you." He pulled out a bundle of carefully folded music paper: it was the first few pages of his handwritten piano score.

She appreciated the gesture and was touched. "You couldn't have given me a nicer present." Suddenly, she realized that she held in her hands only part of the score. "Who gets the rest of it?"

"You. I'll send you—or give you, which of course I would prefer—every year, on this day, another page. In that way, in time, you'll have the lot."

"I see." She was a practical girl. "How many pages are there?"

"One hundred and two. It should do us nicely."

"How many pages have I got, then?"

"Look and see."

She looked and exclaimed, "Twenty-one!" How did you find out?"

He was bland: "Find out what?"

"About my twenty-first birthday. Somebody told you."

He nodded.

She attacked him at once. "I know your nods. Less than three nods, you're lying. Tell me!"

"It started with those flowers from your admirer Mr. Neston Sydney. It was obviously a special occasion. How many special occasions are there for a girl away from home? Christmas? Too early. Engagement to be married? You wouldn't dare offend the boss. Birthday? Aha!"

She knew the answer at once: "Trigorin's office. They have my passport. Very clever, Mr. Sherlock Holmes."

"Elementary!"

"Incidentally, how do you spell Sidney? With an I, or with a Y?"

He looked at her. "There's a catch in it. I can see that. With an I."

"Wrong. With a Y. Sydney, Australia. My aunt, Lady Neston, is out there. She sent me the flowers. Do you believe me?"

He nodded. Three times.

* * *

SATURDAY ARRIVED. THE FIRST NIGHT. Ten minutes before the start, Julian, in white tie and tails, was sprinting up to the dressing rooms.

A moment previously, under the stage, surrounded by the orchestra, Livy had asked him: "All right?"

Julian produced a brave smile.

"I only mentioned it because your face just went a delicate shade of green."

"But I'm not shaking." Julian held out his hands to demonstrate. "D'you know why? I'm paralyzed."

"My dear boy, only very young lovers, or very old men, should be scared of first nights."

"May I leave you for a moment?"

"Go ahead. We won't start without you."

He ran up the stairs and knocked on the door marked MISS VICTORIA PAGE.

"Who is it?"

"Me! Julian!"

There was a sound of voices. Then Vicky's voice said, "Faites entrer!"

He backed into the room, announcing, "I thought I'd give you a chance to see your conductor's back before the audience does." Then he turned round and was struck dumb. It was the first time he had seen her in full makeup and costume. Her glorious hair sparkled and shone, her frock was peach-colored, and she wore a blue velvet ribbon around one of her slender wrists. Her dresser and dressmaker were giving the finishing touches. When she looked at him, he forgot their jokes and quarrels and only said, "I, who am about to die, salute you! Good luck, Vicky. Don't get stagefright!"

"Don't get orchestra fright!"

The callboy rapped on the door. "Cinq minutes!" Lights were flashing. Somewhere a bell was ringing. He ran down the stairs.

Livy was waiting for him, and gave him a keen look. "You look better." At any other time, he would have asked the name of the remedy his protégé had taken. As it was he led the way, saying, "Time to go down."

They crossed the stage, meeting Ljubov in his costume and makeup as the Shoemaker. It gave Julian a physical shock as his eyes met the eyes of the great artist, dark and cavernous under the wild mop of hair, his face pale as ashes. He was moaning, "Chaos! Chaos! Chaos!" He passed them without seeing them. Behind a flat stood, docilely enough, Ratov's donkey, and his little cart, his owner grooming him for the hundredth time in a high state of nerves. Lermontov appeared, doing the rounds, calm, immaculate, as usual.

"Good luck, Mr. Craster."

"Thank you, Mr. Lermontov."

"Nervous?"

Julian gulped, "No." The two musicians went down the steps and crossed under the stage. They could hear the thumps of the dancers practicing their leaps overhead. Livy stopped at the open door to the orchestra pit, where the conductor's podium could be seen in the full glare of the lights.

"Best of luck, Craster. I'll be praying for you."

"I'll need your prayers if it's a flop."

Livy surprised him. That sarcastic, irritable man suddenly seized him by the arms and shook him, saying into his astonished face, "What have you got to worry about? It's a fine score! A fine score! I wish to Christ I—" He broke off, literally pushed Julian into the orchestra pit, and walked back beneath the stage to join Lermontov. He could tell from the growing applause what was happening. Julian had appeared on the podium. Now he was acknowledging their welcome. Now he had turned his back to them. Now he was raising his baton to rap on the stand and collect the orchestra. . . . Now . . . The Overture to *The Red Shoes* had started.

Backstage, chaos reigned supreme, as Ljubov had said. The new prima ballerina was in a panic. Ratov was storming at the stage carpenter. Ivan Boleslavsky was sick to his stomach. Ljubov had lost the red shoes. Only Lermontov moved like a god among distracted mortals, calming here, giving orders there, the cool breeze of his passing bringing relief to nerves as taut as piano wires.

Once again Vicky, watched by her anxious dresser, counted the bars of music up to her appearance. "Good God! I can't remember my entrance! If only Julian were here!" But Julian was in front conducting the orchestra. . . . "Cherchez M. Ljubov, s'il vous plaît!"

Ljubov was raging around the Shoemaker's shop. He couldn't find the red shoes. "Mon dieu! Ou sont les chaussons rouges? The red shoes! Where are they?"

Julian was taking the overture at a vertiginous speed on the other side of the curtain. "Queer," thought Lermontov, "how little of the orchestration penetrates the front curtain—the piano parts are inaudible." He heard Ljubov's despairing cry—"Where are the red shoes?" —and said, "Are you sure you haven't hidden them yourself?"

"*No!No!No!No!No!* . . . YES! FOOL! FOOL!" Ljubov took two leaps to a secret hiding place in the prompter's corner. He returned in triumph with the shoes in his hands.

Lermontov crossed the stage. Panic was spreading like the plague. "Good luck, Ivan!"

A hollow groan was followed by nervous pacing up and down.

At the green-painted door to the Girl's house, Ratov was in tears: "Elephants! Clumsy elephants! They have ruined my décor! Look at it, Boris!"

"It looks all right to me."

"But the door! The door! It won't shut!"

"Somebody must hold it."

"But who?"

"The callboy. He'll be doing nothing at the time."

Vicky's dresser appeared at his elbow. "Monsieur Lermontov! Miss Page vous demand!"

Calmly he followed her to the back of the set. There was less than a minute before curtain. Vicky, looking perfectly ravishing, was shaking with nerves. Nothing serious. Calmness from him was essential. No hurry either.

She wailed, "I can't even remember how my entrance goes."

"You mean you *think* you can't remember. What's this?" He hummed the opening bars.

She breathed a sigh of relief. "It's all right when I hear the music...."

"Then as you are undoubtedly going to hear the music, it is undoubtedly going to be all right."

This was the critical moment. If only she could be reminded of something entirely different.... He compelled her to look at him. "If I had any doubts about you at all, I should be nervous tonight. Am I nervous?"

She searched his face. "I don't think so."

Not enough, he thought. He went on speaking, piling up the reassuring words. "You are not dancing for an audience. You are dancing for Ljubov, Ratov, me—people for whom you have danced many times before...." Her cheeks were losing their pallor. She nodded. He went on, "I believed in you from the beginning, but tonight we all believe in you. Tonight I want you to dance with the same ecstasy that I have seen in you only once before...."

She took him up: "At the Mercury Theatre!"

"Yes. At the Mercury Theatre. On a wet—"

". . . On a wet Saturday afternoon." She was smiling now and quite calm.

He relinquished his grip on her wrists, which he had been holding as one holds the bridle of a nervous horse. He looked around for Livy and saw him watching a few feet away. He had his watch in his hand. "Twenty seconds, Boris. Good luck, my dear young lady."

The two men hurried off to the pass door, through it to Lermontov's box.

"You're a magician, Boris! To have produced all this in three weeks! And from nothing!"

"My dear Livy, the best magician in the world cannot produce a rabbit from a hat, unless there is a rabbit already in the hat."

Ratov was in the box, to view his creation from this, for him, most important angle. He whispered triumphantly to Lermontov, "We could have filled the Albert Hall tonight!"

"But what these few see tonight, the whole world will want to see tomorrow!"

As they slid silently into their seats, the overture ended in bold chords. The audience clapped, but the applause was at once curtailed by Julian's raising his arms afresh.

Livy murmured in admiration, "Good boy!"

Onstage, Ljubov had taken up his place dead center. Trust Grisha Ljubov to find center stage. He held the precious Red Shoes in his hands. He was as calm as he had been frenzied twenty seconds before. He winked at Vicky, nodded to the stage manager, and faced the auditorium.

The cue light on Julian's desk glowed. The audience hushed. The curtain rose in silence. But where Vicky stood, in the wings, the swish of the curtain as it passed overhead was like the crack of doom . . . the most exciting and the most frightening sound a performer can hear.

Her heart gave a jump. She waited for the music. It started. A thin mocking little tune, the Shoemaker's tune. Ljubov never allowed anybody to see him creating or rehearsing his part before the final dress rehearsal. As far as Vicky knew, he has given her all his time. Yet, when the moment arrived, he had a movement, or an attitude, a solo step or a piece of mime, precisely to every note of the music. With his performance, it was not a question of sympathy with the role, still less of inspiration. In that marvelous brain there was a conception of the part that nobody else could have invented: it was the way that his body, his cavernous eyes, his plastic movements, his long fingers, his shock of black hair, were animated, puppetlike, by the music that made the shopworn word "genius" the only possible word to apply to his performance. In a few seconds he had the entire audience hypnotized. They couldn't take their eyes off him. He showed the red shoes he had created; he gave a little dance of triumph; he scampered across the stage of his shop, stage left, and placed the shoes in his window, where they burned, to entice the customer he wanted.

Vicky's entrance was at Bar 42. She rubbed her feet in the rosin as she stood there counting. Behind her was her dresser, Poupette, with the towel and the tray with makeup and the glass of water. She watched her door, that the callboy stood holding. Out of the corner of her eye she could see Nadia and Nora come on, dance in front of the Shoemaker's shop, implore him to sell them the shoes. Bar 40! He refused. He intended them for a special customer. He pointed with his knife across the stage to the green door. It opened on cue!

THE BALLET OF THE RED SHOES

Bravo callboy! I, Victoria Page—I'm on!

The music is all that matters. How right Lermontov was! I flame into the doorway, one arm high above my head in greeting. Ivan, my partner, is waiting for me. He's thirty-eight and not as strong as he used to be, but he's a generous, considerate partner, and a true artist, wonderful to dance with. He's a good actor, too. He plays a teen-age boy and is getting away with it. His movements have all the spontaneity of youth, his admiration for the Girl is so simple and heartwarming! She fancies him, but she fancies the red shoes more. This is my favorite bit. I see them, there, in the shop window where they shine, a tempting bait, while in the shadows the

Shoemaker lurks, watching to see me take it. The Boy tries to dissuade me. Useless! I dance in front of the window. I stretch out my arms to the wonderful red shoes. They must have me! I must have them! I can see myself reflected in the window, as if I were wearing the red shoes. If I had the red shoes I would never stop dancing! I would be the greatest dancer in the world! I must have them! I must! Boy is forgotten. Give me the red shoes!

Ljubov snatches the red shoes from the window. He dances out of the shop. He holds the red shoes in his hands. He lets them drop to the full extent of their red ribbons. He dangles them in front of me. He tempts me. He mocks me. Then quite deliberately he places them on the stage and invites me to jump into them. One-two! One-two! The red shoes are on!

Julian starts to conduct the Dance of the Red Shoes. That diabolical tune comes fresh to me every time I hear it. It is impossible not to dance to it: it is the red shoes themselves dancing. I have them on, and they dance with me. The Shoemaker laughs and picks his nails with the point of his Finnish knife. He's got the customer he wanted.

The Boy sees the red shoes winning. He is losing me. I dance as I have never danced before. It isn't me. It's the red shoes. They scintillate. They are enchanted. Everyone is looking at me, as I dance in the red shoes. More! More! I need more people! More admirers! Off to the Fair!

Girls love the Fair; it's brash, vulgar, idiotic, vital. Anything goes! We dance with anyone who asks us. We dance with top hats, cloth caps, brown derbies ... with striped pants, blue jeans, riding breeches, white tie and tails ... with big bellies, with slim hips ... the red shoes dance them all down. The red shoes never stop dancing. I never danced like this. I can have anything I want! Anybody!

The Boy is following me through the crowd. I've left him behind. A long way behind. He was only a boy after all. And I'm the wearer of the red shoes! Come on, Old Boy! Let's see the color of your money! Come on, Big Boy! Help me to spend it! The night is made for loving! The night is made for dancing! On and on! From hand to hand! From one pair of arms to another pair of arms! From one pair of shoes to another pair of shoes! But the red shoes dance on! They never stop. They never wear out. Like me! I'll never grow old. I'll never stop dancing. Like the red shoes!

The town is asleep. The Fair is over. Memories litter the streets. Balloons collapse in the gutters. Streamers pluck at my hair. All the men have gone. Time to go home. Mother will be sitting up for me. Time to go. Come on, red shoes! Carry me home. The moon is shining. The streets are quiet. The houses throw long shadows on the cobbles. My shadow dances ahead of me, happily, dreamily home. There's the green door I've known all my life. Mother! I'm home!

But the red shoes have no home. They belong to the Shoemaker. I've only bought them. They obey him, not me. Those shadows, those long arms, reaching out to touch them! These are magic shoes! He's a magic shoemaker! A magician! Mother! Mother! Help me! Don't let the red shoes carry me away!

This scene has always frightened me. There is something about it that scares me. There is something in Julian's music that is sinister, that seems to cry out, "Beware, Vicky! Beware!" Ljubov, even, was affected by it. He wouldn't show us what he was going to do. Not even at the dress rehearsal. It was as if he said, "No. I cannot show you. This is too real. This is too frightening." Only Lermontov was allowed to see it.

Step by step I leave my home behind me. I know I'll never see it again. I'll never see my mother again. The red shoes won't let me! They're taking me into the power of the Shoemaker. He seizes me; he dances with me. He can do what he likes with me. I'm under a spell. The spell of the red shoes.

His eyes burn into mine. His hands are like claws. His hair is like wire. He isn't flesh and blood; he's a puppet! A mandrake! His eyes are like a wild animal's. This isn't acting! It's terrifying. I feel my head turning. They've cast a spell on me! All of them! Lermontov! Julian! Ljubov! I'm dancing for them. Only the music can save me! Julian! Save me!

Waves of music catch me and bear me up! Wonderful sounds ... harmonies ... vibrations ... carry me along. I'm floating! I'm rising! I'm falling! I'm weightless! Bodiless! I'm flying! I'm falling ... falling ... fallen ... into a sleeping town at night. A wind blows a torn newspaper towards me. It flaps about as if it were alive. It is alive! It wants to dance! It wants to dance with me. I'll dance with you, newspaper! Dance with me! Newspaper! Dance, you gossip writers! you columnists! you critics! Write that I'm wonderful! Write that I'm great! Write so that my mother can read it! So that my boyfriend can read it! So that he can read about my other boyfriends! So that he can still keep on loving me! So that everyone can keep on loving me! So that everyone knows I'm the greatest dancer in the world!

It isn't true! It's the red shoes that dance, and I follow! It's the spell of the Shoemaker that makes me dance. What's that shape against the moon? It's the Shoemaker! It's he! What a leap that was that Ljubov made! He soared up from the stage as if he were airborne. He seemed lighter than air. He really is a magician! We dance together and the town explodes in colored lights! The sky crackles and flames with all the colors of the spectrum. Dance! Dance, little lady! You can't escape the

Shoemaker! You can't stop dancing! The red shoes carry you on!

Lamplight! The streets! Love for sale. Under the street lamps the garish girls. Faces I knew at home and at school. Scarlet lips! Beaded lashes! Shadowed eyes! White arms like lepers reaching for me as the red shoes dance by. The light dazzles. Out of the shadows leaps the Shoemaker! He's got me by the wrist! There's a wall in front of us. There's a narrow gap and he drags me through!

What are you doing here, Boy? Why do you appear in my dreams? Yes! I loved you once. I think I did. I can't remember. They tell me you never married. I? I'm married to the red shoes!

Darkness! Monsters! Faces in the dark! More and more of them ... Ratov and his wonderful masks ... coming nearer and nearer. All around me. Every way I turn, more and more of them. Faces like sponges! Faces like dead leaves. Faces like bad dreams. Faces like nothing on earth. I shut them out with my fingers. They are still there. I try to dance them away and they dance with me. They seize me, lift me into the air. Into the spotlight.

I'm alone! Alone on a bare mountain! I'm dancing on an airy island no bigger than a tabletop. A sheer cliff on every side. I pirouette on the edge. I lean over the abyss. I'm not afraid. Why should I be afraid? The red shoes aren't afraid. Now I'm at the top. At the top of the world! I'm the greatest dancer in the world!

I can have anything I want. I want a ballroom. A yellow ballroom, blazing with candles. A few guests. Just to dance with. I'll invite the Boy and his friends. Just to show him what he missed. The orchestra plays. The music swells. What a wonderful tune to dance to! What a wonderful composer Julian is! He's conducting his own music as if he were making love to me. He's there! In the pit, behind the blaze of the footlights. What a wonderful theme! It seems to unite us. My dancing! His music! I can almost imagine he mounts on to the stage and takes me in his arms . . .

Ivan takes me in his arms. It's the pas de deux. I'm smiling as I dance it. I'm thinking of Julian. His clouds, his flowers, his white birds flying! I can hear Ivan grunt as he hoists me into the air. And yet . . . and yet . . . the music is airborne. I've left the earth. I'm sailing through the air. I'm a cloud. A flower. A white bird flying! And then I hear a sound I have never heard before. At first I think there's a sudden storm; a storm from the mountains lashing the sea into great waves. I can hear the breakers. They curl in thunder on the rocks. Ivan leaves me. It's my solo. I can hardly hear the music for the storm. It's not a storm. It's applause! The audience is applauding. Without waiting for the end of my dance! I can see nothing there, beyond the footlights. Only the figure of Lermontov in his box. Lermontov, who believed in me. Lermontov, who gave me this chance. Lermontov, with the waves of applause beating around him on his lonely rock.

One final leap I'm in the wings! They're still applauding out there. Hullo! What's happened to Ratov's donkey? They're going away! Ratov's sent them away! Ljubov must have persuaded him to change his mind! Poupette hands me a towel. I dry off. Quick change! Riches to rags. Julian's chorale. The Church scene. It's started already. The company is moving to the church. Ivan looks good as the Priest. There's my cue! I'm on!

Poor girl! I'm always sorry for her in this scene. I feel for her. More than any other scene. The red shoes dance on. They're good as new! They're redder than ever! And she! She's finished! Used! Still lovely but no longer loved. Soiled! Ragged! Rejected! I break through the lines of solemn churchgoers. I run to the Priest. He bars the way to the church. I hang on his arms. I fling my arms round his neck! He'll save me! He'll save me from the red shoes. He'll save me from the Shoemaker!

But the red shoes start to dance again. My feet have to follow. They dance me away from the church. They haven't finished with me yet. The Shoemaker hasn't finished with me yet. The Priest leaves me. He goes into the church. Help me! Someone! Help me!

Who's that? The Shoemaker! What's he holding out? His knife! His Finnish knife. With the handle of reindeer horn. It's a magic knife! I can cut the tapes of the red shoes! I snatch it from him. It's a birch twig! I drop the twig. It's a knife! He's mocking me. The red shoes hold my feet fast. I'm damned forever! I must dance till I die!

Ljubov seizes me. He's like a whirlwind! A flame! A tiger! I feel he could snap me in two if he wanted. I dance faster and faster. Useless! Useless for the Girl! Useless for me! Ljubov isn't a dancer. He's dance itself! Dance in the way the Greeks understood it. Maenads! Furies! Ljubov's a Fury!

If our dance lasted two more bars I'd collapse on the floor. The Boy comes back. I break away from Ljubov and run to him. I hang on his neck. I implore him to help. Take off the red shoes! I leap into his arms. But the red shoes dance on! I'm dying . . . dying . . .

Gently he puts me down on the steps. He touches the tapes and they obey him. They come undone. He takes off the red shoes. His love has conquered the red shoes.

Through my eyelashes, as I lie in Ivan's arms, I can see the face of Ljubov as he watches his prey escape. What a face! What an actor! What a mime! What a dancer! I hope the audience is as frightened as I am!

The theme ends. I'm dead. Ivan lifts me in his arms. I make myself as light as I can for him. He carries me into the church. The red shoes lie on the stage, abandoned. The Shoemaker pounces on them. There'll always be *plenty of customers for the red shoes. He carries them back to his shop.*

The curtain is coming down. Slowly. In breathless silence. Ljubov pauses in front of the Shoemaker's window. He faces the audience. He laughs at them. He holds them with his eyes. He dares them to applaud. On the last bar of music he presents the red shoes to the audience. The curtain closes. Now they can applaud the Red Shoes.

Eight

NEXT MORNING, EARLY, BEFORE TEN, Vicky arrived at class. She was the first to arrive. She took off her beach robe. A certain amount of Monégasque informality, not to say license, had crept into the classroom recently: a whiff of garlic and sunshine. She wore black shorts over flesh-colored tights and a short-sleeved shirt that left a bare midriff; her hair was tied up with a gay piece of cotton. She looked workmanlike and charming, as slim as a boy but by no means the shape of a boy. She stepped up to the bar and started work, as a loud whistle was heard approaching, a cocky, confident whistle, an air from Rossini's *Barber of Seville*. It was Ljubov, a dapper figure, cane between finger and thumb, a beret perched on his mane of black hair, his legs in tight trousers, his chest tough as a board under his striped sailor's jersey. Half a pace behind came Ivan Boleslavsky.

At the sight of the girl limbering up they both stopped and exchanged a look of approval which said "Of course, our Vicky would be first at the bar, even after thirty-nine curtain calls. . . ." Ljubov stopped beside her with "Ça va?" She smiled and nodded, without stopping working, as he continued: "Any swelling? I mean the head." She shook her head again. He rammed the lesson home: "All that clapping . . . Bravos! . . . Roses! Pooh! All that's nothing. But when I, who have seen Karsavina . . . Pavlova dance, tell you that last night you were not bad, not good, but not ba-ad"—he underlined the words, pulling out the vowels like bubble gum—"that-a-at's something!"

And it was! He looked a little longer at her serious face and a rare smile irradiated his own. "Now I tell you the truth. It was—good!"

"Thank you, M. Ljubov."

"My name is Grisha."

"Mine's Vicky."

He extended a courtier's paw. "How do you do?"

They shook hands, as if it were the first time they met. She was on her points, poised on one foot, her body leaning forward in an arabesque. He automatically corrected her position: "Arm straighter. So!" Suddenly he lost all his good humor: "Boris Lermontov wants to see you in his office. Why in classtime? Why?" He turned and cannoned into Ivan, who was waiting to embrace Vicky, which he did without a word. By now others had arrived and surrounded her, and, suddenly, they were all clapping.

DMITRI HURRIED INTO LERMONTOV'S office with another sheaf of cables and indicated that he had managed to hunt down Julian Craster. The young man followed close on his heels. The room was flooded with sunshine and the smell of success. Lermontov, busy on the telephone, swept earlier telegrams aside to clear his desk for the new lot. He glanced at Julian, who intimated if it had to be, he would, like the telegrams, await the Big Chief's pleasure. Lermontov gave him an appreciative glance and directed him to the soft black leather easy chair. Julian realized that he was getting special treatment, although he missed the whiff of perfume and the gentle warmth. He lit a cigarette; soon he realized that from the moment of his entering the room, Lermontov had started to slant his part of the telephone conversation to suit Julian's presence. It was a long-distance call. Somebody rather important was calling to congratulate Lermontov on last night's triumph, and that subtle man was using it to impart simultaneously all sorts of information to Julian as well.

"Thank you! Thank you, mon cher! You're not disturbing me at all. One always has time for congratulations. . . . Yes! I agree! The music"—he beamed at Julian—"oh, yes! a most distinguished score. Yes! He's under contract to me. He's starting work on a new ballet at once." This was news to Julian as well as to the caller, who was yelping with curiosity. "The title?" He thought for an instant, then committed himself. "*Rendezvous Beach.* Yes. Modern. Marvelous characters. Full of charm and humor. . . . Yes, I thought you would." The more he said the more he liked it. He looked at Julian for acknowledgment of this information and got it, before he returned to his receiver. "Oh, yes!"—his tone was caressing—"There will be a wonderful role for her. Not this season. Next! Thank you! Thank you so much, mon cher Jean! À bientôt!"

He hung up and turned to Dmitri, who had ready a typescript bound in a yellow cover. "No more calls! Not even congratulations! Where are the Paris papers?" To Julian: "That's all, Mr. Craster, thank you. I'm proud of you!" He held out his hand to Dmitri, who put the yellow script into it.

Julian did not understand how an interview could end before it started. He stammered, "I would like to tell you, Mr. Lermontov, how very grateful I am to you for—"

Lermontov stopped him with a charming smile. "Another time, Mr. Craster." He handed him the yellow script. "You read French?" He saw the young man's hesitation. "Then get it translated. Read it. We'll have a talk. Now! Go and see Trigorin. He's got a new contract for you."

In the anteroom, Vicky was waiting, standing as all dancers stand; she was wrapped in her beach robe, straight from Ljubov's class. As Julian closed the door behind him they smiled at one another. She saw the yellow script under his arm.

"How was it up there?" he asked.

"Not too bad. How was it down there?"

"Not too good. Adequate."

Their own words were far from adequate, and they both felt it. But what are words? She said, "How do you feel?"

"I don't know. You?"

"I don't know either." She pointed to the yellow cover. "What's that?"

"For me, sleepless nights; for you, days of sweat."

"Our new ballet?"

He nodded. "Our new ballet."

"What's the subject?"

"I'll play it to you every meal you eat. Not this season. Next."

"It's a date."

"Of course, I might see you before then. How about lunch?"

Dmitri appeared at the door. "Miss Page, please!"

He came out. She went in. Julian thought, "What a shocking swap!" and went away.

LERMONTOV STOOD UP AS SHE ENTERED. "Come in, Miss Page." He waved her to the chair. She wrinkled her nose as she sat down in it. She didn't like the lingering smell of tobacco smoke.

"I want to talk to you about your future . . ." He waited for her to speak. She said nothing, so he went on. "When we first met, at Lady Neston's, you asked me a question to which I gave a stupid answer. You asked me whether I wanted to live, and I said, yes. Actually, Miss Page, I want to create: to create is my passion—to make something big out of something little: to make a great dancer out of you." Again he paused; again she was silent. "But first I must ask you the same question: What do you want from life? To live?"

The answer came like a shaft of sunlight: "To dance."

At that moment he loved her: not as a woman, but as an equal. He seized a chair, planted it in front of Vicky, sat down on it, and gripped the arms of the chair she sat in, holding her prisoner. She looked at him, eye to eye. This reserved, secretive, autocratic man spoke, for the first time, with passion: "We have two months left of the season here at Monte Carlo. Not much time, but enough. Then we go on tour. Rome! Vienna! Paris! Copenhagen! Then the United States. Then once more, London! Two months! All the great parts—*Coppelia! Lac des Cygnes! Giselle! The Sleeping Princess! La Boutique!* We will create them all afresh with you! You shall dance and the world shall follow. We shall—"

She was about to speak, but he would not let her: "Hush! Not a word! I shall do the talking! And you . . . you, Miss Page . . . shall do the dancing!"

DURING THOSE TWO MONTHS, JULIAN couldn't make out what was wrong with her, or with him. She refused his invitations; she didn't give reasons; she shook her lovely head, and that was that. Of course, he knew she was working hard with Grisha on the great classical parts. He had conducted her himself in *Coppelia* when Boleslavsky played Doctor Coppelius: together with the audience, he had been doubled up with laughter by the scenes with the Doll; and when Livy took Grisha and Vicky through the Can-Can in *Boutique*, Julian had been in the wings for every high kick. But, most of all, he loved her performance as Odette-Odile in *Swan Lake;* that most romantic of all ballets, that most ambivalent of all theatrical parts, seemed to awaken something deep in Vicky: her Odette, torn from her lover's grasp by the power of the Magician, tore audible sighs from the glittering audience: her Odile, diabolical and sharp as a sword, held them in suspense from her first entrance. There were two Vickys, Julian realized: one of them soft and pliable, the other hard and glittering.

Once or twice a week, *The Red Shoes* was performed, and then Julian felt again the warmth of contact that had existed between them during their musical luncheons. With a fine instinct, Livy had insisted that Julian take over the conducting of some of the classics, but had never suggested replacing him in his own ballet. Julian was grateful. So long as the link of his music held them together he had a feeling that he was not forgotten. Meanwhile he worked hard on *Rendezvous Beach,* with its ensemble of sandflies and mosquitoes. It was fun creating a thoroughly modern score. But sometimes, after the lonely, hardworking life he was leading, composing dances for frolicking mosquitoes, he felt the urge to alight on some sweet-blooded flank himself.

One of these evenings, after the show, Livy said, "Got anything on for tomorrow?"

"It's a Stravinsky program, isn't it?" Julian knew very well that it was and went on eagerly, "You want me to take over?"

"Am I conducting?"

"Of course you are!"

Livy digested this piece of information, then said, more to himself than to Julian, "Fair enough." Then, after a pause: "My ex-wife has turned up in Monte Carlo and I'm obliged to take her out. Come and join us."

"Oh! All right."

"Bringin' anybody?"

"I've got nobody to bring."

"What about Vicky?"

"Vicky?"

"Yes. You know. The redheaded girl in your ballet."

"Oh! Her!"

"Yes. Her."

The two Englishmen looked at one another with straight faces. But there was a twinkle in Livy's eye. Julian laughed, in spite of himself.

Livy remarked, "I thought that you and Vicky were—what do they say now?—going together."

"What on earth gave you that idea?"

"Deductive elimination. You are never seen anywhere when you're not working. She is never seen anywhere when she's not dancing. Ergo, you must be together!"

"Well, we're not!"

"I can count on you, then."

"Where do we meet?"

Livy looked hurt. The Café de Paris without Livy at his favorite table would be like Piccadilly Circus without Eros. Of course this was Craster's first season. He couldn't be expected to know that. Still, Livy put a good deal of gentle reproach into the monosyllabic reply: "Here."

When Julian got back to his hotel it was after 1:00 A.M. He heard the telephone ringing in his room as he walked down the corridor. He fumbled the key, left the door open, ran to the phone, grabbed it, and threw himself on the bed: "Hullo!"

A pause. Then a female voice, crisp and precise, said without preamble in his ear: "I saw you from my windows leaving the Café de Paris. Did Livy ask you to a party tomorrow?"

"Yes, he did."

"Are you going?"

"Yes, I am."

"Oh! What a pity."

He held his breath and waited. She'd called him. She should jolly well speak first.

She did. "I wanted to invite you."

"Invite me? To do what?"

She ignored his question. "You've asked me out so often. I wanted to reciprocate."

"But you never accepted!"

She started to laugh. "Don't hold that against me! The fact is I have to go to Antibes tomorrow afternoon. I've got the evening off and I don't want to go alone."

"Oh!"

"It's only forty minutes in the train. Say yes! Please!"

"Yes."

"Oh, good! Don't tell anybody. You know—in the company."

"Not a soul."

"Let's meet at the station. Six-ten train."

She wore dark glasses and a hat, with a green linen dress, tan shoes, and matching accessories. He didn't recognize her.

"Do you think anyone else will? The guard gave me a good stare."

"Only because he thinks you're prettier than the others."

In the train she asked him what excuse he had made to Livy.

"I told him my ex-wife turned up in Monte Carlo and I felt obliged to take her out."

"You didn't!"

"I did."

"Livy wouldn't swallow that."

"It's the story he told me, and I swallowed it."

"You aren't old enough to have an ex-wife."

"As a matter of fact, I've got three. I say! There are a lot of tunnels on this line. Tunnels make me nervous. Do they make you nervous?"

"No. Besides, I have a very long, sharp hatpin to defend myself with."

"May I see it?"

"There you are!"

"Hm! It *is* very sharp. Do you know what Livy said about us?"

"Livy? No."

"He says that all the company think we're going together."

She was speechless with indignation.

Julian grinned and proceeded to cash in on his statement. "As it's useless denying it and as they've already made up their minds—"

"Well, I haven't!"

"Which means you might decide either way. For or against. Hullo, here's another tunnel!"

She checked a giggle in the darkness. When they came out into the sunlight, he had changed seats: "Do you play chess?"

"My aunt does."

"D'you know what checkmate means? Good. Let's play another game. Your move."

She paused as if choosing a gambit. Then she said, "Don't you want to know why I'm dragging you to Antibes?"

"No, I'm happy to be dragged." He put his feet up.

"You remember I told you about my aunt being . . ."

"Lady Neston. Yes. I remember. She's in Sydney."

"No. She isn't."

He looked at her. "Are we playing?"

She nodded.

"All right. There is no aunt. She doesn't exist."

"She does, but not in Sydney."

He snapped his fingers. "She's in Antibes! Right?"

"Wrong. But you're warm."

"She's got a villa there!"

"A yacht."

He groaned. "I might have known it. I'm a bad sailor."

"Don't worry. She's tied up."

"Lady Neston?"

"The yacht."

He worked things out. The train stopped. "Where are we?"

"Beaulieu-sur-mer. His villa's up there."

"Whose?"

"Lermontov's. Up there. In those clouds."

"That's where we met. Remember? In the clouds."

"I suppose we'd seen each other before."

"I suppose we had." They were both silent, remembering that evening of miracles. The train rumbled on. Julian announced, "I've got it! Your aunt's on the yacht, the yacht's in Antibes, and you're going to present me to your aunt."

"Wrong. My aunt's on her way home, somewhere in the Pacific. I'm going to present you to the yacht."

They got out at Antibes into a grove of olive trees. The station was only an olive-stone's throw from the port. She led the way, stumbling over the tracks, to the harbor. Julian looked curiously up at the high walls of the Old Town. They went in through an enormous arch. The Bar de la Marinière was on the corner—a crowded bistro, much patronized by fishermen, yacht owners, and their crews. They were expected. The Patron and his wife had been telephoned by Vicky as soon as she got her aunt's cable: "JUST PUT IN AN APPEARANCE DARLING. SHOW THE FLAG. TELL THEM I'M COMING."

They squealed with delight when they saw Vicky, whom they knew as the niece of Lady Neston, who had spent two summer holidays with her aunt on the yacht. "Tiens! C'est Victoria! Jeannot! Jeannot! Viens vite! C'est elle! C'est la nièce de Miladi Neston!"

Madame Joséphine embraced Vicky. The Patron embraced Vicky. A boy called Jean-Paul was summoned to embrace Vicky. Julian held out his arms to embrace Vicky and was told not to be silly. He wasn't French. He appealed to M. le Patron. He loved France! He wanted to be French! As soon as possible! "Pour baiser Mademoiselle à la française!" Jean-Paul got the giggles and rushed out into the street. In a moment, with typical French flair, the Patron had conjured up a brother-in-law from the kitchen, a big, amiable, shambling creature, whom he introduced as the mayor of a commune in the mountains. "Way back there!" With a gesture. The mayor had the power to create honorary Frenchmen. Obviously. In the mountains it was like that! A simple thing. The newly enfranchised Frenchman held out his

Two hundred one

arms. Vicky was marched up to him. They embraced, amidst loud applause.

Madame Joséphine, leaning on the zinc counter, watched the two young people closely as Vicky turned her cheek away. There's no smoke without fire. She smelled something burning.

Half an hour later, with several drinks under their belts, Jeannot jangling the keys, they walked along the jetty. The fisherman's harbor was on the other side. There were only big boats here: ships of the French navy, cargo boats, coalers, and some private yachts. They came to where a long, graceful, schooner-rigged ship thrust tall masts up into the sky. Jeannot unlocked the gangplank and they ran it out and went on board. Julian took in the size and beauty of the vessel.

"Holy smoke! Your aunt doesn't do things by halves."

"Three hundred fifty tons."

"How many crew?"

"Nine."

"Where are they?"

"They join us later. Five come from Portsmouth. The others are signed on here."

Jeannot had suddenly become a respectful employee.

"Alors! à toute à l'heure, Miss Page!"

"A bientôt, Jeannot."

He went, leaving them alone. Vicky showed Julian around, casually naming the various cabins, finally returning to the main saloon, where they sank into huge, comfortable chairs and stared at one another. Julian wondered what was coming next.

"Hungry?"

"Mm!"

"You haven't seen the galley."

It was all electric. Vicky selected from a collection

of cans and terrines: "Pâté de fois gras?" She grinned. "Pot of caviar?"

"Let's forget the Russians for a bit."

"Chicken à la king . . . Hearts of artichoke . . ."

"Perfect. What's for afters?"

"Sherbet."

He said, opening the wine, "There's not a soul on the ship except the two of us. Just us two alone. Do you trust me?"

She shook her mane of hair—she was setting the table—and said, "No."

Nine

ON A CERTAIN SULTRY NIGHT TOWARD the end of the Monte Carlo season, Lermontov and Boudin were, as usual, going over the receipts and advance bookings. The director-general was bubbling over. "What a season, M. Lermontov! What a season! Et toujours Victoria Page! You'ave a first-class star, M. Lermontov! Du premier ordre."

Someone was whistling Rossini on the landing. The door was kicked open and Ljubov danced in, singing, "Good night, Boris! She was not bad tonight!"

"Good night, Grisha. She'll be all right."

The whistle became triumphant as Grisha turned, with a flourish, and danced his way out, colliding with Ratov coming in. Meanwhile the floodgates of M. Boudin's enthusiasm burst open: "All r-r-right? Not bad? She is a spirit, a flame, une Coryphée! We should reconstruct the theatre!"

Ratov stood beaming in the doorway. He was like an old dog, a great, bony Borzoi, who needed this nightly glimpse of his master, with whom he had shared the perils and triumphs of a lifetime.

"Good night, Boris."

"Good night, Sergei."

"Vicky was wonderful in *Boutique*. She was born to wear garters."

Lermontov, smiling, returned to M. Boudin's remark: "What's wrong with the theatre?"

"*Too small!*"

In the Ballets Lermontov there were certain customs, almost patriarchal in flavor, one of which was the ceremony of saying good night to Lermontov. This was not only a duty, but a privilege. You showed respect to your superior, true. But you were admitted to the hierarchy only if you were important enough in your own sphere of achievement. The privilege was jealously guarded. It is a measure of the success of *The Red Shoes* that Julian and Vicky were at once advised, Julian by Livy, Vicky by Ratov, what was now expected of them.

Now it was Livy strolling in, his cane between his strong fingers, his hat on the back of his head. "Good night, Lermontov. Her timing's a miracle."

"Good night, Livy. Keep her up to it."

Down below, at the stage door, Vicky and Julian were rushing out together. She stopped suddenly. "I haven't said good night to Lermontov!"

She turned to go back, but Julian was a rebel, not the good-night-wishing type, irreverent, impatient. "So what?" He had seen his first talkie the week before. It had enriched his vocabulary.

"So I've got to go back!"

"All right, go back, like a good little girl, and drop your curtsey to the Squire! I'll say good night to Achille."

He knocked at the stage-door keeper's window: "Bonsoir, Achille!"

"Bonsoir, mes enfants!" He looked inquiringly at Vicky's filmy dress, Julian's white dinner jacket. "Où allez-vous?"

"Au dancing!"

Achille laughed uproariously and made a crack. She translated it to Julian: "He wants to know if we haven't had enough dancing."

Julian replied to Achille with emphasis, "Jammy!" He turned proudly to Vicky. "How's that for accent?"

"Spoken like a trueborn Englishman. Let's go into the Casino! Let's put something on twenty-one! I feel lucky tonight." She had already forgotten about saying good night to Lermontov.

Julian shook his head. "You can't. People who work for the Société can't gamble at the Casino. It's a regulation."

"Oh, bother! How would they know?"

"Know? You have to show your passport! You have—" He realized he had said something silly and shouted, "They'd recognize you, Carrot-Top!"

VICKY'S DEFAULT DID NOT GO UNNO-ticed. A couple of nights later she danced the waltz in *Les Sylphides* with Ivan and again left the theatre without saying good night. All the other good-night wishers had come and gone. Lermontov decided to call it a day, to M. Boudin's delighted agreement. But the surprise of the week was had by Dmitri, who, with the car standing by and the prospect of an early night, heard his lord and master ask Boudin, "Which restaurant is esteemed the best on the Coast this season?"

Jealous of local expertise, Dmitri interposed swiftly, "La Réserve."

M. Boudin agreed: "Oui, oui. C'est exact. La Réserve de Beaulieu."

Lermontov reached for his hat, gloves, cane. "Book me a table."

Dmitri hesitated. "For two?"

"For two."

The functionaries of the Société des Bains de Mer all knew Dmitri; they respected his influence, but they didn't like him. When the telephone at the Hôtel de Paris was answered by the elegant second porter, he said that Miss Page was out. No, he didn't know where she had gone. M. Ratov? M. Ratov was out, too. So was M. Ljubov. No, it was not a conspiracy. The dialogue grew heated.

The head porter snatched the receiver from his subordinate, harshly whispering to him, "Mais tu sais bien! Ils sont tous allés à Villefranche, voyons!" To Dmitri, he cooed, "Yes, M. Dmitri. They have all gone to la Mère Germaine at the Old Port of Villefranche. They are invited by M. Ljubov. It is his birthday!"

THE LONG TABLE HAD BEEN LAID ON the quay, on the very edge of the black waters of the inner harbor, where fishing boats, with hissing gas lanterns suspended over their sides and reflected in the sea, were unloading their nightly catch of squid and octopus. A narrow strip of concrete remained between the table and the water, where a famous local "turn"—an acrobatic cyclist of astonishing virtuosity, whose bicycle seemed always to be on the point of disintegrating and plunging its rider into the harbor—did his stuff to amuse Ljubov's guests. There were no glaring lights, only naked bulbs in red concertina-shaped Chinese lanterns, hanging from makeshift wires above their heads. The hour was late, the night was warm, the blood was hot, and the wine was cold. If you have never had a birthday party at midsummer in the south of France in the Old Port of Villefranche, with the mosquitoes shrilling, the frogs croaking, the crickets chirping, with your companions around you, with the sound of tarantellas from the Old Town blending with jazz from the yachts and mouth organs from the fishing boats, while the scents of olive oil and garlic hang heavy on the air, you haven't lived.

Or evidently so Ljubov thought, as he climbed back onto his rickety throne (a decrepit chair placed upon a superannuated table), from which he could survey his guests. Boudin and Rideault were approaching from the restaurant, escorted by Mère Germaine and her boyfriend, carrying on a tray a most enormous cake, ornamented with dozens of electric bulbs. This was a surprise from the technicians of the theatre, "les machinistes," and Ljubov was loud in his appreciation of this gesture from a group who had, after all, no cause to love a perfectionist. As bows were exchanged with the master electrician, a long black car nosed its way through the archway to the harbor. The archway had been held successfully against Barbarossa and his corsairs four hundred years ago, but it failed to keep out Lermontov and Dmitri. Blinded by the headlights, Ljubov recognized the new arrivals only when the lights were switched off and he saw an elegant figure descending on to the quay. With a cry of "Tiens! Boris Lermontov!" he bounded like a chamois from his perch, the table going one way, the chair another, and galloped to meet him.

When Lermontov, in search of Vicky, had been reminded by Dmitri that it was Grisha Ljubov's birthday, he at once made up his mind to join the party. He had been feeling a bit under the weather and he felt that he could have been nicer to his regular (and faithful) good-nighters. He felt like sitting down with his whole family and sharing their warmth and friendliness for an hour or so. Perhaps he would say to the great Miss Page, quite openly, while they all looked on, that he had intended to take her out to supper that evening but that, thanks to Grisha, he had saved a few thousand francs by finding her here. So with more than his usual charm—and keeping a safe distance between himself and the blazing birthday cake—he said: "Bon anniversaire, Grisha! May I be permitted to join your party?"

In a moment he had become the evening's most honored guest. Grisha was overwhelmed. "What a pleasure, Boris! What a pleasure! A chair for Boris Lermontov!"

"Two chairs for Boris Lermontov," cried Ivan Boleslavsky, already a little tight. "Make way there! A throne!"

Nobody minded Ivan's enthusiasm, least of all Lermontov. After midnight Ivan was always a little tight.

As soon as Lermontov was seated, his eyes moved in search of Vicky. A shadow of disappointment crossed his face. He accepted a glass of Château Grisha and said, "It seems a long time since I sat down to supper with my entire family." He raised his glass to Grisha and took a sip. "It appears that the great Miss Page is not with us tonight."

Ivan rushed in, delighted to be the first with the news. "Don't you miss another member of our happy little family, Boris?"

Lermontov's eyes narrowed. He glanced negligently around the table, meeting familiar faces everywhere. Ivan, swaying slightly in the breeze of scandal, refused to help him.

"No, I can't say that I do," Lermontov said.

By now the responsible members of the party could see what was brewing. Livy did his best, moving in front of Ivan, treading on his feet, cutting in to answer Lermontov's reply. "Why should you? You're a busy man, Lermontov. Have another drink! Grisha! Your health!"

Ivan pushed him aside. "Of course! We all know you're a busy man, Boris Lermontov, but do you mean to say you have noticed nothing?"

"Don't exaggerate, Ivan!" It was Ratov trying to bring him to his senses: with the sweetest of sweet expressions he appealed to their inwardly raging god. "We've a little romance in our midst, Boris. Just one of—"

But Ivan was unstoppable. He interrupted Ratov with a grand gesture. "Little romance! A great romance! Dante and Beatrice! Paolo and Francesca! Cupid and Psyche . . ."

". . . Romeo Craster!" This was Grisha's contribution.

". . . And Juliet Page!" Livy completed the couplings, hoping against hope that this way of breaking the news might have a happier result. He was watching Lermontov closely. He saw the look of fury which appeared and disappeared in a flash; the smile was there, for everybody to see.

"And when did this great romance begin?" Lermontov asked, unconcernedly, conscious of the eyes watching him.

"With *The Red Shoes,*" the obliging Boleslavsky volunteered.

Ljubov, bubbling with goodwill to all men and women, remarked, "You really must have your eyes attended to, Boris."

Lermontov, still with polite surprise in his smile, still with the look of granite fury in his eyes, pursued his inquiry. "And where have they taken themselves to, tonight?"

Ratov saw that all was lost. He spoke quietly: "What does it matter where they have gone? They are young, they are together, and they are in love."

Ten

LE CHEMIN DE LA VIERGE—THE ROAD of the Virgin—runs by the sea and out to the Cap Saint Hospice, where one of the watchtowers built by Philibert, Duke of Savoy, stands scowling at Corsica. Beside the tower is the bronze statue of the Virgin and Child which was intended to be placed on top. Once having got it as far as the tower, the day being hot, the Committee evidently spent the rest of the subscription money on refreshment. Now everyone is used to the statue being at the foot of the tower, although visitors get a shock when they meet the huge faces of the Mother and Child peering at them through the cypresses. The statue, nearly ten meters high, is said at St. Jean to be the work of the sculptor who made the Statue of Liberty. But at St. Jean people will say anything.

The promontory is low and rocky, covered with pines, olive trees, and cactus. The narrow road is never far from the sea. It winds between villas and gardens, their walls washed by the Mediterranean. The rocks are fierce and sharpened by winter storms. On moonlight nights the sea is full of fire. The great bulk of Tête du Chien, the Dog's Head Mountain, with its sheer precipices, provides a backdrop; and the bay twinkles with the lamps of fishermen's boats. It is a landscape made for lovers—but what lovers ever looked at a landscape?

An open fiacre clop-clop-clopped its way along the white surface of the dusty road. The driver dozed on his box. He had no lights, only a red paper lantern fastened fore and aft. Those were easygoing days. If he had looked around over his shoulder, he would have seen a tangle of arms and legs where Vicky and Julian were lying. But of course he would never be so unprofessional.

At long last the silence was broken by Vicky's languid voice: "Cocher!"

The horses twitched their ears. The coachman dozed. Julian murmured, "Sh! You'll wake him."

"I want to know where we are. I want to remember always! I want . . ."

He covered her mouth with his mouth, smothering her protests. She gave a long sigh, then her hands went round his head and she returned his kisses. Far away there was the sound of a horn. The horses raised their heads. They were approaching the crossroads.

Dreamily, Julian began to speak: "Someday when I'm old, I want some lovely young girl to say to me, 'Where, in your long life, were you most happy, Mr. Craster?' And I shall say, 'Well, m'dear, I never knew the name of the place, but it was somewhere on the Mediterranean. Not far from Monte Carlo. I was with Victoria Page—' 'What!' she will say. 'Do you mean the great dancer?' And I shall nod and say, 'Yes, m'dear, I do. But she was, at that time, quite young and comparatively unspoiled. . . .' " Vicky smiled and snuggled up to him. His grasp tightened. " 'We were, I remember, very much in love.' "

The sound of the horn became loud and insistent. The driver woke up. The horses shied. He pulled them over and the car passed in a cloud of dust. It was Lermontov.

ON THE FOLLOWING EVENING THEY were presenting *Coppelia,* preceded by the pas de deux from Act Four of *Swan Lake.* Vicky was dancing both Odette and Swanhilda. When Lermontov met his associates in the stage box for the performance, it was obvious that he was in a filthy temper. Julian was conducting *Swan Lake,* Livy *Coppelia;* and one of the purposes of the evening was to discuss the repertoire and to decide whether Craster could be trusted to handle Tchaikovsky among other classics. Livy soon realized that there would be no worthwhile discussions about such trifles as the art of conducting an orchestra, or interpreting a score. From the start of the pas de deux the tension was building up between the two men. Lermontov did not want an unbiased opinion. He wanted someone of Livy's authority to discover the same shortcomings in the young conductor that he himself now found.

Vicky and Ivan were dancing the scene with the Magician, played with relish by Ljubov, who adored the Gothic villains. The immortal theme swelled and filled the theatre with color and emotion. Julian, in the orchestra pit, felt his own heart swell as his beloved was torn from her Prince's arms. Lermontov's eyes, over his clasped hands, darted from one to the other. "Did you see that? She smiled at Craster!"

Livy grunted: "I don't think so."

Behind him Ratov peeped into the box. Lermontov continued to belabor Livy with his observations: "Look at her dancing!"

"With pleasure!" In order to give weight to his defiance, Livy clapped and called "Bravo!" He knew from long experience how to handle Lermontov in a rage. Never lose your temper! Never show you're afraid of him! Say what you think! Keep calm!

Lermontov exploded, as the curtain descended, "A debutante at a charity matinee!"

Livy and Ratov exchanged glances.

"Dmitri has Paris on the telephone, Boris," Ratov interjected. "It's about your business trip tomorrow."

Lermontov, leaving, said, "Livy! When you take over, send Craster to me."

Livy adored *Coppelia*. The members of the orchestra knew of his soft spot and waited in anticipation of those hilarious moments which their conductor could not watch without giggling. Boleslavsky, abandoning noble roles for the eccentric Doctor, hammed the part up gloriously. The dancers swore that he invented new and outrageous business solely for Livy. The scene of winding up the Doll, played by Vicky, who had a flair for comedy, had been worked out by the two of them to perfection: the antics of the real girl impersonating the Doll, the winding up of the Doll. Boleslavsky's suspicions that all was not in apple-pie order invariably made Livy reach for his handkerchief. What added to the fun for the orchestra was that they could see nothing of what was happening on stage. But they could follow every gag on their conductor's face.

WHEN JULIAN SAW THE PILE OF ROUGH manuscript sheets of *Rendezvous Beach* on Lermontov's desk, it confirmed his suspicions of why the boss wanted to talk to him. He was looking forward to it. When he entered, Lermontov was talking on the telephone as on a previous occasion, but his mood was very different. Dmitri hovered as usual.

The omnipresence of Lermontov's factotum had recently begun to irk Julian; to talk of your work, of the distillation of your blood and sweat, of the essence of your talent and emotions, was too intimate a thing to share with a wide circle. Lermontov seemed to assume that Dmitri's presence, so unobtrusive and so essential for his own comfort, was equally comfortable for others. He was wrong.

It was obvious that the great man was on edge. On the telephone he sounded harsh, peremptory: "No. I never fly. I detest airplanes! Very well. That's understood. I shall take the early-morning train. I shall see you in Paris on Thursday."

Imagining that the conversation had ended, Julian approached the big desk, but Lermontov's interlocutor still had something to say. Lermontov brushed him off: "Yes, yes, *yes!* Thursday. Good-bye!" He banged the instrument down and looked at Julian, who smiled and touched his score, like a father expecting praise for a favorite child.

"It was a bit of a rush, finishing the pencil score," he said. "Have you had the time to look at it?"

Lermontov picked it up, looked at it, then contemptuously let it drop on the desk again. "Yes, Mr. Craster, I have looked at it."

Julian stopped smiling.

"However," Lermontov proceeded, "it is not about your music that I wish to talk at this moment. So, to get to the point, what is all this that I hear about you and Miss Page?"

His words were so unexpected that Julian needed a

moment to readjust himself. He said, "I see." Then he glanced at Dmitri, who, blind and deaf, was busying himself with some files. "Can Mr. Dmitri leave us?"

Dmitri looked at his master. Lermontov nodded. As soon as he was gone, Lermontov said, "Well, Mr. Craster?"

Julian felt a bit of a fool, but he expected this experienced man of the world to understand that such things do happen. He said, "Yes. We're in love."

"I see." It was clear from Lermontov's expression that he found the news distasteful. "Did you see Miss Page's performance tonight?"

Julian felt his hackles rising. "I was in front. I was conducting."

"Did you enjoy it?"

Resentment was piling up in Julian. "Yes. Didn't you?"

The answer came like an axe on the block: "It was impossible. And shall I tell you why it was impossible? Because neither her heart nor her mind was in her work. She was dreaming. And dreaming is a luxury I have never permitted in my company. Miss Page wants to be a great dancer. Perhaps she has spoken to you of her ambitions?"

Julian resented the tone, but he was studying the man. He preferred to let him complete his attack.

Lermontov obliged him. "She is not, however, a great dancer yet. Nor, if she allows herself to be sidetracked by idiotic flirtations, is she likely to become one."

Julian still had himself under control. He was thinking for both of them as he said, with all the sincerity at his command, "You don't get the point. We love one another."

Now they were man to man. Lermontov once more disregarded Julian's words and shifted the weight of his attack to another front. He picked up the score, handling it like a doctor who regretted that he hadn't put on gloves before touching a patient in the last stages of leprosy. "And, Mr. Craster, I have had time to look at your latest effort and find it also quite impossible."

In spite of himself, Julian's answer was truculent. "Oh! Do you?" He knew that this was some of his best work.

Lermontov was beating his child into insensibility: "Childish . . . vulgar . . . and completely insignificant!"

Lermontov knew very well what effect such brutal handling could have on a creative artist, before the general acceptance of original work. But he had overdone it. He had lifted the score and was about to throw it down on the desk when Julian snatched it from his hand, his blood boiling. "In that case, allow me to relieve you of it!"

"There are, of course, so many first-class ballet companies to which you may take it with advantage!"

Julian ignored the sarcasm and replied, as he tucked the score under his arm, "To write the score of a ballet is not necessarily a young composer's dream, Mr. Lermontov. Some of us consider it a rather second-rate activity."

Lermontov pressed one of the buzzers on his desk.

"Mr. Craster is leaving the company. Pay him two weeks' salary against a receipt."

LJUBOV WAS WORKING LATE THAT night and alone, except for a bored electrician. When he caught the working disease, as Ratov called it, there was no remedy and no cure. He would start on stage at 6:00 A.M., break for class from 9:30 A.M. onward, coach Vicky until lunchtime, give a performance, and stay on, after everybody had gone home, trying out new steps, new choreography. Boudin had complained to Lermontov about these late rehearsals: regulations required the attendance of two firemen, a stage-door keeper, an assistant stage-door keeper, and an electrician. Ljubov had been told, "Of course, Grisha, you must be able to work when you want to, but it's costing too much to keep four men up until all hours."

"Then send them home! All except the electrician."

"But he's the most expensive of the four."

"Look, Boris! The two firemen, they play cards. The stage-door man is asleep. His assistant does nothing but use the telephone. But the electrician handles the spot. I need him. Tiens! I pay him myself!"

"Done! And I'll pay for the others."

So it was that Lermontov, on his way out, heard voices onstage: "Spotlight! Sur moi! Toujours sur moi!"

He looked in. His demoniac friend was executing a complicated series of steps, while the electrician, up on the bridge, was trying to anticipate the next move. It was a bit like hunting a grasshopper. The spill light revealed Lermontov as he crossed the stage. Ljubov, continuing to work, called out to him, "I was just coming, Boris, to say good night!"

"Good night," replied Lermontov, continuing on his way.

Something in his tone caught Ljubov's ear, and he moved after him. The faithful electrician kept him centered.

"Is anything the matter, Boris?"

"No. But while I remember, Grisha, don't do any more work on *Rendezvous Beach*. I've decided to scrap it."

"Scr-r-r-rap it? What do you mean? I've worked out half the choreography already. That boy Julian is un maître! It's one of the finest scores we *never* had!" Whenever Ljubov lost his temper he lost his words as well. Accustomed to work in six languages, he ended up with none.

Lermontov replied in his most imperious tone of voice: "Julian Craster is leaving the company, and I don't wish to discuss the matter any further." He walked away.

"Oh! You don't!" Grisha's heart flooded with emotion. He rushed after Lermontov—the electrician still keeping him in the spot—and shouted, "Well, I do! Do you think I don't know a brilliant score when I hear one? Do you think I have been working, night and day, pendant des semaines, for the pleasure of being told I am wasting my time? I tell you, Boris, I have had enough of this lunatic asylum! I am through with it! I resign!"

Caught in the edge of the white spotlight, Lermontov looked at him; it was a cold, remorseless look that struck a chill into Ljubov's innocent heart. His voice matched his look. "I think you have made a very important decision."

He walked away, leaving Ljubov, hurt and bewildered, staring after him. The finality of Lermontov's tone had sobered him. He looked up to the spotrail and called, "You can go home, mon ami."

The light went out.

IT WAS A DISASTROUS NIGHT BY ANY standard.

Livy was at his usual table at the Café de Paris, but his usual waiter was missing.

Where was he?

The maître d'hôtel came over in person to explain and to apologize. Georges, the famous bock-carrying waiter, was at the police station. He was being held for assault and battery.

Georges! Incredible! What was it all about? Whom had he assaulted? And battered?

Two hundred twenty-one

That was the incredible part of the story. The victim of Georges's homicidal attack was a new assistant waiter. Assistant to Georges, voyons! Only arrived that morning from Ventimiglia. A boy from a family that the maître d'hôtel knew personally. Georges had set the boy to clean up—dishes, glasses, cutlery—and when he'd finished that, anything else that needed it. The chandelier! Even the steps he used to clean the chandelier! The boy set to with a will and Georges went for a nap. He returned at five-thirty as usual. He took a look around . . . and then without a word of warning he made a murderous attack on the poor boy. Incredible? Yes! And not a word of explanation! The boy is young—assez solide— he defends himself. Naturally. But Georges . . . you know, monsieur, how strong he is. All those trays! All those dozens of glasses of beer! He half-kills the poor boy before eight of us drag him off. The agent comes! The gendarmes come! The ambulance comes! The boy is taken to the hospital. Georges is at the police station. M. Livingstone has a new waiter at his table. And all because of a few old dirty marble tabletops which Georges, for some reason, had stacked in a corner of the terrace and which the boy in his zeal had started to clean off! Figure to yourself! Marble tabletops! There were forty-six of them, all covered over with graffiti. Forty-six! No wonder the boy got to work! He had cleaned thirty-eight by the time Georges came back from his nap. Garçon! A bottle of Lanson 1925 for M. Livingstone!

The new waiter brought the new bottle of champagne and filled a glass for Livy, who sipped it meditatively. It was his way of contributing to the solution of Julian's problem. Julian refused champagne, but accepted a cognac. He was angry, in love, and spoiling for a fight. Vicky sat beside him, quiet, practical, and as much in love as he was. It was a council of war.

Julian slapped down a wad of French francs. "Two

weeks' salary. About all I've got in the world. No use saying he can't fire me. He has!"

"Look how often Grisha starts packing!" Livy commented.

"That's different. He doesn't hate Grisha."

"Why should he hate you?" Vicky asked.

"Because I take your mind off your work."

An uneasy look passed between them.

"What will you do?"

"Leave tomorrow. Back to London. Work on my opera."

"What about me?"

"That's up to you, isn't it?"

"Oh, Julian . . . help me!"

"Come with me!"

"How can I?" Her voice trembled.

There was a chance of persuading her. Perhaps . . . "You know I had to refuse Covent Garden. Ever since Palmer got them to accept my opera they've been on to me about Act Three. Well, now I'm free to discuss the changes they want. Owing to unforeseen circumstances . . . correction! Owing to circumstances only too foreseeable, I'll work day and night. Palmer will help! After all . . . an opera by Julian Craster at Covent Garden! It's nothing to laugh about."

"I'm not laughing," she said tenderly.

He went on, fiercely: "What do you care where you dance? You can dance where you like."

"Not in *The Red Shoes.*"

"I'll write you another ballet. There are other ballet companies."

"Yes . . ."

"Well?"

"It's not the same. The top's the top." He looked sullen. She stretched out her hand to touch him. "I'd always be dying to go back."

He took her hand. "I hoped you'd be dying to go with me!"

"I don't seem to have much chance of living, do I?" This made him grin. She knocked back her cognac. "I'm going to talk to him!"

"Oh, no you don't!" He tightened his grip.

"So it did start about me!"

"Yes. But keep out of it."

They were still holding hands. Vicky said, "Do you want us to break up?"

"That was a damn silly question!"

Perhaps it was. But she had to ask it. And was happy with the answer.

Livy had been silently taking their conversation in; now he looked up, and they followed his gaze. They saw Ljubov coming, no longer jaunty, covered in gloom: gloom furrowed his face, bowed down his shoulders, leadened his pace. As if they hadn't enough gloom in their little circle already, he seemed bent on importing more. While they stared he ordered a railway timetable and a Fernet Branca—a black potion which only a dyspeptic masochist thinks of drinking. The order given, he sat and stared at the ground, shaking his head when Livy proffered a glass of Lanson as a cure all. He was waiting to be asked a question.

Vicky obliged: "What happened, Grisha?"

He groaned.

Livy tried: "Why are you drinking Fernet Branca?"

"I have a bellyache."

"And why the timetable? Are you going to take a cure?"

Ljubov exploded: "I am escaping from this lunatic asylum! I don't like the methods of the head keeper. He should be inside and the patients OUT!"

Julian applauded. "Hear! Hear! I've got the sack too!"

Ljubov glared: "Nobody can sack Ljubov! I have re-signed! This time definitivement! And no matter how many times he asks me to return it will be: No! No! NO!"

Vicky murmured in despair, "Oh . . . Grisha!"

Almost in tears, he opened his heart to a fellow sufferer: "Does he think the Ballets Lermontov is the only ballet company in the world?"

"For you, Grisha . . . for us . . . yes!"

"But why for him?" Grisha pointed to Julian, happy to record that one cuckoo, at any rate, had escaped from the nest. "Why for him?"

"Because of me. We love each other. Perhaps you didn't know. . . ."

Ljubov nodded. He did know. Who didn't? Since that little affair of the Montagues and Capulets, nothing had caused so big an upset. With dignity, and a full helping of self-pity, he declared, "Fortunately, I have no ties of that kind. No one is in love with me."

Vicky put her arms around him. "Everyone is in love with you, Grisha. . . ."

The waiter slapped down the Fernet Branca and the timetable. Ljubov swallowed the black decoction with a horrible grimace, then picked up the timetable.

Julian bent over him. "I'll pick you a good train."

But the arrival of Ratov changed everything. As he loomed up, Ljubov forgot his dignity. He was pathetically eager as he asked, "Well? What did he say?"

With a motion of his hand Ratov indicated that Ljubov had nothing to worry about, then collapsed into his chair with a sigh. "Of course he doesn't really want you to go, Grisha. . . . He's very sorry. . . ."

"Ah! well . . . in that case . . ." Ljubov beamed with relief and gratification. Then he remembered his dignity and said, "I'll think about it!" He shut the timetable and tossed it to one side.

Vicky asked the question that Julian wouldn't. "What about Julian?"

Ratov was embarrassed. He looked at them both as they sat holding hands. "I have never seen him quite so bad as this. . . . He talked a great deal about ingratitude and disloyalty . . . and he said that when personal relations started to interfere—"

Julian couldn't help interrupting. "Yes. I know that bit!"

Ratov made a helpless gesture. They all understood the meaning of it. "I'm sorry. . . ."

"Boris may feel different in the morning," Ljubov offered.

But Ratov knew otherwise. "In the morning he leaves for Paris."

THE EARLY-MORNING TRAIN TO PARIS was popular at Monte Carlo, judging by the crowd on the platform. One lost a morning's sleep, but had the advantage of dinner in Paris. Dmitri had booked a first-class compartment for his master, who was buying a sheaf of newspapers and magazines at the newsstand. As Lermontov strolled back to his carriage he saw a familiar slim figure in the crowd and altered his course to approach Vicky.

"Has the great Miss Page come to see me off?"

"I want to talk to you," she answered gravely.

He indicated his compartment, she mounted the steps, and he followed her in. They sat down opposite one another. She knew that time was short and she didn't waste it. "I want you to tell me why you have quarreled with Julian."

"May I suggest, Miss Page," he said icily, "that such matters are hardly your business? However, since you have gone to all this trouble . . . Mr. Craster has been unwise enough to interfere with certain plans of mine; and that is something I do not permit."

But her eyes were staring into his quite fearlessly. It was a new experience for him. She did not raise her voice. "I thought, once, Mr. Lermontov, that there would be no room in my life for anything but dancing. . . ."

"You will think so again, my dear."

She ignored the remark. She continued, "But if Julian goes, I shall go, too."

"I see. And what will you do?"

"I shall dance somewhere else."

"Yes. With the name I have given you that should not be very difficult. But will it be quite the same?"

This was the crux of the matter. The ease with which he picked up the scent frightened her. She answered in a low voice, "I have never pretended to myself that it would."

He pressed his advantage: "I could make you one of the greatest dancers the world has ever known. Do you believe that?"

She was very moved. When she spoke her voice was almost inaudible: "Yes. I do."

Both of them ignored Dmitri's knocking on the window, his "The train is leaving!" They were locked in combat.

"All that means nothing to you?"

She had difficulty in speaking. "You know . . . exactly . . . how much it means to me. . . ." She stood up, fighting to control her emotion. On the platform a whistle blew. Another answered it.

Lermontov became angry. He called out: "Miss Page is coming!" Then, to her, "Go then! Be a dutiful . . . *housewife!*" He made it sound like a woman of the streets. Her head came up. The two antagonists stared at each other in silent defiance. Lermontov did not rise.

She put out her hand. "Good-bye."

He ignored the hand. He looked at her as if she were a complete stranger. Then she was gone.

As she walked away, the train started to move. Suddenly, she heard her name: "Vicky!"

She turned like a shot. Lermontov's face, at the open window of the moving train, showed defeat, exhaustion, complete surrender.

"Tell him he may stay!"

He pulled up the window and disappeared from sight.

She stood staring after the train, long after it had vanished into the tunnel. She had seen what it had cost him to admit his defeat; and she knew what it had cost her to win. Dmitri vanished with a sidelong glance at her as he went. Still she stood there, remembering the look on Lermontov's face, the tone of his voice, his words, "Tell him he may stay!" Why didn't she run to the telephone kiosk, ring up Julian, tell him their troubles were over, as easily solved as Grisha's? Why did she still stand there on the platform remembering the look on her beaten adversary's face, before she turned at last and went slowly back to the hotel?

At class, everything was the same and everything was different. At rehearsal she met all the well-known faces—Grisha, Sergei, Livy, Ivan—all the members of the family into which she had been accepted. They had been her brothers and sisters for weeks and weeks and yet . . . the possibility, the speculative notion, that Julian might no longer be with them was enough to turn them from members of her family into hospitable strangers. She could have cried when Julian came in to say goodbye to the company. Ljubov stopped rehearsal to shake him warmly by the hand. But that was all; a few seconds later they were all at it again. She had no idea what she had expected—perhaps Grisha could have paused a little longer. . . . He could have asked Vicky if she wanted to pass the few remaining hours with her friend. But he didn't. Ratov came to Julian and took him warmly by both hands. But then Ratov would often do that. He asked what time his train was and promised to come and see him off if only he could get away: there were some costumes to be checked, numbered, and packed that afternoon. . . . Livy was the kindest of all. He said he had every intention of seeing Julian off, but he'd only be in the way when two young people were saying good-bye to one another. . . .

And still she hadn't told anybody what Lermontov had said. And Dmitri kept his counsel.

Half an hour before train time, Julian had almost finished packing when he heard her voice calling his name. He went out onto the balcony, a bunch of ties in his hand. She was there below him, in the street, in a fiacre, piled high with baggage.

"Julian! I'm coming with you!"

He roared out "Hooray!" and threw his ties in the air. They fell like confetti into the street.

Eleven

THE TELEGRAM READ:

> BORIS LERMONTOV HOTEL CRILLON PARIS
> MISS VICTORIA PAGE MARRIED MR.
> JULIAN CRASTER IN LONDON THIS MORNING
> RESPECTFULLY
>
> DMITRI

It lay on the cloisonné table beside Lermontov, among a welter of telegrams and messages relating to the calamity at Monte Carlo.

He was convinced that if he had stayed in Monte Carlo he would have averted the catastrophe. After all, Vicky was tied by contract. He was lying on a low divan, his eyes open, staring straight in front of him. The daylight was failing. The noises of Paris—the constant klaxoning, the deep horns of the buses, the shrill whistles of the traffic police in the Place de la Concorde—filtered through the closed windows. He felt half-stifled. He was wearing a thick velvet jacket, of Russian pattern and cut. He tore it open as he got up. He walked about the big room, his feet making no sound on the thick pile of the carpet. . . . Fools! Fools! Fools! He struck one hand with the fist of the other. He caught sight of his contorted face in the mirrored wall behind the fireplace and struck it with his fist, splintering the glass and injuring his hand.

The action and the pain brought him to his senses. Once more he was the cold, controlled being that held so many people's destinies in his power. He had seen disasters before; the question was, what could be salvaged from it.

He bound up his hand with a strip of linen ripped from a table napkin. The telephone rang. The porter announced that M. Boisson was below.

"Qu'il monte!"

Boisson was a famous show-business personality and Lermontov's personal lawyer. When the knock came at the door, Lermontov switched on the lights. Before he greeted Boisson he glanced again in the mirror. He was not pleased with what he saw.

The two men had known each other a long time. They shook hands in the casual French manner, Lermontov with his left hand. The lawyer's eye flicked from the starred mirror to the injured right hand. He said nothing, but started to open his briefcase.

Nursing his hand Lermontov watched him. "Well, René. What do you think of this whole situation? What do you advise?"

"Now? Or in the future? You have always told me to expect a thunderbolt or two. Like this one. And I have always told you that the best things for thunderbolts were lightning conductors. You should take out an insurance policy for each contract you sign. You wouldn't listen to me then, but I hope you will in the future."

Lermontov shook his head. "I don't believe in lightning conductors. In fact, after the experience I have just been through, I don't like any kind of conductors. I'm a highway robber myself and prefer to trust to my wits to defend myself against other robbers." He looked at the formidable mass of papers extracted by Boisson. "I hope you haven't been working too hard."

"All finished. I have the injunction with me."

"Have a drink?"

The question aroused the lawyer's suspicion. "Why? Don't tell me you've changed your mind again?" Lermontov nodded. Boisson closed his eyes in despair. "I'll have that drink!"

Lermontov poured a gin and vermouth. "I don't want to stop her doing anything. She can dance when and where she wants to."

Boisson made a helpless gesture.

"But not *The Red Shoes!*"

Boisson brightened somewhat. "What about the boy?"

Lermontov's tone changed. "Everything he has written while under contract to me is mine. That is in his contract. *The Red Shoes* and his work so far on *Rendezvous Beach.* I am not interested in anything else he may write."

The lawyer sipped his drink. "But if you keep *The Red Shoes* in the repertoire, you'll have to pay him royalties."

"*The Red Shoes* is no longer in the repertoire."

Boisson was trying to guess Lermontov's intentions. He knew him too well to think he would accept failure. The next question enlightened him.

"Is Charles Trevelyan in Paris for the races?"

"Yes." Then, answering Lermontov's unasked question: "Boronskaya is with him. Any message?"

"Is their marriage a success?"

"Charles seems to think so. Do you want me to arrange a meeting with Irina?"

Lermontov shrugged. "Not 'arrange' ... by chance . . ."

IRINA'S LITTLE HORROR OF A DOG DID the rest. In an elegant small courtyard, off the Rue François, a famous dressmaker was showing his collection. The poodle yapped. A man in sunglasses looked up from his program. He rose. She came to him, as overjoyed as a child.

"Boris! Nobody told me you were in Paris!"

He raised her hand to his lips. She had a lot of new rings. She looked at him. She knew at once that this was not a chance meeting.

"Where's Charles?"

"At Chantilly. At the races. His horse is the favorite."

"Aren't you interested in horses?"

She laughed. "Not to that extent. You?"

"No. I know that one horse will run faster than the others. But whether he is called Oo-La-La or Mousse au Chocolat doesn't interest me. Have you any plans? Are you going anywhere this season?"

She gave it a thought, while he watched her, with the hint of a smile. Then she nodded, lazily. "Somewhere without horses. . . ."

Twelve

WHEN A GENERAL DECIDES UPON HIS objective, he first studies the terrain and plans his campaign accordingly. First of all he eliminates side issues. The easy recapture of Boronskaya had restored Lermontov's confidence. He always said everything could be achieved if time was on your side. Now, he had time.

Boronskaya's was a name fulfilled: tested and proven. The Ballets Lermontov had made it famous. Audiences all over the world admired her artistry and flocked to see her. Compared with her, Victoria Page was only a promise, but a limitless promise. True, both had committed the unforgivable sin of forsaking the art they had once dedicated their lives to—but one had done it lightly, as lightly as she had forsworn her other vows, and would probably do so again; the other had done it only in desperation and was left defenseless. He launched the whole crushing weight of his main attack on her.

Instead of returning to Monte Carlo, he made Paris his communications center. He telephoned Professor Palmer in London and asked him to come over to discuss *Heart of Fire.* He was prepared to add the ballet to the repertoire of their world tour if the composer would consider writing an intermezzo, before the finale, which would give Irina and Ivan a pas de deux in the grand manner. Palmer swallowed both bait and hook. Lermontov bought him dinner at le Grand Véfour, asked very few questions, let his guest talk.

He learned that the young couple were staying in Lady Neston's house, and had spent the previous weekend visiting Julian's father in East Anglia. Now they were back in London again. Julian was working day and night. "I expect you've heard his opera has been finally accepted for the Garden. He must deliver some alterations in Act Three by the tenth of this month. The first night's planned six weeks later."

"That's about when we start our tour," said Lermontov. "How's Lady Neston taking it all?"

"She is delighted. She's disembarking at any moment. She's giving a triumphant homecoming party the following Friday. I've the invitation already."

"I hate to think of the little party she'll throw for Craster's opera," observed Lermontov. He sweetened the remark by adding, "I wish them well. All of them." He studied the wine list, asking carelessly, "And what's Vicky doing while all this is going on?"

"She goes to class. Does one or two guest appearances. I know there have been a lot of inquiries. A few offers. I'm amazed how well known she is already. She has quite a reputation."

"Doesn't surprise me at all. These performances of ours in Monte Carlo are news. Like the fashion shows here in Paris. Has she accepted any of these offers?"

He proposed some Armagnac with black coffee. The professor was slow with his answer. "I don't believe so. Since she has been working for you she is—or, rather, I should say, working for you has made her—what shall I say?"

"Choosy?" asked Lermontov, always helpful.

"Not choosy. A perfectionist."

THE LAST FEW WEEKS BEFORE THE BALlets Lermontov went on tour were always hectic, and tinged with madness as well. Spring and autumn are two of the loveliest seasons of the year—but lovely for the ballet company for entirely different reasons. Spring meant coming home, travel-stained, triumphant, full of ripe achievement, after a grueling world tour. Autumn meant a new repertoire, new costumes, a new beginning; it meant old friends leaving the company, scattering to join other ballet companies, getting married, or going home; it meant new friendships, new ballets, new worlds to conquer.

Boronskaya was back! The chasseur of the Hôtel de Paris, who took her little dog for his morning promenade, had a lively imagination and chatted with him as they strolled from post to post. "Can you imagine all the little dogs waiting for you? The Fascist dogs in Rome, the Nazi dogs in Berlin, the Gangster dogs in Chicago! You are a lucky dog, aren't you? All those assorted smells! Can't you imagine?"

The little thing yapped back at him, happily. He could.

The boy who brought him every evening to the stage door had quite another line of chat. "Did the little chap sleep on Madame's bed? And, if he did, was he allowed to creep between the sheets and lay his head on

Madame's pillow?" Always, when Irina came out, he picked the dog up and whispered, "Write your memoirs, little chum! And let me edit them. Here she comes!" He got a special tip for being on such excellent terms with her baby.

She had just wished Lermontov goodnight. He had seemed tired and world-weary. He was working too hard and had too little pleasure in life. "Ah, well," she thought. "You can't have everything."

LERMONTOV WAS, AS USUAL, WITH Boudin. The door to the anteroom was open and Livy sat there, reading a letter, absorbed in its content. Lermontov glanced at Boudin. He knew him well. Boudin expected praise. He always did. Lermontov obliged: "All this adds up to a good season, mon cher Boudin. Felicitations!"

Boudin beamed and returned the compliment: "With the Ballets Lermontov, always!"

The outer door opened and Ratov looked in. "Good night, Boris."

"Good night, Sergei," Lermontov acknowledged automatically. Then he remembered. "Sergei!" Ratov stopped in the door. "Could you wait a moment?"

"Of course." He came into the anteroom and found Livy with his letter.

The outer door opened once more—Ljubov. "Good night, Boris!"

Lermontov asked him to join the others. They were both reading letters and Grisha resented it. "Nobody writes to me!"

"Not true." Ratov handed him a sheaf from his own letter. "For you. From Vicky."

Lermontov's pen checked for a moment on a column of figures.

"How's that girl?" Grisha asked.

"Read!" insisted Ratov. "You'll see."

Not to be outdone, Livy held up his letter. "This is from Julian. All about his opera. He describes the whole structure. Enormous talent, that boy."

Lermontov began signing checks. But his whole attention was concentrated on the talk of his associates.

Livy made a noise between a sigh and a chuckle. "He says she's an inspiration. A miracle. He says she never talks about dancing. . . ."

"Never talks about dancing!" Ljubov looked up from his letter. "The boy is an idiot! A criminal! A crétin! This letter is full of words! And all about dancing! She goes to class every morning! She—" He stopped suddenly and looked at Lermontov.

Boudin was going. As he passed the three friends he whispered, "If you write to her, give her mes hommages!"

They went in. Lermontov was in his most charming mood. He lit a cigarette. "Well, I see it's mail-day."

"From our two young rebels." Ratov pocketed his letter.

"Deserters," corrected Lermontov. But he did not sound very bitter.

Grisha offered his letter. "Read it, Boris!"

"Mine, too," Livy added. "It will make you sorry you lost that boy."

"I doubt it. But that reminds me . . ." He picked up a large score in a gray folder, similar to that of *The Red Shoes*. "Georges sent me yesterday the new score of *Rendezvous Beach*. I like it. I would like you all to hear it without delay."

They were excited and interested.

"We might open with it in London, next season."

"With Irina?" demanded Grisha.

Lermontov saw clearly on every face the same expression. "Vicky's part." He handed the score to Livy. "Would you care to glance over it?"

Livy nodded and took it.

"And no prejudice, please!" Lermontov added.

Livy had opened the score at random and without looking up from it, he grunted, "I hope you say that to yourself sometimes."

Lermontov smiled. "Every day." His three children were going. He held them for a moment longer: "On second thought, I would like to read those letters."

One by one they laid them on his desk. But when it came to Ratov, the old man said, "My letter was meant to be read only by me. Good night, Boris." Outside, he explained, "I could hardly let him read it. She calls him a monster—a gifted cruel monster."

Livy stopped, as if he considered going back. "But he'd have liked that!"

The others laughed and they disappeared down the corridor.

Ratov could have safely left his letter with the others. Lermontov did not read them. He looked at them, contemplated them . . . but that was all. Julian's letter was in pencil. It was more a score than a letter, full of hastily scribbled music notations, explaining, quoting some of the phrases familiar to Lermontov from their first meeting. The letter in ink was from Vicky. Of course, she *would* write to Grisha: not because she had spent more time with Grisha than all the rest of them put together; not even because Grisha had given her freely all the fruits of his genius; but because Grisha would appreciate a letter more than anybody. He would never answer it. Not in words. He might dance an answer one day.

LATER, MUCH LATER, WHEN HE ANA-lyzed the succession of events, Lermontov realized it was at this time that he began to draw the wrong inferences which, step by step, added up to the dreadful conclusion. He assumed that Vicky's letters to Ratov and Ljubov meant "I miss you terribly," that all she needed was a little encouragement. He did something contrary to his whole nature: something which, he would have said, had never won a battle. He stretched out his hand, picked up a pen and wrote "Dear Vicky." He got no further. He had always used people: he couldn't communicate with them. He sat staring at the two words.

Suddenly, there was a knock at the door, and without waiting for an answer Dmitri entered. He made no apology, in fact he was jubilant. Lermontov stared. He knew something of vital importance had happened. Dmitri came up to the desk. "Lady Neston was in front tonight!"

Lermontov waited for more.

"That was her yacht, the big one in the harbor. She arrived today."

They exchanged looks.

"And Miss Page?"

"Is joining her next week for a short holiday."

Lermontov picked up the piece of notepaper, crumpled it, and threw it in the wastebasket, while he said, "Find out the telephone number of her yacht."

"I have it, Boris Lermontov. The *Ottoline* is in Number One berth at the Yacht Club quay. Shall I get her for you?"

Lermontov glanced at his watch. If Lady Neston had been in front it would not be too late to call her. . . .

It wasn't; and she sounded delighted. "Dear Mr. Lermontov, what a lovely performance tonight! I enjoyed the ballets so much. Especially the one with Columbine and Pierrot and that enchanting Harlequin. What a gorgeous boy!"

He suggested they have a bite to eat at the Café de Paris.

"Come down here!" She proposed. "My chef will find us something to eat. There's a cool breeze from the sea. I'm sure you'll enjoy it after that stuffy theatre."

When Lermontov's car rolled down the quay, dance music was coming from one of the big yachts, and there was a party going on. He went on board the *Ottoline* and found Lady Neston waiting for him. She was seated aft, under an awning that protected her against the night dew. Beside her stood her chef, with a benevolent smile under his chef's hat. He was presented as M. Martin-Pêcheur. Like the kingfisher, his namesake, he was on the small side, quick, agile, with bright colors about him. He took off his tall hat with a flourish and bowed to Lermontov. He was obviously enchanted to meet the Tsar of All Ballets, and hurried off, after compliments had been exchanged, to prepare something adequate to the occasion.

"He took the job on approval," Lady Neston confided. "Don't misunderstand me. *He* isn't on approval. I am! He was very impressed when he heard you were coming. If he approves me it will be to no small extent thanks to you! Have good cooks always been in such great demand?"

"Always."

A steward brought two sparkling, icy champagne cocktails.

"All right?" she asked.

He smiled: "How did you guess my favorite aperitif?"

"From someone who knows you. Perhaps you would prefer yours with orange peel? Some people recommend it."

He laughed outright, remembering his first meeting

with Vicky. He turned his glass round and round. "How is she, Lady Neston?" He did not look at her.

"Extremely well," she answered cheerfully. "They both asked to be remembered to you."

His sharp ear detected the slight hesitation before "both" and smiled. "How much truth is there in that, Lady Neston?"

"The usual amount," she admitted, without embarrassment. "Fifty percent. Julian wasn't there when she saw me off. His opera is in rehearsal and he has so little time. Poor boy!"

Lermontov enjoyed his drink. With lemon peel. He was pretty certain that this clever woman, whom, at their first encounter, he had treated so ungraciously, wanted something from him, and he could turn it to his advantage. The natural way for Vicky and her aunt to behave would be to avoid him. They knew that in a very short time, Lermontov and his company would have left Monte Carlo. And yet, here was Lady Neston! And Vicky was to join her in a few days' time. Why hadn't they arrived together? Was this genial lady acting as scout for her talented niece? If she would only give him a lead, he would soon get at the truth! He dared not make a wrong move, so he said, "How do you find the newest member of your family, Lady Neston?"

She teased him: "I don't have to praise him to you, of all people, do I?"

"Why not?" he answered, taking his tone from her.

"He's your discovery, isn't he?"

"Not as a husband."

They both laughed. The steward announced that supper was served. They went below to the saloon, which was kept fresh by giant electric fans moving the languid air. The chef served the first course himself: blinis, piled high with gray Beluga caviar, presented on a silver dish, accompanied by sauceboats of clarified butter and sour cream. Lermontov tasted his: the pancakes were made with Russian corn flour. He caught the chef's eye on him and nodded.

Lady Neston was talking of Julian all through the course—how talented he was, how much he and Vicky were in love. "You know, we discovered that we'd known of him for years before we met him, thanks to dear Professor Palmer. It was in all the papers."

"Really?" Lermontov helped himself to more caviar. He was not overanxious to hear Julian's praises sung.

"You know, of course, that he was the professor's pupil?"

He nodded and thought, *I could a tale unfold, my dear lady. But I won't.*

"Apparently they were all in the students' canteen one day," she continued, "and one of the students told about Mozart—the composer, you know ... well, of course you do! It seems that in those days, sacred pieces were played in churches, never outside them, and the bishops had forbidden anybody to copy their scores."

Lermontov knew the story. It concerned Mozart as a child who, having listened to a long cantata, had written down from memory the full score, every note correct, each allocated to the correct instrument in the orchestra. Julian apparently was such a prodigy!

"I remember now," he said. "Weren't they experimenting with selective hearing? A number of people each of them shouting different words at the same time? And the student has to identify as many as he can?"

"I knew you must have read about it. None of the other students managed to hear more than four words. The average was three. Julian scored nine out of ten!"

She looked at him for a reaction. He was prepared to endure wading knee-deep through an unsavory morass of praise for Julian if it would get him nearer to

Vicky. Lady Neston chattered on: "Julian claims that different people have different qualities of hearing. Not because they hear sounds more clearly than other people, but because their ears select them. Fascinating!"

Lermontov reserved his opinion.

"For example, you might be standing in front of a closed door, behind which someone says something. For most of us, the words are lost among the other sounds of everyday life: traffic, the wind, a dog barking, flies buzzing, a chair creaking, someone coughing, I think he said. But someone like Julian could not only identify all these other sounds, but hear what was being said behind the door as well."

"And what *was* being said behind the door?"

Lady Neston chuckled: "You are kidding me, Mr. Lermontov. Or are you kidding Julian?"

"You see, Lady Neston, it does depend, after all, on what is being said. There is so much rubbish being talked in the world. Don't you agree?"

The steward had cleared the plates and brought the main dish. It turned out to be a French orchestration of a Russian classic: Boeuf Strogonoff, au Martin-Pêcheur. Lermontov tasted it and expressed the wish to congratulate "The Kingfisher." That bright bird must have been hovering near at hand. He made a brief appearance, murmured his thanks, cast a beady eye on the serving table, raised the lid of the casserole, gave the contents a masterful stir, and disappeared again. The menu had obviously been inspired by the famous Russian's presence, but when was this inspiration born? And how had it been carried out? Not in the half hour or so since he telephoned his hostess, whose chef would find them "something to eat." Boeuf Strogonoff takes hours to prepare. He saw his question mirrored in her eyes, but he did not oblige her. Instead, he said, "Do you approve of their marriage, Lady Neston?"

"Why, yes, I do! Two true artists, with great respect for each other's talent. . . . Two young people, very much in love, with a big achievement behind them already. . . . Why shouldn't I approve?"

He chose his words carefully. "Craster is an arrogant young man, proud, obstinate. You don't think their very different backgrounds might create difficulties?"

"With Julian? Not at all. How little you know him! He never thinks of such things."

"He doesn't mind living on his wife's money?"

"Certainly not. He's a modern young man. He doesn't worry about trifles."

Lermontov looked incredulous. "No?"

"Why should he? If the money is there. Isn't it bad enough that young people worry about it when they are poor? Should they have to worry about it when they are rich as well? Julian tells me he thinks the rich have no imagination. We have enough money to do what we like. And what do we like to do? Make more money!"

Lermontov was enjoying her sudden eloquence; and the Boeuf au Martin-Pêcheur was very good. He encouraged her to continue: "I see he has converted you, Lady Neston. What do you propose to do for him?"

"You're teasing me, Mr. Lermontov. I'm not an expert on music. I'm not an expert on anything—"

"Except on living—"

"—Except on managing people, perhaps—but I think I would like to set up for Julian something like what those rich landowners set up for Haydn, in—was it Romania?"

"Hungary."

"Of course. The Eszterházys. The princess is always telling me that you can ride for three days over their land without ever leaving it. But who would ever remember the Eszterházys if they hadn't financed Mr. Haydn?"

Lermontov smiled politely. "My dear Lady Neston, I almost expect to hear from you that you have made a bid for the Ballets Lermontov, with the intention of appointing Julian Craster as president. In that case I would not be prepared to bet much on the future success of the present artistic director."

The chef produced his final act of homage to the distinguished guest: a Charlotte Russe, as light as a feather, with Crème Chantilly. Lermontov shook hands with him. "If we still had a tsar in Russia, M. Martin-Pêcheur, you would out-Carême Carême." The chef understood the reference and bowed in acknowledgment. Lermontov explained it to Lady Neston: "The French chef, Carême, gave the tsar notice after one year's service. 'But why, M. Carême?' 'It's too cold in Russia, Your Imperial Majesty.' The tsar tried to get him to change his mind: 'But, M. Carême, if I can stand the cold, why can't you?' The chef replied: 'You have no choice, Your Majesty. I have.'"

Lady Neston had risen and was adjusting the speed of the electric fan. "Bon soir, chef! At any rate, you won't leave me because of the cold."

She led the way to the deck. The dance music had stopped. An American voice was strumming a ukelele and singing "Blue Skies." The sound of low voices traveled over the water; there were sudden bursts of laughter. On the dusty square, where in the daytime they unloaded the cargo boats from Genoa and Corsica, they were showing a motion picture in the open air. They had only one projector, so there were long waits between the reels. It was von Stroheim's *Greed*. Old women walked up and down the audience with trays, crying out, "Pochettes surprises! Eskimobrics!"

They sat under the awning and drank black coffee, enchanted with each other. By now, they were old friends.

Lermontov congratulated her on her souper à la Russe. "And all in half an hour. Your chef is miraculous."

She looked at him, doubtfully, in the half-darkness. "How much do you know about cooking?"

"I know this much, that no chef in the world—not even M. Martin-Pêcheur—could have produced the meal we had in the time he had."

An admission of guilt, when it was unavoidable, was one of Lady Neston's favorite ploys. She sighed. "Have I been caught out again?"

This time Lermontov did not smile. "I owe you a confession, too, Lady Neston. I didn't accept your kind invitation to supper for auld lang syne."

"And I didn't come all the way from London to cook you a Russian meal."

They were like two old campaigners, sparring for an opening. It was Lermontov's turn to lead. "How did you know I would accept your invitation? If it comes to that, how did you know I would call you?"

"You want to know too much, Mr. Lermontov."

"Let's start again. How is Vicky?"

Her reply was emphatic. "Wretched!"

"Did she know you were coming here?"

A nod.

"Why didn't you call me?"

She was silent.

"Would you have telephoned tomorrow?"

She shook her head.

"You travel down from London, you order your yacht from Antibes to Monte Carlo, you go to the theatre and rely on the chance that someone will know who you are and tell me you are here. . . . Why?"

She marched out with colors flying.

"I promised Vicky that I wouldn't get in contact with you unless I had a clear sign that you wanted her back."

"I made no sign."

"Oh, yes! You did. I knew somebody would report to you that I was in Monte Carlo, or that my yacht had been seen. After all, neither one of us is inconspicuous. If you didn't want Vicky back, you would have ignored me. If you did, you would get in touch with me. You did. And—here you are, Mr. Lermontov."

They fell silent. It was delightfully cool. The dance music in the Café de Paris had stopped long ago. The last gamblers had left the Casino. Even the croupiers had gone home. A long freight train was hissing and snorting its way toward Italy without stopping at Monte Carlo station. As it came out of the tunnel, there was a muted clanking, followed by a short, shrill, rasping noise as it passed through the cutting beneath the Casino terrace. Although Lermontov knew the sounds and smells of Monte Carlo as well as any native, he had never noticed it before.

Lady Neston accompanied her guest to the gangway. The sailor on watch touched his finger to his hat and held a lantern to light him to the quay.

He kissed the hand of his hostess and murmured, "Lady Neston, in some ways you are like me. You never give up."

She took it as the compliment it was meant to be. The car, waiting for Lermontov only a few yards away, seemingly dead, sprang into life. A few seconds later he was gone.

He had a lot to think about. He was like a card-player, busy arranging the cards in his hand, guessing what the other hands contained, and how they would be played. Lady Neston would telephone Vicky, who would come to Monte Carlo for a week. The two ladies planned to return together for Julian's first night. Lady Neston was giving a party for the young couple on that night in London. What followed after that lay in the lap of the gods.

That was what Lady Neston's hand contained. Lermontov thought he could trump it. He leaned forward and wound down the window between him and Dmitri, as the car climbed the hill to the Casino Square. He told Dmitri to ring Trigorin early and ask him to be in the office at nine.

"Trigorin intends to go to Brussels tomorrow," observed Dmitri. He was driving carefully through the floods and cascades of water, disgorged nightly into the square after 2:00 A.M. by men with hoses, so skilled at their job that they could drop Niagara at your feet, and the Zambezi over your head, without letting a drop fall on you, while they washed flagstones, asphalt, flowerbeds, the leaves on the trees—everything, including yesterday—down the drain.

"Brussels? Whatever for?" asked Lermontov.

"Some problem about rooms."

"Can't he do it by telephone?"

"He says not. Every day there's three to four hours' delay on long-distance calls, and it's getting worse. Belgium worst of all."

"Why Belgium?"

"Unexploded shells from the War. They went off and destroyed some cables."

Lermontov nodded. Brussels was the first stop on the tour. And Trigorin was certainly right about the French telephone system. It was an international joke. No bombs could make it any worse.

"He'll have to take a later train," he said aloud.

NEXT MORNING TRIGORIN WAS GLOOMily pacing up and down the office when his chief arrived, punctually and full of good cheer.

"My dear Igor, I need your help. It's a matter of the greatest delicacy and importance."

Trigorin raised his right hand to his waistcoat, more or less in the region of his heart—which beat only for the company—meaning "My life is at your service!" He said it with words as well: "That's what we're here for, Boris Lermontov!"

"What relations have we got with Thomas Cook's in London?"

"Excellent. The best."

"I want them to do us a favor."

THREE DAYS LATER, ALMOST TO THE hour, the Blue Train steamed into the station at Cannes, fifty kilometers up the line. In a first-class sleeping compartment, Vicky put down her book to watch the crowd on the platform. She could hardly believe her eyes when she discovered Boris Lermontov among them. He was counting the numbers of the coaches and, as the train stopped, he came directly toward her. She could hardly doubt that he knew exactly the number of her coach and compartment. For an instant she was paralyzed. Then she jumped up, looked in the mirror—she was glad she had asked the attendant to make up her bunk at St. Raphaël—and sat down again. There was a knock at the door.

Lermontov entered. He closed the door and bowed over her hand, as if his magic wand could transform three months into three minutes. "We are destined, it seems, to meet at railway stations."

He was as elegant as ever, leaning against the door, his hat and cane in his hand. He glanced at her book, at herself, waiting for her to speak. It was for want of something better that she said at last, "What are you doing in Cannes?"

"I was looking for you, of course."

"For me?"

"Yes. For you know, my dear Vicky, I am always looking for great dancers."

"Not even my aunt is expecting me. I'm a day earlier than I said."

He shrugged his shoulders. The magician who explains his tricks is no magician. He continued in the same tone: "We have all missed you. I was hoping by now you would have begun to miss us a little."

"I have."

He spread his hands. "You have only to say the word."

Her eyes sparkled. "How is everybody?"

"Including me?"

"Including you."

"Never better."

"And Grisha?"

"Always fighting with Boronskaya."

"And she?"

"Always fighting with Grisha."

"I wrote to him. Did he show it to you?"

"I never read other people's letters."

"And old Sergei? How is he?"

"Getting younger."

"And you?"

"Getting older." There was a private reservation implicit in this last remark. He was angling for a superb dancer and he would have sacrificed mother, father, best friend, and reputation for that.

"Are you happy?" he asked.

"Yes. Very happy."

"I mean as a dancer."

At first she didn't answer. The train started up. She said, "I haven't danced much, you know."

"Yes, I know. I know every time you have danced. But you've never stopped working?"

"Never."

"And never stopped going to class?"

"Never."

He fired his sharpest arrow: "Why isn't he with you?"

"His opera is opening at Covent Garden. It's in rehearsal. The first night is a week from today."

"Would he give it up if you insisted?"

"I wouldn't ask him."

"Then why is he asking you?" The train gathered speed. He sat down beside her. "Does he know what he is asking?" His tone became seductive. "We are preparing a new ballet. We have all been working on it for weeks. The décor and costumes are the best thing Ratov has ever done. Grisha is full of enthusiasm. . . . And you know what that means. . . ."

It was the serpent and the apple all over again. What chance did she have against this devilish man, who held in his hand the key to everything she longed for? What was he saying? "Nobody else has danced *The Red Shoes* since you left us. Nobody else shall ever dance it but you. Put on the red shoes, Vicky, and dance for us again!"

She could hear Julian's music in her head. In spite of herself she started to smile. The man's effrontery was as cool as ever, his maneuvers as forceful, devoted to a single end. She heard herself saying, "How am I going to tell Julian?"

He relaxed and smiled broadly. The battle was won. "Would you like me to do it?"

She shook her head. "I must do it. He wouldn't listen to you."

Two hundred fifty-three

Thirteen

VICKY'S RETURN TO THE BALLETS LER-
montov was no less a sensation than Boronskaya's.
Ratov gave her several fatherly kisses, Grisha some
brotherly ones, while Livy's kisses had very little to do
with family feeling.

"Julian coming?" Livy asked her.

"Perhaps sooner than we think."

She had rather dreaded meeting Irina again on equal
terms, but that lazy, goodhearted lady made things easy
for both of them. Lady Neston asked Irina to tea on the
yacht—"Just the three of us"—and she gobbled down
petits fours and marrons glacé in a way that would have
given Boleslavsky heart failure if he had seen her. The
hostess told her how, only a few months ago, at Covent
Garden, she had had to remove her niece by force from

applauding the great Boronskaya. In return Irina confessed that, one night during the season, she and her Charles—"He is my Charles, but I am not his!"—had penetrated the Monte Carlo theatre in disguise to see Vicky dance *The Red Shoes.* "It was very wonderfool. We were crying."

Naturally, Vicky wanted to know how they were disguised.

"My Charles said I was disguised as Boronskaya in low heels. It was a joke. He makes very English jokes. I am vairy lit-tel in low heels. No one 'as recognize me in the theatre, because we came in the dark, during the ouverture. But outside, people 'as ask, 'Are you the ballerina Irina Boronskaya?' and I 'ave open my eyes, like this, and ask, 'Who is she?' "

"But what about your Charles?" Lady Neston wanted to know. He was an old friend of hers.

"He was disguise as my father."

"How?" asked Vicky, very intrigued. "How did you disguise him as your father?"

"By addressing him as 'Oui, mon père!' and 'Non, mon père.' And outside the theatre as 'Papa'!"

They laughed until tears ruined their makeup, and eternal friendships were sealed.

Two nights later, Lady Neston sat in Vicky's cabin holding her hand. She had been crying. Julian had not telephoned. He had not answered her letter. She had written him pages and pages, telling him how dancing was her life, just as music was his, and telling him how she had longed for him to say that he understood this, how desperately she had wanted to discuss things with him; but that when he came home dog-tired and upset about rehearsals she hadn't had the heart to bother him with her troubles. She had told him what it meant for her to be with the company again and she had asked him to telephone her, so that they could talk to each other.

"That was five days ago, Aunt Ottoline. What shall I do? I can't get him at rehearsals. It's much easier for him to telephone me, than me him."

Lady Neston soothed her: "I'm sure he'll understand. He'll come after his first night. You're both a bit overwrought."

"In the past, he's always been so understanding about my dancing. Now that I've agreed to dance once more, once only with the company; they are going away for eight months after that . . ." She was crying again. "I know I shouldn't do it without talking it over with him again, but when have I had the chance to? I haven't said I would go away with them. But once they're gone, what have I got without him? I need him! I need his encouragement, his love, his understanding. . . ." The tears were streaming down, now.

Her aunt stroked her hair. "Put through a call in the morning, darling, from here."

Vicky shook her head. She had a rehearsal.

"Telephone him from the theatre, then. We'll put through two calls—one to the house, the other to Covent Garden. We're bound to get him at one or the other. I'll book the calls now, while it's quiet, and you must try to sleep. Would you like one of my sleeping pills?"

Vicky shook her head again. She cried herself to sleep.

Fourteen

LIFE IS QUITE SHAMELESS IN THE WAY it imitates art and gets away with it. The telephone call to Lady Neston's house and the call to Covent Garden came through simultaneously at eleven-fifteen next morning, while Vicky was rehearsing with Ljubov and Julian with his orchestra. The call to Belgravia disclosed that he had left for the Royal Opera House before nine o'clock. The call to the theatre established that Mr. Craster was certainly there, but too busy to take telephone calls. Both of the calls had been booked person-to-person, but it took the combined efforts of the French, English, and Monégasque operators to establish that the call was urgent, that it came from Monte Carlo and that the caller, Miss Victoria Page, was actually Mrs. Julian

Craster. By this time two rehearsals had been disrupted: the leader of Julian's orchestra snapped two fiddle strings in the first hour; and Ljubov's nerves were on the point of snapping. As for Vicky, after not having had enough sleep, breakfasting off coffee and an aspirin, and running to and fro between a crackling telephone—"Ne quittez pas! Ne quittez pas! C'est bien Madame Crastaire?"— and a raging Ljubov—"Concentration! Miss Victoria Page! What is the matter with you, MAY I ASK?"—she was building up for the grand scene of hysteria that all Ljubov's pupils dreamed of creating, when they would yell back at the maestro, scream their head off, and burst into tears, before running off to their dressing room.

The new first night was to be next day, Tuesday, and it did really seem like another first night, as this one was like another dress rehearsal. She knew they were sold out only hours after the posters went up in Cannes, Nice, and Monte Carlo. "Return of Miss Victoria Page in *The Red Shoes* for one performance only." The box office telephone had never stopped ringing. . . .

"Miss Page! You are supposed to be expressing ecstasy!"

"I'm sorry, M. Ljubov!"

"Concentration, Miss Page! Again! From Figure Ten! Boy! Go away!"

"If you please, Miss Page, you're wanted on the telephone. . . ."

"What? What? Get out of here, you silly boy! Again! Miss Page! So! So! . . . Brisé! . . . Grand jeté! You see, Vicky, you can do it when you concentrate. . . ."

"Oh please, Grisha! May I go? It must be Julian. I must speak to him!"

She ran off without waiting for permission. Ljubov caught the terrified boy with his arms of tempered steel and shouted, "Criminal! Bandido! Asticot! How dare you interrupt my rehearsal?" He shook him, then relaxed his grip and said, in quite a reasonable voice, "Go after her! Tell her you made a mistake."

The boy scurried away like a mouse from a tormenting cat. With a pointing finger, Ljubov announced, "That boy hears nothing but telephone! And he hears them all the time! He has telephones in his head! Ivan! A moi!"

The telephone Vicky was using had been designed during the period of decadence of Art Nouveau. It was so covered in curlicues of metal and pieces of varnished wood that it was next to impossible to get the receiver to your ear. The designer must have realized this when he supplied yet another receiver, hanging on a hook like an Egyptian amulet, which could be unhooked and pressed to your other ear, making it doubly impossible to distinguish anything clearly. Vicky heard several voices talking simultaneously, then the Paris operator (a female with a voice that could cut through glass) asked the London operator, "C'est lui qui parle, Londres?"

The Monte Carlo operator's contribution (a contralto) overlapped Paris: "Ne quittez pas, Londres! Elle attend! Voici Miss Victoria Page!"

"Julian!" shouted Vicky. "Are you there?"

There was dead silence, like the moment in *Alice in Wonderland*, when Alice shouts at the animals; then the London operator (a man) assured everybody concerned: "Personal call to Mr. Julian Craster from Miss Victoria Page. Our party's here at this end. Go ahead, please."

As nobody went ahead, Vicky tried again: "Allo! Allo! Julian! Are you there?"

This time he was there. "Hullo! Vicky! This is Julian!"

"Oh! darling!" The relief was so great she could hardly speak. "Oh! Julian! Is it really you?"

At the same time: "Hullo! Vicky darling! I'm here! Can you hear me?"

Two hundred sixty-one

"Not very well."

"What? What did you say? You're not very well?"

"No. I'm all right. You're very faint!"

"I can hear you all right. Is that better?"

"Yes. That's better. I couldn't get you at the house. The telephone's very bad here. I'm speaking from the theatre."

"So am I. From Covent Garden."

"I know. You've got a rehearsal. So have I!"

His voice changed. "I know. For *The Red Shoes.*"

"Are you angry? Do you mind?"

"Yes."

"Did you get my long letter, which I wrote you on the train? Didn't you read the letter I left behind?"

But he was very angry: "Letters are no good to me. I want you back."

"Oh! darling . . . How can I? . . ." She was desperate to make him understand. "It's only this once, darling. It's a special gala performance. It's tomorrow, and then I'll come back to you. Oh, darling! Try to understand! It's life for me. I thought I could live without it. But I can't!"

"Apparently you can manage without me. . . ."

The moment he had said it he was sorry. He wanted to qualify it, was going on to say more, but he heard Ljubov shouting in the background, "Miss Page! How much longer have I got to wait for you?" and Vicky's voice answering, "Go away, Grisha! I'm talking to London."

"Vicky! Are you there?"

"Yes, Julian. I'm here! I wish I was with you! I'll be back for your first night, darling!"

"Don't dance, Vicky! Come back now! While there's still time to cancel it. I need you here!"

"Oh! darling . . . I need you, too! Half of me is here and half of me is in London. . . ."

"Vicky! Listen!"

"Julian! I've got an idea! Listen! Couldn't we—"

She heard a click, like the latch of the guillotine, and was cut off in midsentence.

Julian was left alone, more lonely than he had ever felt in his life, at the stage door at Convent Garden. He could see Jerry's back as he stood sneaking a smoke on the sidewalk. He had vacated his lair while Julian talked. The young man tried and tried, in utter despair, to breathe new life into the cold mouthpiece.

"Hullo! Hullo! Operator!" He heard a female voice—a long-drawn-out "Ye-e-e-es?" "I've been cut off! I was talking to Monte Carlo!" A pause. Then the English operator: "Number, please!" "I've been cut off. I'm through to Paris. Don't cut me off!" Then to Paris: "No, Madame! Someone was calling me! Zero, zero, zero, seven! Oui! Monte Carlo . . ." A long pause. Then the English operator again: "They cut off! Hang on! I'll try and get them back." "I can't hang on. Will you book me a call? For twelve noon. Monte Carlo zero, zero, zero . . ." Then a new voice, one that had not been a party to the previous game, announced, impersonal, god-like: "Five hours' delay, all calls to France."

One day, perhaps, say in the early 1980's, we may find an association formed of Devotees of Old-Fashioned Telephoning, like Associations of Enthusiasts for Steam Engines, Veteran Cars, and Ancient Sailing Ships. A generation that communicates by computer and satellite will find it an endearing experience to stage transcontinental hookups by the sole aid of human fallibility and the human voice. Vicky and Julian, alas, will not be of their company.

She dried her tears and went back to the stage. Everybody was hanging about, waiting for her. If Ljubov had given her a good old-fashioned bawling out, as he usually did, she would have been all right, but instead he looked at her and said, pointedly, "I hope you are with us now. Both halves!"

He signaled to the pianist, who started to play the Girl's solo. She started to dance, then she faltered. A murmur like a groan swept around the watching company. Boleslavsky took a step forward. The pianist kept going. Vicky took a few unsteady steps, raised her hands to cover her face, and collapsed.

Lermontov was alerted. The doctor was called and gave her a thorough checkup. His verdict was, "Nothing serious. Overwork. Nothing in her stomach. Young people seem to think they can go on forever without taking a rest or having a proper meal. No damage to her limbs. She'll be up and about in three to four hours, ready for light work. Tomorrow? Tomorrow she'll be as good as new." Lermontov's car took her back to the yacht.

Lermontov sent for Trigorin, who had returned from Brussels: "Is everything arranged for Sunday?"

"Yes. The company entrains at noon."

"What would you say if I asked you to move us one day sooner? If you can."

"It won't be easy."

"What is?"

The doctor had given Vicky a sedative. Shortly after three o'clock she woke up in her cabin on the yacht. She felt much better. Her aunt telephoned to Lermontov, who sent the doctor and offered to come over himself. Vicky would not hear of it. She was perfectly capable of going to the theatre. The doctor confirmed her decision. He accompanied her and Lady Neston to Lermontov's office.

They were all there. Lermontov was deliberately allowing a situation to develop full of uncertainty and hysteria. He had, as yet, made no decision about the gala performance of *The Red Shoes*. Obviously there would have to be a change of program, involving Boronskaya, should Vicky be unable to appear. When she arrived with her aunt there was a confusion about chairs for the ladies.

Meanwhile Ljubov, with his one-track mind, rushed up to Vicky. "Ça va?"

She nodded.

"Come on, then! We can still get in an hour's rehearsal. Then you can rest. And there needn't be any more talk of canceling the performance!"

His words stunned Vicky. Cancel tomorrow's performance? When she had come for it from London! When she had risked breaking up her marriage with Julian by even mentioning it! She'd sooner die! Besides the doctor had said she was fit!

The doctor intervened: "Ah! Pardon, madame. Fit, yes! But to dance tomorrow night? And *The Red Shoes*? No! I could not accept that responsibility."

This was where Lermontov showed what a superb actor he was. At the doctor's word he exclaimed, "Voilà!" and clapped his hands together, accepting the verdict without further discussion. Aesculapius had spoken! There could be no arguing with such advice.

There could be no performance! Vicky was crushed, annihilated. Everyone looked at the floor. There seemed no solution. Suddenly they heard him say, as if he had just snatched it out of the air, "But after all . . . is it really necessary to cancel? Why not postpone?"

Postpone! The word gave new life to everybody—to Vicky most of all. Her heart overflowed with gratitude. "Postpone it till Wednesday?"

"Even better than that. Until Friday. It is the closing night of our season here. And you and Grisha would then have all the time you need to make it a memorable performance."

Lady Neston spoke up.

"Friday is Julian's first night. Of his opera at Convent Garden. We planned to leave on Wednesday to be there in good time."

But Vicky's eyes were fixed on Lermontov. He gave a shrug of despair, indicating that he had done all he could do. Even that needed Boronskaya's consent. Because of course she would have to swap performances with Vicky.

"I would have to know tonight at the latest," was his conclusion.

They were all puppets, dancing on strings, giving a performance, breaking their hearts, while he, the master showman, held the strings.

On Wednesday morning Vicky and her aunt arrived at the railway station, for the early-morning train to Paris and London. But only one of them was traveling. Lady Neston had decided to return to London and talk to Julian. She approved of this marriage and was prepared to make a personal effort toward making it work. Of course it was a bore that Julian seemed to dislike that clever Mr. Lermontov so much . . . but some people don't like Boeuf Stroganoff—she didn't like it herself, but she didn't burn the house down to avoid eating it. On the whole she felt fairly confident.

Vicky looked as radiant as a girl should look who, on Monday, has made an important decision, which had, through Tuesday, so far resisted the ravages of time. Nothing more had been heard from Julian. Lady Neston was carrying a letter, which was to be delivered to him with the least possible delay.

It was a pathetic document, this letter from the fly explaining how much she needed the spider, how she needed fresh air in her struggle to survive, how she must dance or die. She spoke of the other flies, of those famous dancers, designers, and choreographers, with whom she had been given the chance to work. Why was it wrong to stick to them? She would dance because she had given her word she would dance this single performance, and then she would sit down, with Julian's arms around her, and discuss what could be done. "You don't like Lermontov. I know that. But he gave you your chance, too, darling. Every artist needs people to believe in him and criticize him, and the greater the critic, the more he believes in himself. Why desert the Number One name in ballet for a possible Number Two, or Three?"

Cupid and Psyche was to be broadcast on the BBC. Vicky would be on stage through most of Act One, but she would keep her radio set on in the hope of picking up something from London.

She was full of reminders for Lady Neston. "You won't forget to tell him that we can have the yacht for our honeymoon?"

"Of course not."

"There's a special reason for it."

As her aunt failed to ask why, she told her anyway. "It was on board the *Ottoline* that Julian Craster kissed Victoria Page. For the first time ever!"

"You said it was in the bistro."

"I mean ... for keeps! In the bistro it was half a joke. Remember to kiss him for me as well as for yourself."

"I don't go around kissing my nieces' husbands." She remembered something. "It seems as if I shall never see *The Red Shoes*. When am I to see it? And where?"

"We'll let you know." A whistle blew. "Good-bye, Auntie, good-bye!"

"Good-bye, my dear. I'll bring him back to you, as soon as I can."

"Auntie! Tell him this—it's very important—I won't believe anybody anymore who doesn't nod three times!"

The train was already moving. It was doubtful whether Lady Neston got the gist of Vicky's last message to Julian. But she nodded cheerfully and struggled with the window until the attendant came and fixed it. By then the train had plunged into the tunnel.

And that was that.

Fifteen

THE RUSH TO THE MONTE CARLO BOX office was tremendous, as soon as it was announced that *The Red Shoes* would be postponed from Wednesday to Friday night. The telephone started to buzz and never ceased the whole blessed day. It brought tears to Monsieur Boudin's eyes. It was an international sensation, a public event! People called up the box office demanding, not asking, to buy any tickets that had been returned after the announced postponement. They were told apologetically that no tickets had been returned. And when they expostulated that there were always people who couldn't arrange to alter their engagements, they were told, not so apologetically, "Not in this case!" For once the law of averages was suspended in Monte Carlo.

A famous travel bureau in Paris rang up twice to buy out the whole auditorium, including the boxes, for a private performance on Saturday on behalf of a New York chain of fashion shops holding their convention in Paris. Although they offered seventy-five percent of the gross takings and later raised their offer to double that, they were told that it couldn't be done. The Ballets Lermontov was leaving on Saturday for Brussels. The heat was turned on to Brussels now that the rumor had been propagated that the Ballets Lermontov would arrive one day earlier than their announced date. The request came back to Lermontov, who promised to give his answer in Brussels.

Late Friday afternoon, Vicky and Boronskaya were sitting in the bar of the Hôtel de Paris eating Café Liégeois. Irina was in full plumage. Her Charles sat beside her, minding her little dog in his lap. Irina had introduced her husband to Vicky, and Vicky had thanked her for playing her part in the swap. Irina opened those famous eyes: "But I suggested it to Boris! First he have wanted Wednesday. But after I have agreed Wednesday he rang me and asked me to change it to tonight. To Friday. I tell him, 'Je m'en fou! It is all the same to me.'"

Vicky sighed. "Wednesday would have been perfect. I could still have got to London in time."

"Easily," agreed Charles.

His proprietress, fishing for a delicious blob of cream at the bottom of her glass, asked, "You think, Vicky, that Boris chose Friday, so that you cannot go to Julian's first night?"

Vicky was quite shocked. "He wouldn't do a thing like that!"

The eyes closed to lustrous slits, as Irina purred, "Oh! wouldn't he, just!"

* * *

IN EVERY CORNER OF THE THEATRE
there were new notices, as well as in hotels, bars, cafés,
and restaurants frequented by the company:

RE: DEPARTURE TO BRUSSELS

OWING TO UNFORESEEN
CIRCUMSTANCES the departure will
now take place, not on Sunday, but at
midday on Saturday. Any questions should
be directed to MR. TRIGORIN.

Nobody knew why these unforeseen circumstances
couldn't have been foreseen. Those who had thought
they had plenty of time to pack, or say a fond farewell,
had to get down to it at once. Appointments for Saturday had to be canceled. Luggage to be shipped had to be
handed in to Trigorin's office. To quote Ljubov: "Chaos!
Chaos! Chaos!"

The switchboard of the Opéra had been warned not
to put through any calls to Miss Page's dressing room,
owing to her recent illness. Her radio set had been
connected with a new, specially installed, aerial which,
according to the Monte Carlo post office engineer, in-
creased not only the reception of static, but also the
range of the set. In any case, the quality of reception
would improve after sunset. What Vicky did not know
was that Lermontov also had a set available, which was
more powerful than hers.

He came to wish her well for the performance and
remarked on her quiet confidence. "You are a real old
trouper in our company now, Vicky. Do you remember
what nerves you had the first time?"

"I still have nerves. But now I know how to cover
up."

He smiled. He seemed in an excellent mood. As he left he said, as if he had just remembered it, "Oh! Vicky, I would like to have a word with you after the performance."

"In your office?"

For a moment he seemed to consider it. "Mm . . . no! Somewhere we can talk."

"On the yacht?"

"With pleasure. I'll have my car." At the door, he stopped again. "You know, of course, that we start later here than at Covent Garden?"

"Only half an hour."

"I'll see you onstage."

Poupette helped her into the Girl's frock. Carefully and solemnly Vicky tied the ribbons of a new pair of red shoes and started to break them in. She had already darned the toes herself. She wondered how many pairs of red shoes the company had in their baskets . . . She thought of the pair, of ordinary peach-colored satin, which she would change into for the first scene, before she bought the red shoes from the Shoemaker. She nodded approval when she saw that Poupette had them already in her hand. The two girls chatted. The transmission of Julian's opera would begin any moment now. Poupette knew as much about it as Vicky did.

The announcer's voice came over loud and clear above the static. He gave a résumé of Julian Craster and his work, mentioning the ballet of *The Red Shoes,* the Ballets Lermontov, and Monte Carlo, so that Poupette exclaimed "Ah! Ça!" and clapped her hands. Then there was a pause.

Radio never has liked pauses. Vicky could not only sense the nervousness around the microphone, she could actually hear it. Sheets of paper were changing hands, somebody whispered, then, once more, silence.

At length the announcer spoke again: "We regret to announce that Mr. Julian Craster, the composer of *Cupid and Psyche,* who was to conduct his own opera, has been suddenly taken ill. Sir Hartley Menzies will take his place." Already polite clapping acknowledged that the replacement conductor was mounting the stand.

Vicky stared at the radio. A dozen possibilities, each one worse than the last, were flashing through her brain. She heard Poupette's question: "Ou'y a-t-il, Madame?"

She heard herself say, "Something has happened to Julian," as in a dream. The overture to *Cupid and Psyche* began. The door behind Vicky opened. Someone was standing there. She turned.

It was Julian.

They stared at one another.

Vicky whispered, "Laissez-nous, Poupette!"

The dresser hesitated whether to obey. Then she went. Julian stood aside to let her go. An image of their brief, well-remembered glimpse of one another on the first night of their ballet—he immaculate in white tie and tails, she as the young girl going to her first dance—flashed through their minds. He was travel-stained and tired. He had come the best part of a thousand miles without food or sleep. He had dined on hate, breakfasted on jealousy. He shut the door and walked up to her. He did not kiss her. He looked at her, long and earnestly.

"All the way I wondered whether I would find you here." She made no answer, so he went on. "And here you are!"

She said, gently reproaching him, "You left your great night."

"Yes. Why didn't you?"

"Oh! Julian, darling . . ."

He couldn't resist the pain and love on her face. The

crest of bitterness broke and he took her in his arms. When he felt her slim body, he crushed her against him, caring nothing for the fragile dress or the velvet ribbons. Nor did she. They kissed passionately. He had already forgiven her. Now that he was as sure as ever of her love, he took for granted that everything was the same. Still holding her tight, he whispered in her ear: "It's all right now. It's all right. The train goes at eight o'clock for Paris and we'll be on it. It'll be our honeymoon."

He felt her stiffen. She drew back in his arms. "You can't ask me to let down all my friends here! And all those people!"

"Why not? I did!"

He let her go. In seconds, disapproval built into rage. "Haven't you any pride at all?"

"None of the kind you mean. How could I be proud of walking out on the company? On the people who have come to see me dance?"

"And on Lermontov!"

"Yes! And on Lermontov!"

"Right!" he said. "Stay, then! And dance!"

She stared at him, keyed up for the performance, obsessed and unapproachable, like one of the Greek maenads who tore Orpheus to pieces. There were no tears. The moment was too deep for tears. He turned to go, then saw the radio and said, "Without my music!" He struck the clumsy box a blow that knocked it to the floor and silenced it. Together with his music vanished his love, his hopes, their life together.

But she still whispered, "I love you, Julian."

"That's what you love!" He pointed to the red shoes on her feet.

It almost seemed as if the red shoes glowed as he went out of the door.

Lermontov had known from Poupette of Julian's arrival. He had guessed what to expect when he heard the radio announcer in London. A lesser man might have given orders to keep Craster out, to refuse to let him see his wife until after the performance, to lock him in a dressing-room if necessary, with all the consequent violence and scandal that would ensue. Lermontov simply gave orders to leave them alone. Let Craster hear the truth from her. He would never believe it otherwise.

Lermontov was a gambler; he would not have risked a centime at the tables, but he would bet his fancy against the world and the critics without hesitation. Nothing but the best would do for him. He never wasted money, but he spent it like an Indian prince when it was necessary. The events of the last fortnight had seen him in his element. Steadily he had raised the odds on Vicky—on dancing against domesticity, on theatrical glory against the humdrum life of wife to a famous man, on *The Red Shoes* against Julian Craster. What was going on now was the final struggle. He sent word to the orchestra pit. Hold the overture! When the stage-door keeper reported that Monsieur Craster had just stormed out of the theatre, Lermontov congratulated himself. He had won. It was true that in a bunch of horses, one horse must be faster than the rest. But he who said that it didn't matter which was a liar! He called the stage and told them they could start the overture. He was going to fetch Vicky himself.

VICKY OPENED THE DOOR TO THE COR-ridor. She could hear voices from below. One was Lermontov's, the other Poupette's. She thought, She'll have told him that Julian was here. He would know by now that Julian had gone. *Where are you, Julian, my darling? Where are you?* They were coming up. Nobody else was with them. She could hear Poupette grumbling. She was complaining that she had not been told about Brussels, that she would not have time to pack her own and Madame Page's things. Lermontov was replying, "How could you have been told when I haven't had time to speak to Miss Page herself?" *That's why he wants to see me tonight! He wants to persuade me to go with them. If I agree—and how can I refuse?—it won't stop there. It will mean Brussels, Copenhagen, Berlin, Rome, Paris, America—the whole eight-month tour.* She ventured out into the corridor. She could hear every step they made on the stone stairs, but her own feet in the ballet shoes made no sound at all, only a slight squeak when she turned on the concrete to go the other way, down the corridor.

Julian! Darling, I need you! Lermontov is coming to get me. He'll comfort me and tell me everything will be all right. I don't want to see him. I don't want to believe him. I don't want to be comforted, and certainly not by him. He hates you because you aren't afraid of him. I must avoid the main staircase. This way! The emergency stairs. I can hear Poupette screaming! She's found the open door to my dressing room and the room empty! "M. Lermontov! Venez vite! Venez vite!" Hurry, red shoes! Hurry! You know the way. They fly down the spiral staircase! Round and round and round!

Julian! Julian!

The red shoes are flying! Through the emergency exit! Over the flagstones! Into the late sunlight! It's like a blow in the face. The red shoes know where he is! Down there! Where the train comes out of the tunnel! Where it slows down to take him away from me!

Julian! Darling, wait for me! I waited for you! You threw your ties in the air. Do you remember? They fell like confetti into the street. I ran to pick them up. I'm coming with you!

The red shoes ran across the pink icing terrace.

The red shoes jumped onto the parapet—the parapet over the railway cutting.

Julian felt, rather than heard, her desperate cry. People who are very close to each other sometimes know when they are needed by another ecstatic soul.

Even that leap to death was a work of art. Julian saw her throw her arms up against the sky. Her body made a perfect curve against the smoke of the engine. He ran and ran along the platform toward the train and roared with horror.

The train pulled up with crazy, frightened clanking. It was a freight train, unscheduled, not meant to stop at Monte Carlo station. Julian headed the running searchers, stopping along the tracks, searching ... searching. ... Then he saw a bloodstained bundle of pink tulle and went on his hands and knees and crawled under the railroad car.

IN THE AUDITORIUM OF THE THEATRE, the overture to *The Red Shoes* was finished. There was no cue for the curtain. The people waited. At first, patiently. Then impatiently. Livy put down his baton and folded his arms. The audience whispered, rustled, asked questions. The footlights came on. Livy prepared for his cue, his eyes on the curtain.

The spotlight came on—the big, main spot that followed Vicky and Grisha wherever they danced. The curtains trembled, were parted, by hand, and Lermontov appeared. Livy exclaimed out loud at his appearance. He moved like an automaton and had a ghastly color. He stood there, in the flat light of the spot, trying to speak and failing. A solitary laugh was heard in the audience and was angrily hushed by the others. Silence. With a visible effort Lermontov forced himself to speak.

"Ladies and gentlemen! I am sorry to tell you that Miss Victoria Page will not dance tonight. . . ."

A sigh swept over the audience. They had dreaded it, and now it was a fact. But this man, Boris Lermontov, the great Boris Lermontov, had something else to say, even though the words had to be forced out of him. "Nor indeed, on any other night." He gasped for breath. He looked like a drowning man. Livy was listening with open mouth. Ratov, horrified, left the box. Ljubov, behind the curtain, cradled the red shoes in his arms. The dead, heavy tones of Lermontov's voice, by a huge effort of will, dominated the theatre.

"Nevertheless . . . we are presenting . . . *The Red Shoes* tonight . . . because she . . . would . . . have . . ." He could hardly get the words out. ". . . wished it. . . . It was the ballet . . . which made her name . . . and whose name . . . she made. . . ."

For a long, infinitely painful moment he could say no more. Then he ground out his last tribute to Vicky. And even his intimates failed to realize what it cost him to add those few words: "She was . . . as you know . . . a very great dancer. . . ."

Behind the curtain, Ljubov raised the red shoes in his hands and laid them against his cheek as he said a prayer for Vicky.

Lermontov had done what he came out to do, but he seemed incapable of moving. He stood in the spotlight staring out at the audience, but nobody could say what he saw. Then he stepped back and vanished from sight.

The cue light glowed. Livy alerted his orchestra.

The curtain rose in silence. The music started. Grisha did his dance.

On Vicky's entrance the spotlight centered on the green door. When it opened, there was an audible gasp from the audience. A woman cried out. Although there was no one there, the spotlight seemed to render visible that young vibrant body, that wonderful red hair. The spotlight crossed to Ivan, who danced with a nobility that was his own tribute to his partner. The company came on stage. The spotlight moved in and out among them. It was too much for them. Two of the girls broke down and stopped dancing. The spotlight went on dancing as before.

A SILENT RING OF PEOPLE SURROUNDED Julian, as he knelt by Vicky in the last of the sunlight. Her poor broken body lay on a stretcher. Children, women with shopping bags, station officials, looked dumbly on, as a little fat doctor made her as comfortable as he could. "Pas d'éspoir. No 'ope at all," he muttered to Julian, who threw his face up to heaven and his arms about, as if he were asking God to have pity on a poor puppet with a human heart. The sun beat down on the torn, bloodstained body and the despairing man. A man started to cry with great sobs as Julian stretched himself on the ground beside his beloved as if he were trying to sink with her into her last resting place.

She felt his breath on her face and opened her eyes. She was going. She breathed, "Julian. . . . Take off the red shoes. . . ."

It was her last gift to him. He undid the tapes, slid off the red shoes—now, alas, more red than ever before. He kissed her feet. The doctor put his arms around him.

THE RED SHOES LAY ON THE STAGE IN the full glare of the spotlight.

The Shoemaker danced across the stage, picked them up, and danced with them to the footlights.

Lermontov sat watching in his gold and crimson box, a silent, motionless figure. An idol.

The Shoemaker presented the red shoes to the audience.

The curtain closed.